Spin
the
Golden
Light
Bulb

Jackie Yeager

Amberjack Publishing
New York | Idaho

Amberjack Publishing

Amberjack Publishing
1472 E. Iron Eagle Drive
Eagle, Idaho 83616
http://amberjackpublishing.com

Publisher's Cataloging-in-Publication data
Names: Yeager, Jackie, author.
Title: Spin the golden light bulb / by Jackie Yeager.
Series: The Crimson Five.
Description: New York, NY: Amberjack Publishing, 2018.
Identifiers: ISBN 978-1-944995-44-7 (Hardcover) | 978-1-944995-46-1 (ebook) | LCCN 2017941027
Subjects: LCSH Inventions--Fiction. | Inventors--Fiction. | Schools--Fiction. | Family--Fiction. | Teamwork--Fiction. | Science fiction. | BISAC JUVENILE FICTION / General | JUVENILE FICTION / School & Education.
Classification: LCC PZ7.Y321 Sp 2017 | [Fic]--dc23

Cover Design and Illustrations: Gabrielle Esposito

To my husband, Jim, who will always be my Golden Boy.

TABLE OF CONTENTS

THE AMPHITHEATER

MY SIXTH GRADE class marches into the amphitheater, an outdoor stadium with a crumbly center stage, at the same time the Piedmont Challenge theme song thunders through the speakers. Grandma Kitty said I would freak out when I saw all the banners and balloons, probably chew my nails right down to the skin. But my nails aren't even bleeding, and the amphitheater looks perfect. Just the way I imagined it.

Well, except for maybe one thing. My name won't be listed on any of these bleacher seats. Mine will be marked with number 718 to match my uniform shirt, my books, and everything else at school. And that's so annoying. Just once I wish I'd see *Kia Krumpet* written someplace. It's like my name isn't even real.

Principal Bermuda stands on stage wearing a suit that barely buttons over his belly. Next to him stands a lady in a purple dress. I've never seen anyone's hair piled that high or with so many purple ribbons woven through it. She must be from Piedmont University. I tighten my ponytail and march up the bleachers as straight as I can because Grandma Kitty says winners have good posture and hold their heads high.

When all the seats are filled, Principal Bermuda flings open his arms and a siren blasts so loudly we cover our ears. Before I have time to wonder what's happening, an aero-car zooms straight for the amphitheater, but it screeches to a halt high above the stage. The motor quiets to a hum, whirring like an old-fashioned ceiling fan, and lowers a golden sign:

Welcome to the Piedmont Challenge!
Think More. Work Hard. Dream Big.

I smile as the aero-car flies away. One of the winners of the Piedmont Challenge invented the first flying car like twenty years ago, and she was a girl—a fifteen-year-old girl. I could be like her someday. Only I would be Kia Krumpet, the girl who invented the first underwater bubble bike—at age eleven.

Grandma Kitty always tells me, "Butter Cup, the best inventions come from thinking of things you already know and dreaming up ways to make them better."

Well, I *do* know a lot of things. Like, nail biting is a habit people do when they're nervous, but it's also a sign of being a perfectionist. And when you divide the circumference of a circle by its diameter you'll always get 3.14—that's called Pi. Oh, and I also know best friends can stab you in the back without even owning a knife. Just ask my ex-best friend, Charlotte Montgomery. Her stabbing skills are stellar.

But I didn't know the sun would scorch my head so much that my ponytail would feel like fire. This is the Piedmont Challenge, though. I don't care if these sun-fried bleachers burn my legs right through my uniform skirt. This sunshine is going to bring me luck in the competition; I know it is. The sun *is* one of the brightest stars in the universe, after all.

Principal Bermuda taps the microphone and combs his greasy hair with his fingers. *So gross! Doesn't he know some of us have butterflies in our stomachs?* Mine almost force my morning oatmeal onto Charlotte's lap. It would serve her right for sitting next to me, though, and for being the best-friend-turned-traitor that she is. But I can't throw up. I have to think about solving my first task of this competition, and puking at the Opening Ceremony wouldn't be smart at all.

"Welcome sixth graders, to the 50th Annual Piedmont Challenge!"

The theme song roars through the amphitheater. I'm not looking at Charlotte, but I can feel her looking at me.

"Psst," she says.

I don't answer.

"Kia," she whispers.

"Shh! I'm listening to the music."

"I want to tell you not to be nervous. None of us are going to win anyway."

I glare at her as hard as I can.

"No one from Crimson Elementary School has ever won a Golden Light Bulb."

"I know that."

"Everyone knows this competition is cursed or something."

I barely move my lips. "It's *not* cursed."

"In fifty years, no one from the whole town of Crimson has ever won. Why else would that be?"

Maybe if I ignore her, she'll stop. I stare at the trees towering above the amphitheater and see the shape of a light bulb woven into the branches.

"Well?" she says.

I sit up straight. "That's because no one from Crimson has ever tried hard enough to win."

She stares at me like I just flew in from Mars.

The music fades and Principal Bermuda states the rules of the competition, the things we've all heard a bazillion times since the beginning of the school year. I bet I could stand on that stage and recite his speech myself.

"The Piedmont Challenge is a national event where tasks are given to every sixth grader, including all of you!" He points his finger straight at us and spins in a circle, like a rooster perched on top of a weather vane. "Over the next week, you'll solve a task in each academic category: Art Forms, Communication, Earth and Space, Human History, Math, and New Technology. The scores will tell us what category you'll study in seventh and eighth grade, and high school after that. The process is called 'Programming.'"

I bite my thumb nail hard. That's six whole years of studying one thing. I can't do that! I'll never get to build my sixty-seven inventions—or even one. If I'm forced to study one category for the rest of my life, my best ideas will shrivel up for good. I'll probably have to study math. I'll be stuck in a building with really tall walls. Walls!

"However, the Piedmont Challenge is also a search for the brightest and most creative sixth graders in the country. For that reason, you'll also solve a seventh task: The Swirl and Spark Recall. The Swirl and Spark Recall is a task where anything goes. You won't know what you'll be asked to do until you walk into the testing area."

Charlotte nudges me. "That shouldn't be hard for you, should it, Kiiiiaaa?" The way she says my name makes me want to spit in her face. I know she's talking about all the times I've made up plays for us to perform and games for us to play, and probably all the times I've tried to get her to build inventions with me. Those things used to make us best friends. Now they don't.

"The five elite students in each state with the highest score will travel to Camp Piedmont in Maryland this summer and eventually enroll at PIPS, the exclusive Piedmont Inventors Prep School instead of getting programmed into one academic category."

My knuckle cracks. I don't realize how hard I'm squeezing my hands until I feel the pop. I could go to PIPS instead of getting programmed into math. I could meet kids who appreciate my ideas. I could finally build my sixty-seven inventions. They wouldn't just be incredible ideas on my list. I know my chances stink, but somebody has to win—I pick me.

"At the Day of Brightness Ceremony, most of you will receive your programming placement, but the top five students in New York will be given Golden Light Bulb trophies instead." He flips a switch and the outline of the Golden Light Bulb flashes in the trees. Even in the daylight, it illuminates the amphitheater brighter than the blazing sun. If I could, I'd climb up that tree and let the light pour into me, for luck or something.

He waves a flag in the shape of the infinity symbol. "I now declare the Piedmont Challenge at Crimson Elementary School officially open."

We stand up, turn on our heels, and I'm facing the back of Charlotte's head. But I don't think of her as my ex-best friend who rides aero-scooters without me now. Today she's one of the 200,000 kids that I'm going to beat, and when I do, I'll find someone else to ride aero-scooters with, and, hopefully, underwater bubble bikes too.

THE MERMAID SONG

WE INCH DOWN the bleachers like a bale of turtles. I'm not even sure we're moving at all. Charlotte's messy disaster of a braid is in front of me. It looks like she slept on it. I smooth out my ponytail and straighten the collar on my shirt. That's what the Piedmont people want to see— someone neat and prepared. I picture myself in my perfectly pressed uniform flying over my classmates, swooping down first and grabbing my competition tickets, but instead I wait my turn like everyone else, biting my nails down to their nubs.

I finally step onto the center stage, the very spot where Principal Bermuda stands next to the Piedmont University lady with the ribbons. She hands me seven tickets and looks me right in my eyes. Then she smiles. A warm, knowing smile . . . I think she just sent me her Piedmont good luck vibes.

I squeeze the tickets tight and peek at the one on top.

Student No: 718
Crimson Elementary School
Task 1: Human History
June 1, 2071

Emerald Room J

I tuck the tickets into my shoulder bag as my classmates march past me—*my* competition. Some look nervous. Some look like they don't care about this challenge at all, which is so weird. I can't underestimate any of them, though. That would be foolish.

We head out of the amphitheater, across the school yard, and up to the front archway of Crimson Elementary School. Two teachers dressed in red robes hold the doors open and we travel down the hallway. *Emerald Room J* flashes above my first task room.

I bite the skin around my pointer nail. What year was the Boston Tea Party? What side started the Civil War? What year was the Crossover? I know that's when all the schools changed. Was it forty years ago? No, fifty—in the year 2020. I force myself to focus. I can't let all these facts defeat me. Not when this competition is my only chance to get into PIPS.

I step out of line and into Emerald Room J, a creepy dark room with lights glowing out of stations. At the turn-style, I slide my ticket into the card reader. It tells me to go to station thirty-four, and I find it in the back. I don't go in right away though. I fix the pleat in my skirt and give myself a pep talk: *Just answer all the questions right. Don't mess up. Take deep breaths like Grandma Kitty said, the big kind that will make the butterflies go back to sleep.* I do it, and some of the butterflies in my stomach listen, but not all of them. I can be as stubborn as they are though, so I hold my ticket up to the reader and the door slides open without a sound.

Hmm. It smells like oranges in here, kind of like Grandma Kitty's house.

A voice inside a speaker startles me. "Hello, Number 718. Please sit down at the desk."

I do as the voice tells me and tighten my ponytail again.

"Thank you. On the screen you will find Task One."

The monitor flashes: *No: 718: Task One-Human History.* My eyes blink a bunch of times until they adjust to the light.

"In thirty seconds, you will receive the first of three hundred questions. Use the air pad to select your answers. You will be released at the end of the testing time, three hours from this point. Begin."

AFTER SIX days of tests, experiments, art projects, recitals, and written exams, I'm used to the butterflies that stay awake while I'm solving my tasks. I need to ignore them for just one more though: The Swirl and Spark Recall. This solution is worth triple points so I *have* to make it amazingly good.

I sit in a waiting room trying to convince myself that answering one question to a table full of judges will be easy. I'll walk into the auditorium and act like an idiot if I have to. I'll sing, maybe quack like a duck, whatever I can think of to answer that mystery question better than all the other kids. I bite my thumb nail and then my pointer. I can't help it. If nail biting was judged in this competition, that Golden Light Bulb would be mine.

The clock ticks. 11:11 a.m. I jump out of my seat. A Piedmont usher appears in the doorway and leads me to the auditorium. I walk down the aisle to the judge's table where I swipe my ticket through the reader and step into a taped off area on the stage. Six grown-ups with matching shirts stare at me. Of course I smile like I'm not nervous.

One judge, a man with a long neck says, "Please state your student number."

"I'm Number 718, sir."

"Thank you, 718. Now that you've completed your six academic tasks, you'll solve your final task of this competition—The Swirl and Spark Recall. It's your chance to think up a creative answer the judges will not expect. First, I'm going to read your question. Then, you'll have one minute to think before you are required to respond. You may ask questions during that time only. After one minute is up, I will ring this bell. That is your signal to begin. Do you understand?"

"Yes, sir. I understand."

"Very well. You will have a total of two minutes once the bell rings to respond to the following question: *If you could be anyone else besides yourself, who would you be and why?* Your one minute of thinking time begins now."

My mind jumps all over the place before an idea comes to me. I rush to ask, "Can I use props in my answer?"

"Yes, as long as you do not move outside the taped off area."

"Can I sing part of my answer?"

"Yes."

I reach for my shoes. The straps are tricky but I manage to get them off. I set them down, take off my knee socks, and unfasten my belt. I tug it from the loops of my skirt, wrap it twice around my legs, and then buckle it back together. I pull one sock over each arm. I lay on the floor sideways and prop myself up on my elbow. A tune from a TV commercial pops into my head . . . *If I can just change the words—*

Ding!

"If I could be anything, I would be a mermaid. I would invite human kids to spend their summer vacation with me. First, I'd speak to them in the language of the water world, which, of course, is made up of songs like this:

> *Summer break is here at last and you need something new,*
> *Let me show you where I live and all that we can do.*
> *I'll teach you how to use your mind to breathe first out then in,*
> *and give you water gliders, that work just like real fins.*
> *We'll dive deep down into the sea and find a sunken ship,*
> *Or play some soccer with the squids and take a submarine trip.*

When I'm done singing, I slide across the floor like I'm swimming and hold up my shoes. "Then, I'd present these water gliders to the human kids. They'd put them on, and together we'd explore all summer. I'd have a million new friends, and that's why I'd choose to be a mermaid if I could."

The judge with the long neck dismisses me. I take a deep breath and try to read the expression on his face. *Did he like my answer? Did he think I looked like an idiot?* No luck. His face is stone cold.

The same usher leads me out of the auditorium, down

the hall, and into the Exit Room. "718, now that you've completed your tasks, your scores will be sent to the Piedmont Committee for review. The winners will be announced Friday on the Day of Brightness. Good luck to you."

"Thank you." I chew my pointer nail.

I sink into a chair by the window and stare at the blowing branches beyond the amphitheater. I squint to see if the outline of the Golden Light Bulb is still out there—if the glittery branches are still glowing—but it's too far to tell. I can't tell if I did okay on my Swirl and Spark Recall task either. *Why did I have to sing that stupid song?* It probably didn't even make sense, but maybe the judges give extra points for mermaid songs. Maybe they like when kids swim across the stage.

I bite my pinky nail. I wish Grandma Kitty had seen my solution. She would know if it was good enough. She won the Piedmont Challenge when she was in sixth grade, way before she wore sparkles in her hair like she does now. I hold her shiny Golden Light Bulb every time I visit her, only it's not so shiny anymore. Maybe gold isn't supposed to be rubbed that hard.

At the end of the day, I weave my way through the factory. That's what Crimson feels like to me anyway. We punch our student number cards at the door like we're on an assembly line. Teachers call us by our numbers, not our names, because they want us to focus on the categories we study instead of the kids we study with. I hate that only best friends call each other by their actual names. I like being called Kia. I wish more kids called me that.

Someday I'm going to invent a patch for my uniform shirt that includes my name not just my stupid number. I know that's against the Crimson rules, but maybe there's a sort of substance I can paint on it so if you looked at the digits real close, in the right light, you'd see it—like a secret code. On a sunny day like this, *Kia* would shimmer right through 718. Then everyone would know my name, and I'd know everyone else's too.

I break free of the building and walk past the dogwood tree with the pink blossoms. I pull my yellow aero-scooter out of the rack, zip up my parachute vest, hop on, and crank it into gear. It hovers above the ground by just a few inches until I push the release button. Then, it slowly lifts up to the top of the tree and takes off. The warm breeze blows my bangs away from my eyes and Crimson gets farther and farther away with every house I pass. I could ride through the air like this all day! Mom says it's not good to waste petroleum though, and I know she's right. Maybe someday I'll think up a better fuel to use, like old feathers or discarded pet fur.

I fly over the blue house where Charlotte and her twin brother, Charlie, live. It doesn't look much different from when I used to hang out there—back when they didn't care about what lunch table they sat at. Maybe I shouldn't have told them about my latest inventions, Inventor Ball and Duct Tape Ball, but who wouldn't want to play sports where you race to build inventions or where you wad up duct tape for thirty minutes and see whose ball gets the biggest? They seriously don't have any imagination anymore.

I catch the smells of cinnamon and sugar and slam on the brake. Snickerdoodles! If only I could stop to eat one right now . . . or a muffin. But right then a new invention pops into my head. *Muffin Baking Pants Pockets!* I could make really cool white pants with colorful pockets. The pockets could be lined with special oven material—the hot coals and everything—except they would be insulated so your legs wouldn't burn up in flames. If you wore them, all you would have to do is pour the ingredients into the pockets, shake them up with a dance, press a button to bake, and ta-da . . . muffins made in your pants! No kitchen needed. You could bake muffins anywhere.

Hmm. I'll have to add that to my list of inventions when I get home.

I shoot down to the sidewalk and take the side streets to my house. Mine is the stone one high up on the hill. I think a long time ago, Hansel and Gretel lived here—after they defeated the witch with the crooked finger. Maybe someday I'll write a book about the mysterious creature they hid inside the oak tree in my front yard. That would be a really good story.

My Grandma Kitty is waiting by our fence, right where I knew she'd be. She pulls me off the scooter. "Oh, Lovey Girl. Tell me how it was! Was your question a tough one? Did you stick to the plan? Did you give the judges an answer they weren't expecting?"

My face burns up. "I gave them an answer they didn't expect, that's for sure."

"Then you did amazing!" Her lemon drop earrings swing as she talks.

"Maybe, if they like watching kids act like idiots."

"What do you mean?"

"I sang a song and swam around on the floor like a mermaid."

"You didn't."

"I did."

"Oh, Peppermint Stick! That's wonderful!"

"Really?"

"Yes, of course. In the academic categories, the judges want to see that you're intelligent and can retain information. That's why you study. But in the Swirl and Spark Recall category, the judges want to see that you can be original and think quickly. They want you to give a creative answer."

"Then maybe I did okay?"

"Of course you did okay! Mark my words. Besides, you've inherited all those creative genes from me. Now go inside and see your mother. She'll have my head if she figures out I was here."

I give her a long hug, park my scooter in the scooter port, and find my mom in her office. That's where she keeps copies of her files. She's a chemist. When she's not working in a lab, she's reading her files.

She looks up from her work. "Hi, Honey. How was your task today?"

"I'm not sure. The judges looked stern. I couldn't tell what they were thinking."

"I'm sure you did fine. You always do."

"I better have done better than fine! That was my last task, Mom. My scores are being sent to the Piedmont people right now! What if I didn't make it? What if I didn't score high enough?"

"Then you'll get programmed like all the other kids at school. That wouldn't be a bad thing you know."

"Mom! That would be a *very* bad thing. You know that!"

"Kia, I know you want to go to that camp, and then go to PIPS after that. Grandma Kitty has filled your head with all sorts of unbelievable stories, but, in reality, only five students from each state get to go. Those are not very good odds. Besides, math is a well-respected program. Numbers are important; they're reliable. You'll have a very bright future if you get programmed for math."

"I don't want to get programmed for math! Who wants to study one category for six years?"

"I did. I loved being programmed into the Earth and Space category."

"That's you, Mom."

"Yes, you're right. I just want you to prepare yourself for the fact that you probably won't place in the top five, and later this week, you will probably be programmed for math."

I want to scream but I don't. "I'm going to my room. The Day of Brightness is Friday, and I need to pick out my best uniform."

She shakes her head, but I don't care what she thinks. I could place in the top five. I could be on the New York State Team. I just don't get it. *Why doesn't she want me to win?*

THE GOLDEN FIVE

THE DAY OF Brightness is dark and stormy, with the rain pounding the roof of the auditorium. I don't think that's a good sign for any of us, but I'm wearing my lucky uniform skirt with the ruffled bottom and my favorite black boots. Maybe those will help. I even wrapped a braid around my ponytail. Grandma Kitty said it's good to have an important hair style for important days, and I'm definitely sure this is the most important day of my life.

If wishing with my whole heart could make my wish come true, I'd win the Piedmont Challenge. I'd get my very own Golden Light Bulb trophy, just like Grandma Kitty's. But wishing won't help me win, and I haven't invented a wishing machine *yet*. All I have are the scores on my seven tasks, and I really hope that's enough.

We shuffle in our seats waiting for Master Freeman,

the President of the Piedmont Organization, to pop onto the video screen. Kids from all over New York must be watching on their screens too. Soon, the video flickers to life and Master Freeman walks up to the podium wearing a tuxedo—and a very serious face. I sit on my hands. My nails can't take this pressure.

"Welcome, sixth graders, to the Day of Brightness, the day we honor the brightest thinkers, the most creative problem solvers, students who are able to make any situation brighter!"

I clap along with my eight hundred classmates and all of our teachers. That's when the shivers shoot up my arms, leaving goosebumps scattered all over.

"There was a time in our country's history when our students were the brightest in the world. The most innovative ideas came from the people of the United States of America. Back then, our country was the leader of the free world, but as the world changed, we failed to change with it. Other students from around the globe created things the world had never thought possible. Gradually, we lost our place as the country with the best ideas. That's when Lexland and Andora Appelonia from the Piedmont University stepped in.

"They were young students at the university when they met. She was a science major, and he was a creative writer. They knew the best ideas came from giving young minds the freedom to be creative and study the areas that came naturally to them. But they also knew the importance of focusing an individual's talents, helping them to avoid outside distractions. Not long after they graduated and married, they developed a new educational system. Under this system, students are programmed into their strongest course of study: Art Forms, Communication, Earth and Space, Human History, Math, and New Technology."

Inside, I cringe when he mentions math but try to keep my expression normal as I listen to the rest of his speech.

"Today, each of you will discover what category you'll be programmed into. You'll study that category for the next two years. You'll become a specialist in that category, and by the time you complete eighth grade, you will be fully prepared to enter a specialized high school as well. This is an exciting day for you. We at the Piedmont Organization wish you well in your academic careers."

The clapping hurts my head; I can't get programmed today.

"We also hold this competition to discover the most creative problem solvers in this country—all in an effort to restore our creative greatness. These young people may one day do just that!"

My stomach gets swirly. I'm going to be one of those people.

In one swift motion, Master Freeman pulls a slip of paper out of a red envelope. "The following five students from across the state have received the highest scores in the Piedmont Challenge. They will make up the elite 2071 team from New York who will attend Camp Piedmont in Maryland this summer and move onto the next phase of our competition, The Piedmont National Finals. The end result may be enrollment into the exclusive Piedmont Inventors Prep School, instead of getting programmed."

The auditorium is silent. I think I might throw up. Like right here. Now. All over my lap.

My mother's words pop into my head, *Math is a very good program, Kia. You'll have a very bright future if you're programmed for math.* Grandma Kitty's words fight to take their place. *Oh, Lovey Girl, of course you did okay! Mark my words.*

I don't want to hear Mom talk about math. I just want Grandma Kitty to be right. I press the fold in my skirt and make my silent wish: *Please say Kia Krumpet. Please say Kia Krumpet.*

Master Freeman grins. "The first winner is . . ."

The fold in my skirt won't stay down. The corner is wrinkled, and now it's—

"Number 718. Kia Krumpet from Crimson Elementary School."

He's not going to call my name. It won't be me. I didn't beat all those kids—

Heads turn to look at me. *Wait, what? Did he say 718? Did he say Kia Krumpet?*

Arms are pulling at me and faces are staring, no—they're smiling at me. He did. He said Kia Krumpet! OhmygodOhmygodOhmygod!

I scoot my way across the seats in my row, trying not to step on any feet, but my heart is pounding so hard I almost forget how to move. I walk down the aisle as kids and teachers reach out to slap my hands. My body seems to figure out what to do though, and suddenly I'm running up the steps.

Principal Bermuda greets me on the stage, but I can't hear anything he says. It's like he's talking in slow motion as he hands me my very own Golden Light Bulb. It's heavy and way shinier than Grandma Kitty's! I look out into the crowd and the people come into focus. Their faces are still staring at me, and their hands are still clapping. Principal Bermuda points to a spot on stage where I'm supposed to stand, but all I can do when I get there is squeeze my trophy. My knees are shaking. I feel the zippers of my boots bumping into each other. I can't believe I won. I'm the first kid from the whole town of Crimson Heights to ever win The Piedmont Challenge. Charlotte said I had no chance, and so did my mom, but I did it!

Master Freeman holds up the red envelope. Yes! Now I'll find out who my teammates will be. Maybe they'll come from New York City or Buffalo. Or maybe Albany. I don't actually care where they come from. I just know they're going to be my new best friends. They won't think my inventions are weird because they probably like to think up inventions too.

The auditorium gets quiet again. I stare at the giant screen. "The second winner of the Piedmont Challenge is: Number 122, Alexander Yates, also from Crimson Elementary School!"

Wait. What?

A skinny boy with a huge smile lands on the stage next to me. *How did he win too?*

He pumps his fist in the air. The crowd roars as he dances with his Golden Light Bulb. *What is he doing? This is my moment.* I'm the one who broke the Crimson Curse. He bows to the crowd, so I curtsy. I can't believe I just curtsied.

Master Freeman taps the microphone twice. I'm not standing on this stage alone anymore. I always dreamed of being the first winner from Crimson, but I never dreamed of some dancing kid winning too. Master Freeman calls out the three other winners and everything that happens after that is a blur.

"Number 219: Marianna Barillion, Crimson Elementary School! Number 606: Jax Lapidary, Crimson Elementary School! Number 434: Jillian Vervain, Crimson Elementary School!"

What? Are you kidding me? One by one the three other kids from Crimson run up onto the stage. We stand together stunned.

Master Freeman clears his throat. "It appears as though Crimson Elementary School has made a bit of history today. No two students from the same school have ever won the Piedmont Challenge in the same year. Now, in New York, we have five. Congratulations to this year's New York team—the Crimson Five!"

Principal Bermuda is puffed up with pride. Teachers flood the stage to shake his plump hand. Flashes from cameras that come out of nowhere blind me. My teammates and I dance and jump around the stage. I'm grinning so big my mouth hurts. It's okay that I'm not the only winner from Crimson, I guess. Who cares anyway? I did it. I'm going to Camp Piedmont—with my very own Golden Light Bulb!

I WRAP my Golden Light Bulb inside a sweatshirt and pack it in my suitcase. It should be safe in between all my socks. I can't forget my invention list too. I pull my wooden *Someday Box* off my dresser, lift the cover, and there's my list rolled up a like a scroll. I untie the ribbon and let it unroll. The list is at sixty-seven now starting with the Underwater Bubble Bike. I smile as I skim through it. *Wait until the Piedmont people at PIPS see all my amazing ideas. They'll probably want me to show the list to my new class.*

I think about how far away this camp is, and I wonder if I'll get homesick. Will I miss Mom and Dad, or my sister,

Malin? Will I miss sharing a room with her this summer? I definitely won't miss her make-up and clothes all over my bed. I might miss my brother, Ryne though. He loves hearing about my inventions. But then I move one of the socks, peek at my Golden Light Bulb trophy buried in my sweatshirt, and try to forget about all the miles between New York and Maryland. Besides, I'll see them when they visit at the end of camp.

FOUR DAYS later, even before the sun rises over the amphitheater, my teammates and I meet at Crimson Elementary for our send-off. The grass shivers in the breeze, just like I do. The globes of the tree-high lamps look like halos in the middle of the sky. It feels weird here—like I'm heading off to a secret place, all on my own. No moms. No dads. No grandmas. Just me. Well, me and my teammates, and two hundred and forty-five kids from the other states. I imagine all those kids getting onto their own aero-buses, and the butterflies in my stomach wake up. Why can't they go back to sleep?

Principal Bermuda leads us to our aero-bus. "Safe travels to you," he says. "I know you'll represent Crimson Elementary School well. Now remember, when you arrive at Piedmont University, you'll be given a new task, only you'll solve that task as a team. At the end of training camp, you'll present your solution in the next phase of the Piedmont Challenge—The Piedmont National Finals. The top five state teams will then advance to the Global Championships, an international goodwill competition also created by the Piedmont Organization. The whole community has faith in your abilities, but we'll be here waiting for you if you don't make it that far. And no worries because if that happens, you'll still have plenty of time to be programmed before the start of seventh grade this fall."

"But, we're going to Piedmont Inventors Prep School in September. We don't have to get programmed," I remind him.

"Not so, 718. Of course you'll be programmed if you don't move on in the competition, just like everyone else."

"What do you mean?"

Grandma Kitty stomps over to him, her hair shining under the street lamps. "That's not the way I remember it, Principal Bermuda. Back in my day, after kids went to Camp Piedmont, they didn't have to get programmed."

"Ah, yes, years ago children who won automatically went to PIPS. That's not necessarily true today. Only students who compete at the Global Championships will have the opportunity to be programmed there instead of at their own school."

"Only kids who make it to the Global Championships get to go to PIPS?" I ask.

"Yes, only them." He pats me on the shoulder.

I shrug his hand away, but he doesn't seem to notice.

"Well kids, it's time for your bus to lift off. Once again, good luck to you. We look forward to hearing updates on our Crimson Five."

I think my head is going to roll off my shoulders. My mom whispers to my dad and then to me. "Listen, Kia. Are you sure you still want to go to this camp? I can tell Principal Bermuda that under the circumstances, it's not a good idea. You can give someone else your spot and come back home with us."

"What? No! I don't want to go home. I want to go to

Camp Piedmont!"

"But the rules are different now. You may not get into PIPS after all."

"But there's still a chance, Mom. We might make it to the Global Championships."

She kisses my forehead. "I know. I just want to be sure this is what you want."

"I'm sure." She just wants me to come home so I can be programmed into math, and a part of me *does* want to stay right here. But I can't let her know I'm afraid to go now. She'll sit on me while the bus flies away. Instead, I think of my Golden Light Bulb and hug her quick.

My dad wraps me up like a burrito. "Okay, Little Bear, go get on that bus. Show those Piedmont people all the great ideas swirling in your head."

I nod. "I will."

Grandma Kitty grabs my hand. Her bracelets jingle next to mine. "I know this is a colossal challenge, Butter Cup, but you were born to go to PIPS. I should know. Advancing to the Global Championships can't be that hard for you. Do what you do best and you'll make it. Mark my words."

I don't know what to say, so I don't say anything. I just step onto the bus.

THE AERO-BUS

I CLIMB INTO the bus, and my eyes don't know where to look first. It's like a glittery motor palace! The seats are sparkly couches, and the walls are painted all different colors. Control panels fill the back of the seats. *What kind of aero-bus is this?*

My teammates have already found their seats. Jax is camped out on the couch behind the driver, his head buried in a magazine. Marianna and Jillian are sitting together a few rows behind him with their heads practically touching. I wonder what they're looking at. Alexander is sitting by himself on the other side of the aisle. His legs are sprawled over the whole seat. He swings them off and moves over toward the window.

"You can sit here if you want."

I slide in. "Thanks."

"You can call me Ander. I don't like long names."

"Okay. You can call me Kia. I don't have a long name."

The bus pulls away and lifts off before I can look out the window and wave goodbye. All I see is the empty amphitheater, but it doesn't matter. I didn't want to see my family drift away anyway.

Ander presses a button on the control panel. His seat reclines, and the control panel extends toward him. "I hope my hockey stuff is okay under the bus. I have a brand new helmet in there."

I stare at his skinny body. "You play hockey?"

"Yup. I'm a winger. I always say, if I can get the puck, I can score."

I think he's making that up. "Why did you bring your hockey gear?"

"Principal Bermuda told me they have everything at this camp. If I find an ice rink, I want to pull a game together. Do you play?"

"Me? No."

"No problem. I can teach you."

"I don't think we're going to have time for games. We have a task to work on, remember?"

"How long can that take? I bet we'll have a ton of free time."

He pushes another button on the control panel and chooses a song. Iridescent headphones descend from the ceiling to cover his ears. I hope he's kidding. Six weeks is not a lot of time to solve our task, especially now that there's a chance we'll have to go back home for programming.

I sink down in my seat. I wonder what category our task will be in. I hope it's not in Human History. I look at Ander. He's mouthing the words to a song. I nudge his arm, and he pulls the headphones away from his ears. "Do you want to talk about which task they're going to give us? You know, guess some of the possibilities?"

"Nope. I want to enjoy the ride." He jumps up and turns around in his seat. "Can you believe this bus? Look at it back there."

All I see are rows of couches and a curtain behind them. He pushes another button on the control panel. A map of the aero-bus appears on the back of his seat. "Look! There's a movie theater behind that curtain and an ice cream shop too."

"Really?"

"Yeah, come on. Let's go check it out."

I think about it for a second. "Maybe later. I want to study my task notes."

"What for? We have eight hours until we get to camp. Can't you do it later?"

"No. I'll find you when I'm done."

He takes off his baseball hat, messes up his brown hair, and shoves the hat back on his head. "Okay, see ya."

I quiz myself on as much Human History as I can, but it's hard to concentrate. I feel like Principal Bermuda played a trick on us. In all the years of talking to us about the Piedmont Challenge, he never told us that if you make it to camp, but don't do well in the National Finals, you can still be sent home for programming. It's not fair. I can't study one subject for seventh and eighth grade and high school too! How can anyone expect us to do that? I bite the corner of my thumbnail and the nail polish flakes off. I pick a piece off my tongue.

I skim my category notes but my eyelids flicker when I get to the Revolutionary War. I force myself to read about

Paul Revere's midnight ride, but soon I close my book and make a wish that our task will not be in this category.

I peek down the aisle at the girls. They look like they could be sisters, or cousins maybe. Jillian's blond hair is long and wavy but Marianna's is stick straight. Jillian is pretty. She seems nice, like we could be friends. I like her headband and her flowing skirt. I'm not so sure about Marianna. She seems too perfect. I think whenever she looks at me she's laughing at me. I look up the aisle at Jax. All I see is the back of his head—and the flat top of his haircut. His face is still buried in the magazine. I don't get it. Later today we could find out our task. Why don't any of them care?

That's when I jump out of my seat. I don't even know my teammates. How can we work together when we don't know anything about each other? Crimson Elementary School is really big, and except from meeting them on the Day of Brightness, we haven't even talked!

I change my plan. Maybe getting to know each other is more important than studying right now. I head up the aisle to Jax's seat. "Hi, what are you reading?"

He sits up straight. Now he's way taller than the back of the seat. "It's a magazine of machine parts, all about the way things work."

Hmm. So Jax likes mechanical stuff. Interesting.

"Do you want to go to the back of the bus? Ander said there's a movie theater back there."

He slumps back down. "Nah."

I walk back towards the girls. They don't notice me standing there until I say, "Hi, Jillian. Hi, Marianna."

Marianna giggles. "Um, no one calls me that."

I feel my face get hot. "Oh, sorry. What should I call

you?"

"Mare."

"Okay. Well, I'm going to the back of the bus. Ander said there's movies and ice cream. Do you guys want to come?"

"No, thank you," says Jillian. "We're watching a video my dad made of the crowd this morning at Send-Off."

I try to catch a glimpse, but they don't turn the player my way. "Oh, well maybe later we can study for our task together."

Mare looks at me with a crinkled forehead. "Why would we do that?"

"So we can be ready for whatever task they give us when we get to camp."

"Seriously?"

"Well, yeah. I want to get a head start, don't you?"

She shakes her head. "No."

"Oh. I guess I'll talk to you guys later. Come find us when you're done if you want to."

Jillian smiles. Mare laughs at something on the screen. I walk away. I'm not sure my "Getting to Know My Team-mates Plan" is working.

Behind the curtain I find a small room with a giant screen and a row of seats. Ander is sitting in one of them.

"Ha! I knew you'd change your mind. You have to see this. We can pick any movie ever made, or make our own. What do you want to see? I already started two different ones, but you can pick now if you want. Go ahead."

"Any movie ever made?"

"Or make combinations of movies too."

"Okay!" We scan through the list, pick the funniest ones we can find, and splice them together. Two hours go by like two minutes and the lights turn on by themselves. My ribs hurt from laughing, but I can take it. This is all part of the "Getting to Know My Teammates Plan."

Ander puts his hat back on. "What should we do now? Want to eat?"

"Sure." We step out of the movie compartment and the aero-bus shakes. I reach for the railing. Maybe we drove through a patch of turbulence. We cross the aisle into a restaurant called the *Circle Café*, where colorful rings like hula hoops hang from the ceiling. Each wall is painted a different color: red, blue, yellow, and green.

"Whoever designed this bus must have a thing for circles," he says. "Let's sit over there."

We spin on circle-shaped chairs at the counter and drink blueberry milkshakes while Ander talks and talks about his hockey team. I don't care about that team, but he's so excited that I listen. He plays with the straw paper, and somehow he turns it into a mini sailor hat. "Look, I made a hat for my hockey puck. Let's make some more. We can turn my hockey bag into a ship, and the pucks can be the crew." His smile is big, like he just came up with the most amazing idea ever. Weird. I wonder if he has an invention list too.

"Okay," I say. "I'll get more straws." My insides churn as I walk away. My plan is working. I'm getting to know Ander! Now I just have to convince the rest of my teammates to build the Hockey Puck Hats too.

PILLARS AND STONE

HOURS LATER, OUR aero-bus lands on the Piedmont University campus in front of Piedmont Coliseum, a brick stadium set in a forest of trees. A banner hangs from the eaves.

Welcome State Champions to Camp Piedmont.
Training Center for the Piedmont National Finals.

I'm one of those state champions!

We run down the steps, and it's like we've entered a fairy tale. The buildings surrounding the stadium are old but really pretty! I stare at the grass, the flowers, the stone pathways, and all of the people. Kids with suitcases are scattered everywhere.

I spot a sign in the grass with the Piedmont Challenge

crest painted on the bottom:

Piedmont Training Camp . . . This Way.

"Come on!" I yell and race down the path pulling my suitcase behind me. My teammates can hardly keep up. I can't slow down though. They may think we're not in a hurry, but six weeks is not a lot of time to prep for this competition.

We weave in between the brick buildings. Another sign directs us through a bumpy alley. We round the bend and enter a square, grassy area surrounded by buildings with fancy white pillars. Kids from all over the country have invaded. A band plays under a tent. Flags from all fifty states hang from the buildings. I have to stop for a second to catch my breath. None of us say a word. My teammates must be swallowed up by the sight like I am.

Finally, Ander yells above the music. "Let's go check in!"

The check-in line leading to Piedmont Chamber winds through the square like a snake. We take our place at the end of it, and I look up. The Chamber looks like a castle! I shade my eyes from the sun and imagine what could be inside. Before long, the band music stops and a voice booms through the cobblestones beneath my feet. I jump off the path and realize there are speakers down there!

"Welcome to the Piedmont Training Camp at Piedmont University. To make this check-in process run smoothly, all team members must be prepared to show their Golden Light Bulbs. This is your ticket to camp, and you will not be admitted without it. There will be no exceptions."

I open my suitcase as the music starts up again and unwrap my Golden Light Bulb. No scratches and still shiny.

I trace the plate with my name. It seems strange that the Piedmont Challenge was only last week. I've let myself feel like a princess ever since I won, but now I better forget about all that. I have to start prepping for our task because I'm not a big deal here like I was back home. I'm not really a princess. Here, I have to ace my task all over again—with teammates this time.

Piedmont Chamber is up ahead, but there must be at least twenty teams still in front of us. I clutch my Golden Light Bulb. My teammates haven't even taken theirs out of their suitcases yet. I wonder if they wrapped them up like I did. Ander probably didn't—he seems more worried about his hockey gear. Mare might have placed hers in a safe spot. Everything about her seems perfect. Her packing skills are probably perfect too. I'm not too sure about Jax. He's one of those kids who looks older and more mature than everyone else in our grade. I never let looks fool me though. I bet his mom packed it for him. Jillian seems too spacey to worry about that kind of stuff. I've already had to remind her twice to grab her suitcase as we've crawled along this side-walk.

I tug at my own suitcase. The wheel is stuck in a crack in the sidewalk. I break it free, and we scoot up a few inches. Jillian trips on the crack and bumps into me. My Golden Light Bulb fumbles in my hand, but I don't drop it.

"Oh, I'm so sorry!" she says.

"It's fine," I say. "I didn't drop it."

Ander laughs. "Nice one. That would be funny if you got up to the registration table and had to show them your chipped trophy. You'd be the girl with the broken light bulb for the rest of camp."

That would be horrible.

To pass the time, I study my teammates. I keep wondering how each of them won their trophies. They each scored a ton of points on their seven tasks like I did, but I want to know which category they scored the highest in. I guess once we get to our rooms, I'll try to talk to them again.

I can see now that one team at a time is allowed into Piedmont Chamber. I can't stop staring at the tall stone building. Tiny question marks and stars have been chiseled into the giant door. At the entrance, two matching magnolia trees stand watch as teams from all fifty states pass by.

I can't be sure, but I think the tree on the right just raised its branch, and then lowered it again! *Did it really do that?* Its white flowers look like tiny bowls of vanilla ice cream and smell like it too. I wait to see if the branch moves again until Ander pulls on my ponytail. "Hey, Kia Krumpet, if I had duct tape and a few branches from that weird looking tree over there, I could make us some wings. Then our team could fly to the front of this line."

I laugh. "Or maybe we could make stilts and step over all these other teams."

"What are you guys talking about?" asks Jillian. "This is Camp Piedmont. Aren't you just happy to be here? There's nothing like this place anywhere in New York."

A girl in front of us, with witch-black hair spins around. "New York? Oh . . . you're *that* team."

"What do you mean, *that* team?" Ander asks.

She smirks. "My team has heard about yours. All of you came from the same school, didn't you?"

"Yeah," says Mare.

"It must be nice to be famous."

"We're not famous," I say.

"Okay, whatever you say."

"Where's your team from?" Mare asks.

"Nowhere as exciting as New York." She spins around and her braid whips Ander in the face.

Ander rubs his cheek. "I hope the other teams here aren't that friendly," he says under his breath.

"She's just mad because she has to work with those four dorky boys," says Mare. "Look." She points to three tall boys and one scrawny one with glasses.

I shrug. "Who cares if the other teams are friendly or what the kids are like? We have a competition to win, remember?"

"I care," says Ander. "I want to meet kids from all over the place."

The massive doors open and the girl with the witch hair and her team pass through. They slam shut before I can peek inside. I hear a clicking sound coming from the vanilla ice cream tree. The petals on each flower close and then open right back up again—all at the same time.

That's weird. How did they do that?

I forget about the tree and watch for the doors to open again. I have more important things to focus on anyway. I'm about to walk into Camp Piedmont, one step closer to getting to PIPS. I pull my suitcase and look for my Golden Light Bulb. It was just in my hand. *Wait! Where is it?* I look every which way. It's not here. It's not anywhere!

The doors swing open.

"My Golden Light Bulb! Where is it?" My team stares at me. We freeze in the doorway. "I just had it!"

Ander looks at me, confused.

I blurt out, "I don't have it!"

Mare points to the side of my backpack.

I see it there, shining in the pocket. And then I breathe again.

We step through the doorway and I take an even bigger breath.

The arched ceiling above us must be a hundred feet tall. Now I'm definitely sure this is a castle! In the center of the lobby is a table. A small lady with tiny eyes and a bun on top of her head sits behind it. Her chair may as well be a throne. Behind her is a two-sided winding staircase covered with red carpet. The two sets of stairs curve and meet up in the middle on the second floor. I can barely see up that high.

We stop at the table and the lady's crackling voice surprises me. "Welcome, children from New York State. I am Mistress Andora Appelonia. You, of course are the New York team—all from Crimson Elementary School, yes?" Her smile is warm. Her eyes are accusing.

My throat feels like sand but I answer anyway. "Yes, Miss Appelonia. We are the team from Crimson."

"How refreshing—a team where all five finalists come from the same school. I can't imagine a more peculiar occurrence. That doesn't happen often, you know."

"Yes, Ma'am."

"Well, we will be expecting great things from you this summer. Welcome to Piedmont, the Camp of Champions. May you create a task solution worthy of a team in your situation."

Ander speaks a little too loud. "What do you mean, 'a team in our situation'?"

"You can't possibly think that you won't be set to a higher standard? You come from the same school, so of course the judges will expect more from your team."

"That's not fair! We just met each other last week on the Day of Brightness. We don't have an advantage."

"Well, I would encourage you to change your thinking, Mr. Yates. It would serve you well in this competition."

I can't think of one thing to say. We've been inside here only one minute, and we're already on Andora Appelonia's bad side.

"Now, if I may please see your Golden Light Bulbs, I will give you your room assignments. Ladies, you'll take the staircase to the right. The young girl at the bottom is Miss Seraphina Swing. She will take care of your travel cases. Gentlemen, please take the staircase to the left. The young man on the bottom, Mr. Gregor Axel, will do the same. At the top of the stairs, follow the numbered signs to find your rooms. An itinerary of events for the remainder of the day will be waiting for you."

We show our Golden Light Bulbs to her, and she hands us each a small golden card. Mine, Jillian's, and Mare's all say *Room 1512.*

"Now children, you may be on your way. Good luck to you. I look forward to hearing many exceptional tales of the Crimson Five from New York State."

I smile as wide as I can, but my teammate's faces tell me they're feeling as much pressure as I am. We say thank you, and I walk with Mare and Jillian to the stairs. Seraphina Swing, a tall girl with purple lipstick and platform heels flashes us a smile. "Hi there, girls. I see you've met Andora Appelonia."

Mare giggles. "What's up with her voice? It sounds like she swallowed sand paper." Andora swings around in her chair. I shoot Mare a dirty look. Seraphina straightens her face and whispers. "It's okay. I want to laugh at her sometimes, too. You can leave your travel cases here. I'll see to it that they arrive in your bedchamber within the hour. I hope you're in good physical shape. You have a lot of stairs to climb."

We begin the trek, and I'm sure my legs are going to turn into Laffy Taffy. When we finally reach the top, we see the boys. They take the down ramp to their rooms and we take the up ramp to ours. Ander waves to me as we pass. I feel better when he does it, like maybe the butterflies in his stomach are wide awake too. Soon our ramp levels out. The hallway is like a grand hotel! The doors are gold with red trim and a card hangs on each one. Written in fancy letters are the names of the girls staying in each room. Down the hall, we see our names on room 1512:

The Champions from New York:
Marianna Barillion, Kia Krumpet, Jillian Vervain.

A smile builds from deep inside me as I reach for the golden door knob.

THE BEDCHAMBER

I PUSH THE door open and see a flurry of silver sparkles floating in the air.

"What the heck?" asks Mare.

We freeze, watching the sparkles fall like snowflakes. They land on our bed—or is it three beds? The center purple platform is one big circle shaped mattress full of pillows. Three beds spring out of it, almost like a peace sign or a star. *So cool!*

The sun casts a bright beam onto the pillows as sparkles hover over them. I move closer, hold out my hand, and a silver fleck lands in my palm. "Look!" I say. "I caught a sparkle!"

Jillian spins around and around, letting the sparkles fall all over her. Mare wrinkles her forehead. "What is all this?"

"It's raining sparkles!" I pour mine into her hand.

Jillian sits down on the bed and runs her hand over the

blanket. The sparkles float up and then settle back onto it. She squishes one between her fingers. "These look like they're made of tin foil and glass. I wonder what they are."

I skip over to a huge closet. The inside is filled with three sets of round cubbies that stretch all the way up to the ceiling.

I look at Mare. "What are those?"

She tilts her head. "I think we put our clothes and shoes in them."

I feel stupid. "Oh right. They're clothes cubbies!"

We check out the purple bathroom next. We each have our own dressing tables. I can't believe what I'm seeing. Grandma Kitty was right. This camp *is* a castle.

Through an archway, at the other end of the room, are walls painted in circles—pink, purple, and silver. There's a round table and chairs and a bucket filled with notebooks and pens. I pick up one of the notebooks and see my name engraved on the cover. "This must be our work area. Look at these planning notebooks. We can get started right now!"

Mare picks up her notebook and flips through it. "Get started? We don't even know what our task is yet."

"Oh, right. That would help." It's not *what* Mare says when she talks to me exactly, it's *how* she says it. I can tell she doesn't like me very much.

Before we can explore any further we hear a knock at the door. Jillian answers it and Seraphina stands there smiling. Her teeth are pearly-white, and her light brown hair reaches halfway down her back. I wonder how old she is.

"Hi, again! I see you've found your bedchamber. What do you think?"

"It's beautiful," Jillian answers. "The bed, the sparkles—"

"Yeah," says Mare, "but what are they?"

"Those sparkles are actually the task solution created by the Colorado team who won the Piedmont National Finals several years ago."

"What do you mean?" I ask. "What was the task they had to solve?"

"Their task was to create an object that could eliminate something negative."

"So they made floating sparkles?" Mare asks.

"Yes, sort of. They're Air Purification Sparkles—micro beads that purify the air. The materials inside them make them float."

I catch another sparkle and cup it in my hand before it can float away.

"Wow," says Jillian. "That's really cool."

"I think so too. This next solution came from last year's winning team from Tennessee. They had to create an object that could make light the work of a person. Watch." She snaps her fingers and from out in the hallway, a small robotic monkey wheels in a cart filled with our suitcases.

"No way!" I exclaim.

"Yes, way," laughs Seraphina. "Meet Mabel."

I kneel down to pet her, but I don't know if I should.

"It's okay. She's friendly. I'll teach you lots of commands for her. She's your assistant, well aside from me and Gregor. I've already met the boys. I stopped at their bedchamber on my way here. Ander is a bit of a talker."

I laugh. "Yeah, I know."

"Jax doesn't say much. Maybe I can get him talking tomorrow."

"Are you our coach?" asks Mare.

"I'm your preceptor. I've been through this competition

before, and I'm here to help you any way I can."

First we get a sparkly room, and now Pretty Purple Girl is going to be our preceptor!

She points to a bulletin board on our wall with her shimmering purple nails. "Now here is your itinerary for the rest of today. This will be changed every day by Swissa when she turns down your beds. She's your chambermaid. She'll also be here to wake you each morning so you don't over-sleep."

What? We have a chambermaid? Grandma Kitty really wasn't kidding! I love Camp Piedmont already.

Camp Piedmont Itinerary
June 17, 2071
6:00 p.m. - Welcome Dinner Reception ~ Appelonia Dining Hall
8:30 p.m. - Evening Announcements ~ Bedchamber
9:00 p.m. - Lights Out

Seraphina turns toward the door. "That gives you just twenty minutes to change for dinner. On the bottom cubby of your closets you'll find your purple team shirt for today. You'll also find your team's wrist band with a message I've engraved for you. I want you to wear the wrist bands every day until the competition. I'm a big believer in team spirit. Our mantra is simple. Watch!"

She presses a button near the door, and purple letters light up on the wall:

The Crimson Five:
Be Curious, Be Creative, Be Collaborative, Be Colorful,
Be Courageous.

"And if you don't know what I mean by all that, don't worry—soon you will."

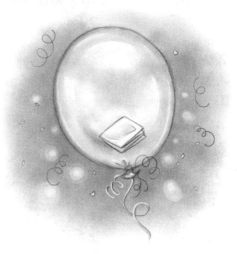

BALLOON MESSAGES

WE MEET THE boys in a living room outside Appelonia Dining Hall. Ander is sprawled on a couch, and Jax is sitting up straight in a chair. Gregor, our other preceptor, stands stiff beside the fireplace. When he sees us approaching, he reaches out his hand.

"Hello, ladies, allow me to introduce myself. I'm Gregor Axel, and I will be helping Seraphina prepare your team for the competition."

Seraphina grins. "Gregor, I present to you the girls from our New York team: Miss Marianna Barillion, Miss Kia Krumpet, and Miss Jillian Vervain."

"It's *Mare*. Not Marianna." Mare whispers urgently.

Seraphina corrects herself with a smile. "Excuse me. *Mare* Barillion."

Gregor bows while we stand there awkwardly. I try hard to think of something to say, something that will make me sound smarter than everyone else on my team, but I just stand there quietly. Gregor doesn't seem to mind the silence, though. He doesn't even change his expression. He seems kind of weird, like he just stepped out of a museum case or something.

We make our way into the dining hall, a colorful room filled with banners that say: *dream, create, explore, and imagine.* My favorite kinds of words! The round tables each hold a sign shaped like a ball. We find the New York table and sit down together. I pick a seat next to Ander, and Seraphina sits next to me. I scan the rest of the room packed with teams from every state and bite my thumb nail. There are so many kids here and all of them must be really smart, maybe smarter than me. They probably have cool ideas too, like the floating sparkles and robotic monkey assistants. Maybe one of them has already thought of how to build an underwater bubble bike. Maybe they have the same idea I have to make flying suits for treetop scavenger hunts.

Ander leans over and whispers, "What's with Seraphina? Did she eat too much grape juice for breakfast?"

I wrinkle my forehead. "What do you mean?"

"Her nail polish and lip stuff—all purple."

I smile. "I love her nail polish."

"Maybe we can borrow some to solve our task. You know, mix some with rusty metal to make recycled paint."

"Ha! Finally, someone is thinking about this competition."

We talk until a million bells ring out, drowning every other sound in the dining hall. Master Freeman and Andora Appelonia stand up like soldiers at the head table; five grown-ups flank them on either side, wearing jumpsuits. They look like they're going to leap out of an airplane.

The bells fade away and Master Freeman bellows, "Welcome, State Champions, to Camp Piedmont on this prestigious campus of Piedmont University. You have accomplished a great deal to earn your place here. I commend your efforts and applaud your achievement!" Balloons drop from the ceiling. One lands perfectly in each of our laps. Mine is yellow. I touch it and it pops, just like everyone else's. It's a symphony of pop, pop, popping. The balloon pieces float away and somehow drift behind a curtain near the head table—as if on cue, a breeze got rid of the mess. I look down in my lap and see a message written on a slip of paper.

Don't be afraid of change.
Have the courage to believe in what you can achieve.

I look at my teammates to see if they've gotten messages too. Before I can ask, Master Freeman bellows again, "You've each been given a message that's for you and you alone. Do not share what it says with anyone. It was chosen for you especially based on your psychological evaluations and is for you to study and understand. When the right time comes, you will know how to use it."

That's strange.

I memorize my message and tuck the paper into my pocket.

"All two-hundred and fifty of you have proven your ability to think through problems in many areas, to think creatively, and to think spontaneously. Now, you must do the same with four teammates. You see, it takes great talent to work with other people, and in this competition, those who form the strongest unions with their teammates will achieve the best results."

I knew it! We do have to spend time bonding as a team.

"Later tonight, you will learn what task you'll be challenged with in this competition, but first, we celebrate with a feast chosen especially for you by Andora. Tonight, we also remember her late husband, Lexland Appelonia, the Founding Father of the Piedmont Organization. He saw the value of creative thinking, teamwork, and children. And so with that, I urge you to nourish your body, which will, in turn, nourish your mind and creative energy."

The ball at the center of our table starts spinning, slow at first and then practically at warp speed. I feel dizzy watching it. When it stops, it breaks apart like flower petals into seven sections. Each one holds a different type of food. The flower slowly rotates, and as it does, each petal slides the food onto our plates! I wonder if this gadget is something a past team invented for the finals too.

While we eat our feast, Gregor and Seraphina ask us questions. Seraphina turns to Jax. "So, Jax, how was your aero-bus ride this morning?"

He gets red in the face. "It was good."

"I'm familiar with the bus you rode in. I hope it was more than good."

Jax looks at his spoon. "Oh, it was. I checked out the engine and the jet propulsion system at all the scheduled stops. I was amazed to see the bus lift off the ground like our scooters back home. The driver showed me how it can switch from driving on the ground on regular roads to driving above it on the expressways. At first, I couldn't see how the system could change like that with just a flip of a switch, but the more I saw, the more I realized that the system is really simple. I can't wait to use something like that for the competition—if we need to use motion to solve our task."

That's the most I've heard Jax say all day.

Gregor leans forward on his elbow. "Yes, of course, it is very simple. I have many more tricks to teach you in that area should you be inclined to hear them."

"I'm inclined. I mean, yes, I'd really like to learn *whatever* you can teach me."

Mare laughs at Jax, but this time I don't give her a dirty look. I feel like laughing too, but then I see the expression on his face, and I feel bad. I'm glad I held it in.

Seraphina smiles. "You're right, Jax. Your task may require knowledge of mechanics and that certainly will help. When I was in this competition, my team used the concept of motion to create our solution."

"How long ago was that?" I ask.

"I was here six years ago when I was in sixth grade."

I put down my fork. "Are you eighteen?"

"Seventeen."

"How did you become a preceptor?"

"If you are able to achieve the status of Threeble, you have the choice of positions here at Camp Piedmont. I chose preceptor."

"What's a Threeble?" Jillian asks.

A Threeble is a person who has studied at the Piedmont Inventors Prep School for two years and then has trained at a Camp Piedmont job for three years after that. Only the brightest students receive jobs."

I feel like a sponge as I listen to her talk, soaking up everything she says. She must be really smart.

"What was your camp job?" asks Mare.

"Oh, I had three different ones. We'll have plenty of

time to talk about me another time though. For now I have more questions for each of you."

"But what were the other choices," asks Ander.

"What do you mean?"

"Instead of being a preceptor, what were the other choices?"

"That's privileged information. You only learn that if you become a Threeble."

Ander laughs. "If? I'll become a Threeble for sure, so why don't you save me some time and tell me right now?"

Seraphina laughs. "Nice try. Why don't you do your best to become a Threeble. That way I won't waste my time if you don't."

Ander jumps out of his chair. "Oh, that sounds like a challenge to me!"

Gregor pulls Ander back into his seat. "You must sit down. We have rules to follow during dinner."

Ander looks over at the head table and slinks back into his chair.

Jillian yawns. "What state are you both from?"

"Why, New York State of course!" Seraphina replies. "You can only be a preceptor for your own state."

The lights dim and the bells return. In a flash, the centerpiece petals reach out, scoop up our dishes, and they disappear into the spinning food flower. Almost just as fast, Master Freeman opens his arms and a large screen rolls down behind him. "State Champions, I now present the official task of the Piedmont National Finals!"

At his announcement, the butterflies in my stomach wake up. Andora opens a scroll, and a hundred circles dance on the screen behind her as her voice crackles into the microphone. "This year, each of our fifty state teams is challenged to find a solution to the following task:

Our home, the Earth, is shaped like a circle.

Your task is to create an object that transforms three times into something else, and then transforms back to its original position . . . creating a circle effect. The object you create must answer a question that is universally asked, but has not yet been answered by mankind. Your solution must include elements from each of the six academic categories and 1 original language. Your presentation to the judges may not exceed twelve minutes.

What? I shove my thumb nail into my mouth. We have to use strategies from all six categories? This task is not fair—it's *impossible!* I rattle off each category in my head: *Art Forms, Communication, Earth and Space, Human History, Math,* and *New Technology.* How are we going to use all six? My brain feels like it's going to explode right here at the New York table.

"Crap, this task is hard!" says Ander.

"What's a universally asked question?" asks Jillian.

"And how do we make an object transform?" asks Mare. "What does that mean?"

We look to Gregor and Seraphina. Gregor's face looks concerned. Seraphina's face breaks into a smile. "What? Are you guys worried? This task looks fun!"

"Fun?" I say. "We have to use skills from all six categories to solve it!"

"Exactly," she says. "That's what makes it fun."

After the five of us mope through dessert, Seraphina hustles us out of the dining hall. "Enough of the pouty faces. Let's go see Ander and Jax's room. Gregor, lead the way."

I tell myself to forget about our task, but I'm not so sure I can. At least Ander's non-stop talking as we pass by all the golden doors distracts me. Eventually, we end up on the boys' floor, and Jax opens their door just before Ander barges through.

"Okay girls, wait until you see this!" He points to a giant board on the back wall. Streaks of color arrange themselves in different positions with each step he takes. "Come in, but then don't move, got it?"

We enter the room, take a few steps, and then freeze. The streaks on the wall change colors and find another spot. "Now, watch this." He doesn't move, but the sound of his voice causes the streaks to move to a new spot.

I squint at the wall. "What are those?"

Jillian reaches out and touches a blue streak. "They don't feel like anything."

"They're sound beams," says Jax. "They display the sounds made in the room."

"Why?" asks Mare.

"It's a way for people who can't hear to know what's going on around them."

"How does it work?" I ask.

Gregor explains, "Many non-hearing people can detect vibrations and beats. The sound beams are harnessed using a computer and laser images. The computer program was designed by a team from California. They found a way to make these beams interpret those sounds and turn them into visual messages."

Mare grins. "So if a person couldn't hear at all, they could watch this wall and know if their favorite song is playing."

"Yes," Gregor replies, "but only if the person knows the

language of the sound beams."

Ander stands up on the desk chair. "This could change how deaf people communicate with hearing people!"

"Yes, it probably will," agrees Seraphina.

Jillian shakes her head. "That's amazing."

Ander jumps off the chair. "Wait until you see our bunk beds."

I pick at my nail polish. I bet it's going to be *another* amazing invention.

We follow him through an archway just like the one in our room. The bunk beds look normal to me. Ander stands before us like he's about to give a speech.

"Now, the girls may think these beds look like any they've seen before, right Jax?"

"Right."

"But they would be wrong, wouldn't they?"

"Yes. They'd be wrong."

"So, girls, you are about to see how unique they are. We'll demonstrate."

Ander sits down on the bottom bunk and Jax climbs up to the top.

"Let's say that I usually sleep down here and Jax usually sleeps up there. One night, I may say to Jax, 'It's not fair that you always get the top bunk. I want a turn.'"

Jax sits up straight. "Then I would say, 'I don't feel like moving my blankets.'"

"Okay, no problem," says Ander. "Let's take the beds for a spin . . ."

Ander pushes a button on the bedpost. The bottom bunk moves out on rails to the right side and the top bunk moves out to the left. Then the bottom bunk slides up to the top spot and the top bunk slides down to the bottom spot.

Ander shouts. "The beds can switch spots!"

"That's so cool!" I exclaim. "Can I try?"

"Me first!" squeals Mare.

Before the boys can protest, Mare and Jillian have pulled Ander off the top bunk and climbed into his spot. Jax looks at me and slowly stands up. I sit down and Ander pushes the button. My feet leave the ground and dangle below me as the beds switch spots again.

Mare laughs, of course. "What team came up with this idea?"

"The Ohio team—four years ago," Seraphina replies.

Ander grins. "This place is awe-some!"

I can't believe the stuff we've seen today. *How will we ever think up something amazing like switching bunk beds and robotic monkeys?* I mangle my thumb nail again.

"Pardon me, ladies," says Gregor, "but it is nearly time for evening announcements, and we must all be secured in our own bedchambers."

"Right," says Seraphina. "We have a big first day tomorrow."

We make plans to meet Ander and Jax in the morning, and when Mare, Jillian, and I get back to our bedchamber, Seraphina reminds us that Swissa will be here to wake us at seven o'clock. I wait for my turn in the bathroom but suddenly all I can think about is sleep. I'm too tired to worry about our solution or to even miss my mom, but I send her a good night message anyway. She sends one back and I promise to call her in the morning.

I wash up as quickly as I can in the purple bathroom, then slip into the star bed full of pillows. My mind jumps around thinking of this fancy bedchamber and the fancy campus and the fancy bus ride that only began this morning. If I can just stay awake until the evening announcements. But just like that, I fall asleep dreaming of Grandma Kitty. I have so many things to tell her about, like blueberry milkshakes, floating sparkles, balloon messages, switching bunk beds . . .

SECRET CREATION

MY EYES FLICKER open. Something is bouncing near my head. I roll over and it's Jillian jumping on the bed—on our star bed.

"Wake up, Kia. Come on, Mare!"

"I'm sleeping," Mare groans and pulls the blanket over her head. I can't pass up a chance for team bonding though, so I scramble out of my own bed and bounce with Jillian. We hop from bed to bed singing Mare's name until she finally crawls out of her blanket cave. "Don't you guys sleep?"

"It's our first day here," says Jillian. "We want you to bounce with us."

"Can't we do it later?"

"Nope!" We grab her by both arms and drag her to a stand. Soon she's bouncing too. Finally, we fall into the heap of pillows in the center of the star.

"You guys stink," she says, her hair covering her face like an old-fashioned mop. "What time is it?"

"Six thirty," I say.

She flips her hair back. "What? Breakfast is at seven-thirty. That only gives us an hour to get ready!"

"It won't take me that long," I say.

"Are you kidding? Didn't you see the boys at dinner yesterday? We might see some today, so we have to look good."

"Where?" I ask.

She looks at me like I just sprouted another head. "Everywhere. Like at breakfast or in the hallways. Come on. Get ready!"

We take turns in the shower and get dressed in shorts, flip flops and the matching blue NY shirts in our cubbies. While I'm waiting for Mare and Jillian to finish, I dig through my backpack for my phone and click on Grandma Kitty's number. Her face smiles back at me.

"Hi, Grandma!"

"Oh, Peanut Butter Cup. I've been dying to hear from you. How is it? Do tell!"

"It's even better than I imagined. I don't know where to start. Our room has sparkles. They purify the air. And our bed is so pretty. And we have this really nice preceptor, Seraphina. And our bus ride was like a movie theater, and I can't even believe it. I feel like we're in another dimension with more surprises every minute!"

"I knew it would be wonderful and amazing and fabulous! So tell me. What is your task about? What category does it come from? Earth and Space? Communications?"

My excitement sinks like an anchor. "All of them."

"All of them? Oh my. That is a different twist."

"Grandma Kitty, it's an impossible twist!"

"Now, don't think like that. Think of it as a chance to show off things you know in all the categories."

"I guess."

"So, I've been wondering, has anyone said anything about your whole team coming from the same school?"

"Well, yesterday one girl said we're famous, and then we met Andora Appelonia, the one who started the camp. She wears this weird bun on her head, and she told us we have an advantage in this competition because we knew each other before we got here."

"Oh, crabapples! You do not have an advantage. I would come right down to that camp and tell her myself if it wasn't against the rules."

"It's okay. We're going to work extra hard so it won't matter anyway."

"That's the spirit. I'm so thrilled you called me. Thank you, Dumpling. Now you go on ahead. I'm sure they have lots of activities planned for today."

"Yes, they do. We have to be at breakfast soon. Bye, Grandma Kitty. Love you!"

"You too, Sugar Plum."

Her face fades away, and I wish I could get her back, but I click on Mom's number instead. She picks up right away, and I hear her calling the rest of my family to the phone. They all squish into the tiny screen. "Hi, Kia!"

"You're all there!"

"How are you, Kia? Did you get settled in okay?" asks Mom.

"Yes! It's amazing here. Wait until you see it."

"So, you're having fun?" asks Dad.

"It's like a fairy tale."

"Your shirt doesn't look like a gown, that's for sure," says Malin.

I look down at the big letters and state map across my shirt. "No, but that's okay. Everything is awesome. I can't wait until you come."

"But Mom said we can't come until the end of camp," Ryne says.

"None of the families can, Ryne—those are the rules. But you can come to the competition in a few weeks and cheer us on."

"Oh, we'll be there," says Dad. "We're counting the days already."

"How's your task?" asks Mom. "Will it be hard?"

"It's impossible! We have to use six categories to solve it."

She laughs. "Well the math portion shouldn't be too hard for you."

"Mom, this competition is not just about math. It's about being good at everything."

"Well that's true but—"

"I am good at other stuff too, you know."

"Of course, I'm just saying you can really focus on using some advanced math strategies to solve the task. That will really show the judges."

She doesn't get it. I huff out a breath.

"Kia, we know you and your teammates will use whatever skills you need to come up with a terrific solution," says Dad.

"I hope so."

"Have fun today, Little Bear."

"I will."

"And call us whenever you want to talk again, okay Kia?"

Mom says.

I doubt I'll want to talk to her again soon, but I don't tell her that. "I will. Bye everyone. I miss you."

"We miss you too. Bye!" Their faces disappear, but I don't mind. I have to stay focused on this camp. I feel bad not wanting to talk to them—especially Mom, but she doesn't really get any of this. Not like Grandma Kitty does.

Mare is doing Jillian's hair in the bathroom. She makes an elaborate braid over the top of her head and down the back. Jillian admires the creation in the mirror and leaps across the room, like she's in a meadow of wild flowers.

We unpack the rest of our suitcases and fill up the extra cubby spots in our closet.

Jillian shoves a colorful skirt into one of hers.

"Is that the skirt you wore yesterday?" I ask her.

"Yes, I made it myself."

"You made it?" asks Mare.

Jillian shoves a pair of shorts in next to the skirt. "Yeah. It was easy."

"Why wouldn't you just buy one?" asks Mare.

"What fun is that?" she replies.

"I think it's pretty," I say.

"Me too," Mare continues. "I just think shopping would be more fun."

"I like shopping too," says Jillian. "Shopping for fabric."

"I've never thought about buying fabric to make clothes," I say. "I wouldn't even know what to do with it." I take out my Golden Light Bulb. "I think we need to find an important place for our Golden Light Bulbs too. How about the windowsill over the sparkle filter?"

They agree, so we arrange our Golden Light Bulbs in a row and stand back to admire them.

"Do you guys think it's weird that all five of us came from Crimson?" I ask.

Jillian sits down in the middle of the floor cross legged. "I don't know. I never thought about it."

Mare sits down next to her. "Me either."

"Well, I think it's weird that all five of us won."

"Why?" asks Jillian.

"I don't know. It's just never happened before. It seems like a big coincidence."

Mare shrugs, but before either of them can respond, we're interrupted by knocking on our door.

Jillian rushes to open it, not quite running, almost floating. She reminds me of a gazelle. A girl appears in the doorway wide awake and smelling like flowers—the same vanilla flowers I smelled on the tree yesterday. "Hi," says Jillian. "We're up already. Are you Swissa?"

Swissa looks startled. She's a teenager, probably Seraphina's age but a lot smaller. "Okay, that's great. I won't have to toss you out of the bed. That saves me a lot of time. Anyway, here are the flowers for your work table. I'll bring more tomorrow."

Jillian takes the vase from her. "We get flowers every day?"

"Yes, that was Seraphina's request for your team. She thinks it will be easier for your creative juices to flow if you have something beautiful to look at while you work."

"You're kidding, right?" asks Mare.

"Nope. I wish I was. I'll be back while you're out of the room to clean up."

"Thank you for the flowers," I say.

She spins around and leaves without saying goodbye.

"So, that's Swissa," Mare says.

"She seems mad," I reply.

"I would be mad too if my job was to clean up all these fancy rooms."

We head down the hall to meet Ander and Jax. They're waiting for us at the bottom of another set of winding stairs. Ander is jumping from the step to the floor, from the floor to the step, and back again.

"What are you doing?" Mare asks.

"We're having a competition to see how many times we can jump back and forth in thirty seconds."

Jax shakes his head. "No, you're having a competition with yourself. I'm just watching."

"Well, I hope you won then," I say to Ander as I walk toward the dining hall.

He catches up to me. "Oh, I did. No one even came close!"

AT THE entrance to the dining hall, we swipe our meal cards through the reader and each take a tray. There's a boy in front of me loading up his plate with something mushy. "Cool," he says. "Scrambled Apples."

"Scrambled Apples?" I scrunch my nose.

"They're a camp tradition, I guess. I gotta try them."

"Me too, then." I plop a scoop onto my plate.

"There's peppermint in there," he says. I look at him, and he's grinning. I try not to melt into the floor. I'm starting to see what Mare was talking about when she said there were cute boys here. Maybe I should have spent more time getting ready like she did.

"I'm Johab from Colorado. What about you?"

"I'm Kia, from New York."

"Do you live near the Statue of Liberty?"

"No, that's about six hours away from my house, but I've seen it. In fact, I dressed up like it one year for Halloween. My costume was kind of babyish but I didn't care. I'll wear anything with a crown."

He squints and moves down the line.

Wow. Maybe he doesn't like Halloween. Whatever. I don't care what he thinks of me anyway. I'm going to kick his butt in the finals no matter how cute he is.

I take some pancakes and pour steaming syrup over them, but once we're at our table, I try the scrambled apples first. The peppermint slides down my throat, warm and sweet. I decide not to bother with my pancakes after all and go back for another two scoops.

We've just finished eating when Seraphina appears at our table. "Hey it's my Crimson Kids! I see you've tried our famous Scrambled Apples."

Ander leans back in his chair. "Those are outstanding."

"You can thank Andora for them. They're her secret creation. But if you're finished eating, we can head out to meet Gregor. He's reserved a private room down the hall for our first team meeting."

"Finally!" Ander jumps out of his seat. "I was wondering when we'd get to the good stuff."

"Me too!" I hurry to the counter to clear my tray, but as I walk away, I can feel someone staring at me. I turn around and see the witch girl from the check-in line yesterday. She's sitting at the table from Michigan. I pass by her on the way back again, but she doesn't look away. In fact, she stretches her head to follow me as I catch up to my team. *That's really weird. She knows I saw her watching me. Why doesn't she look away? No one keeps looking when they're caught staring.*

CRIMSON ADVANTAGE

GREGOR IS PACING when we arrive at Meeting Room Twelve, a large room on the first floor of Piedmont Chamber. When he sees us he stops and stands like an eagle, hands on his hips. His blond, spiky hair scares me. "We've reserved this room for only one hour so we must get to work."

I sit down at the table next to Jillian.

Gregor places his hands on the edge of it. "Now that we know the task you've been given, we must explain the rules for creating your solution."

"And then can we start working?" Ander asks.

Gregor looks at him, annoyed. "This will take a while."

Seraphina passes out packets that contain a description of our task, a list of the rules, and the scoring system.

Gregor speaks in a slow voice. "Rule number 1: No outer team influence. Any ideas that are discussed must be your own. Any work must be your own. In other words, no one else outside of the team may give ideas or assist you in any way. The task must be completed in its entirety by the five teammates and no one else. If the judges feel your team was assisted, you will receive a penalty. The amount will be determined by the judges as indicated in the scoring section of your packet."

Ander sits up. "So you and Seraphina can't help us at all?"

"No, we may not."

"Can you make suggestions?"

"No."

I lean on my elbows. "So the five of us have to come up with a way to complete the task by ourselves and do all the work ourselves?"

"Yes, that is correct."

"What if you gave us a suggestion anyway and we use it?" asks Mare.

"We won't do that. We've taken an oath that we will assist you in other ways like helping you gather supplies, scheduling meeting times, and keeping you focused on your work. The rest is up to you."

"What if we can't agree on a way to solve the task?" Jillian asks.

"That is part of the challenge you face."

"Rule 2: You must follow the camp schedule we give you. We will have set times for work, breaks, meals, and activities. You are required to be on time for every event. No exceptions. You will receive your schedule in your bedchambers each day."

Ander wiggles in his chair. "How long will our breaks be?"

"That depends on the day and what you are working on."

"But will we have time for any fun? I brought my hockey bag."

"This camp will be your fun."

I stare at Ander. He must not be scared of Gregor at all. "Yeah, I know, but we can't work all the time. Will we have time to play tag or ghost in the graveyard or anything?"

Mare giggles.

"Like I said, you *will* have breaks."

Ander slides down in his seat.

Gregor walks around the table. "Rule 3: This is not an official rule, and it does not apply to every team. Only yours. The fact is this: Your team will be more closely watched than any other team in this competition. All eyes will be on you because you all come from the same school."

Ander jumps up from his chair.

Gregor holds out his hand. "Before you explode, please hear me out. It may not be fair that the judges expect more from you. We know that you didn't know each other before this competition, but team spirit is a large part of this competition. It takes most teams a long time to feel at ease around each other. The best teams are able to work together and inspire each other. The judges may score you more harshly because they feel you already had that advantage."

"But we didn't," Ander insists.

"We know," says Seraphina. "But we can't change their minds."

"So there's no way we can win," says Mare.

"Not true," says Gregor. "We feel you can use this as an

opportunity."

"How?" asks Jillian.

Seraphina smiles. "You all come from the same school. That makes your team special. All you have to do is show everyone why that is."

"I don't understand what you mean," Jillian grabs her hair and twists it tight.

"You simply need to create something that will showcase your special team."

"Isn't that breaking the rules?" I say. "I thought you can't tell us what to do?"

Gregor stiffens. "That is called coaching. Of course that is allowed. Now, turn to page three. Here you'll see a detailed description of your task. Please read it through, and when you have finished, Seraphina and I will answer your questions."

Ander flips the page over and groans. "We have to read all of this? When do we get to start working on our task?"

Seraphina smiles. "How can you start working without first knowing the details of the task?"

Ander shrugs and looks down at his packet.

I read through every single page devouring the words. When I finish, I turn back to the first page and read the summary of the task again.

Our home, the Earth, is shaped like a circle.

Your task is to create an object that transforms three times into something else, and then transforms back to its original position . . . creating a circle effect. The object you create must answer a question that is universally asked, but has not yet been answered by mankind. Your solution must include elements from each of the six academic categories and one original language. Your presentation to the judges may not exceed twelve minutes.

Seraphina flips over the packet. "Okay, then. Any questions?"

"I have one," says Jillian. "How do we make up our own language?"

Gregor responds. "You must use the creative side of your brain."

"That sounds hard," says Mare.

"That sounds fun," says Ander. "Maybe we can talk like aliens from Mars."

I sit up in my chair. "Or we could talk like roosters that just came out of the ocean, riding on an underwater bubble bike!"

"Or maybe we come up with something more mature than that," Mare replies.

I slouch back down in my seat.

"Can the object be made out of anything?" asks Jax.

I look down the table at him. He's been so quiet, I almost forgot he was here.

His face turns red. "You know, the object that has to transform three times and then transform again to its original position."

"Yes, Jax," Gregor replies. "You may use any material as long as it does not contain anything deemed explosive or dangerous."

I scoot my chair closer to the table. "It says here we have to present the solution of the task to the judges. But how? Do we write a report and then read it to the judges during the twelve minutes?"

Seraphina spreads her purple nail polish fingers on the

table. "That's for your team to decide."

"That's too boring," says Ander.

I tuck my foot underneath me. "I think so too."

Ander springs up from his chair. "What if we do a play?"

I think for a second. "That could be good. Maybe we'll get extra points for being original."

"No way," says Mare. "I don't perform in front of other people."

"I don't mind," says Jillian. "We'd get to play someone that we're not."

"I bet Jax doesn't want to," Mare says, boring her eyes into his. "Do you, Jax?"

Jax looks away. "I don't care."

"You would do a play?" she challenges him.

His face turns into a cherry again. "I guess so."

Mare scowls. "We have to create an object, not a Broadway play. I vote no."

Ander taps his fingers on the table. "Well, if all of us want to do a play then you have to do it—majority rules."

"That's not fair," says Mare. "I won't do it."

Seraphina holds up her hand. "It may be too early for a team vote. Why don't you think up a few more ideas first?"

"Thank you!" Mare snarls, smirking at the rest of us.

Gregor closes his packet. "Our time has expired. We will gather again here in Meeting Room Twelve for our afternoon session."

I pick at the skin around my pointer finger. I don't want to take a break.

Seraphina stands up. "Well, I guess we can discuss this again later."

"Where do we go now?" asks Ander.

"We go to the Team Building Room down the hall. Our

session starts in fifteen minutes. You are excused until then. Please be prompt."

We pour out of Meeting Room Twelve and into the living room outside the Appelonia Dining Hall. Mare and Jillian fall into the couch. I sit in the chair next to them.

"What do you guys think about our task?" I ask. I'm starting to think the hardest part is getting all of us to agree.

Jillian smiles. "It's better than I hoped for. I can't wait to start working on the language part. We could make up our own handshake or invent our own way of moving—kind of like the sound beams on Jax and Ander's wall."

Hmm. That's a good idea. Maybe I've underestimated her.

"I bet we can think of something better than a play," says Mare.

Why can't she just like the play idea? "Like what?"

"I don't know yet. I'm sure I'll think of something though."

"Well, I think it's a good idea." I'm trying to be nice but working with teammates is hard.

When the boys get up, we follow them down the hall and find Seraphina and Gregor waiting in the doorway. "Come on in," Seraphina says. "This room is where we'll work on your team building skills."

"Team building skills. What for?" Mare crosses her arms.

"Since you'll solve your task as a team, it's important to learn to work together, so let's get to our first exercise. I want all of you to stand in a circle facing each other."

We do as she instructs, rearranging ourselves two or three times, trying to figure out who we should stand next to.

"It won't matter who you stand beside for this activity."

We stop shuffling and I end up between Jax and Jillian.

"Now reach across the circle with your right hand to the person across from you. Grab their right hand. Next, take your left hand and reach across for the left hand of a different person who's not standing next to you."

I look across the circle and take Ander's hand with my right, and Mare's hand with my left. Everyone else chooses hands too.

"Your team has formed a human pretzel. Your task is to untangle yourselves in under three minutes without letting go of the hands you're holding. To successfully untangle, you'll end up in a circle, holding onto the hands of each person next to you, without your arms crossed."

"Oh, man," Ander laughs. "This'll be cool."

"First, the rules: You must not let go of your partners' hands. Your team will have failed the task if you do. Also, you must use positive phrases to encourage your teammates. Your three minutes starts now."

We immediately lift our hands and take turns crawling under and over arms. When we're stuck, Jillian says, "Here, Ander, I'll lower my arm, you climb over it."

He tries, but Mare's arm pulls on mine almost out of the socket. "Ouch! No. I can't bend it that far."

"This is impossible." Mare rolls her eyes. "It's never going to work."

"We can do it," Ander says, his voice full of authority. "What if I crawl over Jax's arm and then Jillian's right here?"

"No," I say. "Jax, you have to lift your arm. Then Mare can go under."

He does and Mare crawls through. Jillian twists around.

Soon, we're more tangled than ever. My right arm is twisted and stuck over Jax's head. I'm facing the outside of the circle but my left hand is pulled behind my back.

"I told you. This can't work," says Mare.

Ander lets out a loud breath. "What if Jax turns around and Kia pulls her right arm under Jillian."

I try that but Mare cries out. "My arm!"

Jax pulls his arm and let's his hand break free of Jillian's.

"No!" Jillian cries.

"Aw, Jax!" Ander yells.

Jax turns red. "I'm sorry, I didn't mean to let go. My hand slipped."

I feel bad. He looks like he might cry.

"It's alright," says Jillian. "I couldn't hold on either."

"We stunk at that one," Ander sighs.

"Not so," says Seraphina. She puts an arm over Jax's shoulder. "It takes a while to learn how to work as a team. We'll try it again another time."

We complete two more team building tasks almost like the Human Pretzel before we stop for lunch. I can tell Jax doesn't like doing them, and Mare thinks they're stupid. So much for team building. Whatever—if we don't start planning our solution, our team will be going home right after the finals anyway.

I examine my nail stubs. Seraphina says we have an advantage but I'm not so sure about that. How can we convince the judges our team is special when we can't even work our way out of a simple pretzel?

BRAINSTORM

I MUST BE in the wrong room, but this has to be Meeting Room Twelve. It's the same place we met this morning except for the flying cloud tunnels, climbing cubes, and airborne trampolines. What the heck? Meeting Room Twelve is a like a space playground!

Seraphina and Gregor stand in the corner whispering. I want to jump on the trampolines, but I'm not sure if we're allowed to. I look at Ander and he looks at me. We make a break for it at the same time. We leap onto a swirly ladder and race for the platform, but when we take our first jump, it tosses us across the room onto bean bag looking blobs.

Mine wiggles, then bounces me so high I can see the fluffy insides of the cloud tunnels. "Come on, guys! This cloud smells like toothpaste."

"Kia, how'd you do that?" Ander tries to lift his blob, but instead it spins at warp speed like the food flowers in the dining hall. "Whoa!" he screams with his cheeks spread flat across his face.

Seraphina strolls over, smiling. "Like the Brainstorming Room?" She pushes a button and Ander's blob suddenly halts. I drop to the ground and my stomach sinks, but not from the bouncing. This whole room is unbelievable, probably full of inventions made by last year's winning team. How can we think up something this good for the finals? I bite my thumbnail and stare at Ander, Mare, Jillian, and Jax. I wonder if they're freaking out inside too.

Ander grins. "That was awesome! What *is* all this stuff?"

"This is the solution that won seven years ago. The team from North Dakota designed a collection of playground equipment using invisible springs and environmentally safe materials. We brought them in while you were having lunch at the dining hall."

I knew it! Those kids must have been geniuses. I bet they moved onto the Global Championships and then went to PIPS. I bite my ring finger nail. We really have to start working now. I'm *not* going to be happy if we waste this meeting playing around.

Seraphina walks around the equipment like a game show host. "Here at Camp Piedmont, we believe a child's imagination is always present, but as we get older, we forget how to let the creative parts of our brains take over and simply have fun. Some of the best ideas are born when you allow yourself to act like a child, like the child you were in kindergarten. Do you guys think you can act like kindergarten children this afternoon?"

"I can do that!" Ander says and springs to his feet.

Seraphina smiles, shaking her head.

"Me too," I say. I really do want to play, but this idea

better work.

"Sure," smiles Jillian. Her eyes are practically twinkling.

"What about you, Mare? Are you up for some kid time?"

She smoothes out her hair and smirks. "Yup." She says it like she thinks she can have fun way better than the rest of us. No chance!

"Jax?"

He straightens up in his bean bag. "Sure, I'll play if you want me to."

"Well," whispers Mare. "If he plays as well as he talks, we're doomed."

I glare at her. *I can't believe she just said that!*

Jax looks over at the climbing cube and I consider making a joke out of what she said or something, but maybe he didn't hear her. I hope not anyway.

We spend the next half hour playing our own version of tag. We make up a game using a yellow pole at the end of the room. Ander is *it,* and the rest of us have to scatter away from him and try to reach the pole without him catching us. I race through the cubes, down the slide, over the swings. I hide under the clouds, inside the cubes, and on top of the trampolines.

"Come on, Kia Krumpet," Ander dares me. "Run for the pole!"

I bounce on the trampoline and aim for the yellow pole. I stumble a few steps away and graze it just as Ander dives for my ankle.

"I got you!" he yells and rolls back up to his feet.

"No way!" I say before Seraphina calls us back to the bouncing blobs. By the time our play time has ended, I've learned that Jax doesn't run very fast but somehow finds ways to trick Ander. Mare squeals a lot. Jillian comes up with the best hiding places and Ander likes to be in charge. That's pretty good information for just one game!

Seraphina pushes a button on a remote control. A door to a low cabinet in the corner opens up. Mabel, the robotic monkey rolls out and zooms over to us. She stops in the center of our circle.

"Cool!" says Ander. "What's that?"

Seraphina smiles. "Hello again, Mabel. Please deliver the cards."

The side panel on her body opens up and five cards slide onto the floor. Mabel picks them up with her robotic hand and passes one out to each of us.

The Crimson Five:
Be Curious, Be Creative, Be Collaborative, Be Colorful,
Be Courageous.

I look down at my wrist. "That's the same message that's written on our wrist bands."

"That's right, Kia," says Seraphina. "These are the very words I had engraved on them. As you think of ways to solve your task, be mindful of what those words really mean because each one will lead you to achieve something amazing."

"What does *collaborative* mean?" asks Mare.

"*To collaborate* means to work together."

"To use teamwork, right?" I say, sitting up straighter.

"That's right," Seraphina answers.

"Then what about *colorful?*" asks Jillian.

"That's my favorite one," says Seraphina.

Ander points to Seraphina's shoes. "Obviously, it means to wear your favorite color. You wear purple all the time."

Seraphina laughs. "Good guess—but no."

"You want us to pick a color to identify ourselves?" he continues.

"Not exactly. When I say *be colorful*, it means that I want you to be memorable."

"What does that mean?" asks Mare.

"I want you to make yourselves known. You're extraordinary kids. Don't stay in the background. Make the judges remember you."

Make the judges remember you.

"I think *Curious, Creative, and Courageous* are pretty self-explanatory, but I think we should talk about them anyway. First, when you think of being curious, I want you to think of the word 'wonder.' It's good to wonder what something is about or what something would be like if you used it in a different way. It's good to be curious about any part of the task in front of you; it's good to wonder. It's good to ask questions too, and Gregor and I will always encourage you to do so. Does that make sense?"

I nod, and my teammates do too.

"Next, when you think about what it takes to be creative, think of making something new or unique. Think of finding a special way of doing something you've done hundreds of times before. The key to achieving greatness is being creative—in other words, creating something only you can, something special."

"Lastly, let's talk about what it means to have courage."

"Well, courage means to be brave," says Ander.

"It does," says Seraphina. "There will be times during this competition when you need to be courageous or brave, like when you're competing for the judges. But there's another way you need to be courageous, and it will happen when you're working on your solution to the Piedmont

Task."

"What do you mean?" I ask.

"In the weeks to come, when you're working, trying to create something special and unique, it will get difficult. There will be times when you want to give up or at least conform—do things the way they've always been done, take the easy way out. But that's when you need to be at your most courageous—have courage to push yourselves to create something special and unique. Being courageous is the opposite of what it means to conform."

Courageous is the opposite of conform.

"Do you have any questions so far?"

None of us do so she continues. "Okay, so now you know why the skills on your wristbands are important to use when solving the task."

She presses a button on the wall, and a red screen rolls down. She speaks the word, "BRAINSTORMING." White letters pop onto the screen. "Now that we've talked about your wristbands, I want to move on to something else . . . Brainstorming. Have any of you tried this before?"

We shake our heads.

"Okay. Let me explain. Brainstorming is a great tool for a group to use when they have a problem to solve together. Remember the game of tag you just invented using the yellow pole? That was great collaboration and very creative. Now, I want your entire team to come up with ideas for solving the Piedmont task in the same way. No idea is bad—in fact, all ideas are important. Something you say may turn out to be the idea that's chosen by the team, or it may be something that reminds your teammate of another idea—an even better one. It doesn't matter whose ideas are chosen. You're a team now. Your idea is the team's idea. The important thing during a brainstorming session is to keep the ideas flowing and also to include everyone. So, please be respectful of your teammate's right to speak. When you have an idea, simply say it and the brainstorm board will record it."

"I have an idea," Jillian calls out, but then leans back in her chair. "Wait. Never mind."

"It's okay, Jillian. All ideas are worth sharing."

"I don't want everyone to think it's stupid."

"We won't," says Ander.

Wow. Ander is really nice.

Jillian looks down. "No, it's okay."

"Okay," says Seraphina. "Maybe you can tell the group later—when you're ready. Anyone else?"

"For the object that rotates, what if we use a giant hockey puck?" asks Ander.

His idea is recorded on the screen.

I tuck both my feet under me. "Can we add the idea about doing a play?"

The word *play* is recorded.

We continue calling ideas out and before long we have a screen full of words and phrases.

"This is a good start," Seraphina says, staring at the screen for a second. "Now, I want you to read through your list silently. See if anything there leads you to think of another idea, something you can add."

Jillian spins her wristband. "I remember my idea. It's about the original language. Maybe we could make up a handshake or way of moving or something."

"Nice," says Seraphina.

The screen records her idea.

Mare snaps her gum. "Can we talk about the play idea?

I don't want to do one."

I lean my head back. Here we go *again*.

Jillian turns to her. "But Mare, I bet no one else will do a play. And we can even make really amazing costumes."

"And write a script," I say.

Ander jumps out of his bean bag. "We could build sets and scenery too. Couldn't we, Jax?"

"Yes. I'm sure we could figure out how to do that. We'd use math for measuring."

"Oh, right," says Ander. "We have to use skills from each of the six categories to solve this thing, so at least math would be covered. Good thinking, Buddy."

Jax turns red. Of course.

"I don't care about any of that," Mare says. "I'm not going to get up in front of a bunch of people and make a fool of myself."

I shake my head. "Why not?"

Mare scowls. "Because."

"What difference does it make?"

"I'm terrible in front of crowds. I don't see why we have to anyway."

I jump out of my bean bag too. "That's what will help us win! If we can perform our task like a play, we'll get extra points for sure."

"How do you know?"

"My Grandma Kitty won the Piedmont Challenge when she was in sixth grade. She's always telling me that to win this competition you have to give the judges something they won't expect. If we read about our solution in a report like everyone else, we'll get average points, but if we can turn our solution into a play, the judges will see we're extra creative."

"Yeah," says Ander. "We can wear crazy costumes if we want to, too."

"Yes!" At least someone here thinks like I do. "We can act like creatures from another galaxy, with flowers growing out of our skin or something."

Mare looks at me like I'm the one from another galaxy. "I don't want to wear some embarrassing, ugly costume, say stupid lines, and make a fool of myself."

Mare just doesn't get it. "You don't want flowers growing out of your skin?" I ask her. Now I don't even care if she gets annoyed at me.

Ander shrugs. "I'd want flowers growing out of my skin. Especially dandelions. You can eat those."

Mare glares at both of us.

I realize making her mad is not going to convince her. "Mare, you don't have to wear a weird costume or say embarrassing lines. We'll write our own script. We can give each other lines we really want to say."

Ander picks up his bean bag chair. "And I can say all the stupid stuff. I don't mind making a fool of myself—especially if I get most of the lines."

Mare does not look convinced.

"Come on, Mare, please," I beg.

"Yeah," says Jillian. "It'll be fun. I promise."

Mare sits there stone-faced. "Nope. I guess we better brainstorm more ideas."

I look at Seraphina. She doesn't say anything; she just shrugs.

Are you kidding me? Why isn't she making Mare agree with us? I hate this. Brainstorming stinks.

RED BOARD

AFTER THE BEST sleep ever in my star bed, we go to the top floor of Piedmont Chamber for a workshop called *Re-imagine It*. We learn ways to take garbage items like candy wrappers and turn them into something new. We clean them up, rub a gel over them, cut, glue, sew, and tape them together, and soon we've made baby clothes and blankets! The Twix and Hershey bars become blankets and M&M wrappers become colorful skirts. I never thought of using wrappers to make clothes. I definitely would have added that to my invention list.

We finish and walk down to Meeting Room Twelve wearing our matching white T-shirts. I like wearing the same shirts. It makes me feel like my teammates and I belong to a special club. Except maybe Mare. If she wore a different color, like black or something, I wouldn't really mind.

Seraphina sits at the table with us as we brainstorm again. Gregor listens in the corner.

"I know how we can agree on this," says Ander.

"How?" asks Mare.

"Well, since four of us want to do a play for the judges but you really don't want to, maybe you don't have to act in it."

"But we all have to be part of solving the problem."

"We will be. What if you worked behind the scenes? You could move the sets around. You wouldn't have to say anything in front of anyone."

Mare scowls. "But I could design the sets and paint them?"

"Yup," says Ander.

"And I could help make the costumes and write the script?"

"Sure," he says.

"But I wouldn't perform?"

"Nope."

"So I'd do all the work and then just sit around like a loser while all of you get the credit? No thanks. Your idea *stinks*."

"Mare!" I shout.

"What? It does. I'm not doing that."

"Why are you being such a jerk?" I ask.

"Kia," says Seraphina. Her face tells me I crossed a line of some sort.

Everyone stares at me and my face feels hot. "I'm sorry. I just think Ander came up with a good compromise."

"Well, he didn't, because I already told you I won't do it."

I let out a breath.

"I guess we have to come up with another idea, right Seraphina?"

I watch her. I'm sure this time she's going to tell Mare she has to go along with our idea.

"That's right, Mare. If you need more brainstorming time then you may have it."

"What?" I shout.

"That's not fair!" says Ander. "It's four to one. Majority rules."

"No, it doesn't," says Seraphina. "The team rules."

"Are you kidding me?" I say. "This is impossible. There's no way we're all going to agree on a way to solve this task. We're just wasting time. If we have any chance of winning, we have to start working!"

"She's right," says Ander.

"Well, Mare's right too," says Jillian. "Her opinion matters as much as ours does. We have to come up with an idea we all agree on."

"Thanks a lot, Jillian," I mumble. I bite my pointer finger and then my thumb. I hate Mare.

Gregor paces the room with his hands folded behind him. I can't tell if he's bored or ready to explode.

"Okay then," says Seraphina. "How else can you present your solution? Does anyone have another suggestion?"

I prop my elbows on the table. Ander slumps in his seat.

"What if we write a documentary?" asks Jax.

"A what?" asks Jillian.

"We could make a movie, only none of us has to act in front of the camera. We could write a report and then take turns narrating pages. That way none of us has to say anything in front of the judges. We just play the video."

The red board records his idea.

"It might work," says Jillian. "The judges would see our technology skills."

I shrug. I don't even want to acknowledge his idea. I feel like falling asleep just thinking about it. Mare doesn't say anything either. Maybe I just don't *want* to like this idea because I really want to do a play . . . but that's not it. A documentary won't get us to the Global Championships. No way.

"Okay, what else?" asks Seraphina.

Jillian taps her pencil. "This idea is sort of like Jax's, but what if we wrote a book? We could tell our solution like a story and then take turns reading it to the judges."

"Or we could make a picture album," says Mare. "We could take pictures of all the parts of our solution—or even draw them and then display them in a giant album."

My teammates nod their heads. But none of us are smiling. None of us are jumping out of our seats. The ideas appear on the red board anyway.

"Anything else?" No one answers. Seraphina looks at her nails. Her once perfect purple nail polish is starting to chip.

Ander jumps from his seat and walks around the table. "Okay, guys. Obviously none of us are excited about these other ideas. A play is the only way to surprise the judges. We want to be memorable, don't we? Isn't that what Seraphina said about being colorful? Mare, can't you just agree to do it? You won't look like a loser. I promise. We'll write our script however you want us to so you don't hate your lines and don't look like an idiot."

I plead with Mare inside my head.

She stares at Ander. He stares back. His big blue eyes don't blink. He's pleading inside his head too. I can tell.

I chew on my pinky.

She waves her hand at him. "Whatever, I'll do it."

Yes!

"You will?" asks Ander.

"But only because the other ideas are stupid. I'm getting bored talking about it."

Ander shrugs. "Okay then. Cool. We're doing a play!"

Finally, we're getting somewhere.

"As long as you all promise we'll have enough time to rehearse."

We agree, and Seraphina jots down notes. Mare and Jillian get up from the table to talk about costumes. Ander and Jax get ready to talk about what object can transform. I stare at the table. I realize that before we can figure out what sets and costumes to make, we need to know what the play is going to be about.

"Hold on a second," I say. "The task states we have to answer a question that all of mankind has been asking but, before now, has not been answered. So, don't we have to decide on the question before we decide the rest?"

Ander comes back to the table. "Oh yeah, that would help."

Again, we call out suggestions while the red board records what we say. After about twenty ideas, we come up with our top three questions.

"Okay," Seraphina says. "This is what we have so far."

Three questions appear on the screen.

1. Is there life on Jupiter?

2. What happens to us after we die?

3. When will the world end?

"Let's start with number one. Would any of you like to

choose, *Is there life on Jupiter?*"

None of us raise our hands.

"Then how about number two? *What happens after we die?*"

All of us, except Ander, raise our hands.

Mare smiles. "Majority rules. Number two wins!"

"Hold on," says Jillian. "Ander still hasn't voted."

"Well, obviously he wants number three," says Mare.

"Well, can't he at least vote?"

Mare shrugs. Ander grins.

Seraphina waves her pointer. "Okay, then onto number three. Would anyone like to do, *When will the world end?*"

Ander raises his hand, but then pulls it back down. "I want to do that one, but I don't mind if we do number two. That one would be cool too."

"Okay, good!" I exclaim. "Our question is: "What happens to humans after they die?"

Gregor walks over to the table. "That's the question you've decided on?"

I sit up straight. "Yes, isn't it a great one?"

Gregor doesn't smile. He presses his lips together instead. *Doesn't he like our idea?* Oh, who cares—we've decided, and it's a good one, so that's all I care about.

BUTTERFLY BRAINS

THE NEXT MORNING, I sit in the dining hall, shaping my scrambled apples into a circle. My teammates are talking about something, but all I can think about is how unfair it is that we have to solve this task using all six categories.

"Kia, what's wrong?" asks Jillian. "Why are you so quiet?" Her hair is pulled over one shoulder into a fishtail braid.

"The teams who competed all the other years only had to use skills from one category to solve their task. Like Colorado, the team who made the floating air purification sparkles. They had to use what they knew about Earth and Space to solve that problem and I'm pretty sure the team from Tennessee who built Mabel only had to use information from their New Technology class. It stinks that we have to use all six."

"I don't think it's a big deal."

"Why not? It's going to take us forever to include skills from all six. I think we should ask Master Freeman to change the rules or something."

"Kia! Are you crazy? He'll think we're lazy or not smart enough to figure it out."

"I am *not* lazy!"

Jillian's eyes get big. "I didn't say you were lazy. I just don't think you should complain to him. We have to work harder, that's all. We can figure it out."

Now I feel stupid for saying it. I'm not afraid of extra hard work. That's what got me to this camp in the first place. Besides, I don't want anyone thinking I'm not smart enough to be here. "I'm sorry. I'm just nervous."

"That's okay. I am too."

"You are?"

Jillian quick looks over at Mare like she's afraid she'll hear what she's about to say. But Mare's talking to the boys, not even listening to us.

"Well, yeah," she says. "I want to win just as bad as you do."

I think about that for a second. Jillian never looks worried about anything. I mean I can tell she likes being here, and really wants to do a play, but I never thought about why she would want to win or if she was worried we wouldn't. "Are you afraid to get programmed?"

Her mouth turns into a frown. "Yeah. I'm probably going to be put into Earth and Space. I always score the highest in that category, but I really want to be put into Art Forms. At least if I win and enroll at PIPS, I'd get to work on some artistic stuff. It would be better than Earth and Space, that's for sure."

I smile and her frown disappears. It's nice knowing she

really wants to win like I do.

We walk down the hall to Meeting Room Twelve with the rest of our team. The same chair I've sat in all week is waiting for me. I'm glad I only have to sit in it for a few minutes though. Seraphina doesn't mind if we sit on the floor or even on the table.

We've already decided on the theme for our play—ghosts! We agree that if we're trying to answer the question, *Where do humans go after they die?* then using ghosts as tour guides will be perfect. We've decided who our characters will be too, and now we're working on what our play could be about.

After our morning meeting, Gregor leads us on a jog around Piedmont University. Ander tries to run ahead but Gregor won't let him. When we get to the pond at the far end of campus, we climb onto a pile of rocks. Gregor says that fresh air and exercise encourage a creative mind. I think he's right. The breeze has filled my head with lots of ideas about our play. So have the butterflies fluttering near me.

If only our team could fly to heaven, then we could spy on the dead people and know for sure if that's where they went—because maybe it isn't heaven. Every single person in this whole world wants to know what will happen to them after they die, and I think I know why we all want to know—because we're scared. Maybe if we knew, then we wouldn't be scared at all.

My brain swirls in fast motion. Maybe we could invent a robot like Mabel who could travel with a dead person and give us the answer. Maybe we could capture a dead person's spirit and analyze it under a microscope. Or we could analyze a dead person's cells under it instead. My ideas are swirling in my brain. As soon as I think of a new one, I forget the old one. I feel like a pinball machine. I could really use a brain organizer.

When our break is over, Gregor leads us on the run back. Seraphina instructs us to work in small groups in our bedchambers until lunch. Mare and Jillian want to start planning costumes. The boys want to plan the sets. I want to do both, but I decide to work with Ander and Jax. We have to come up with an awesome backdrop for our play and there's no way I'm going to miss this part. Besides, Ander will probably take too many breaks, so I think I need to make sure that he doesn't.

When we step into the boys' bedchamber, the laser board jumps to life, and the beams rearrange themselves. It startles me every time I speak. Ander says I'm jumpy. I'm not jumpy. I'm just not used to laser creatures flying around every time I make a sound.

Jax sits down at the planning table and folds his hands. I want to remind him there are no teachers here—he can relax a little bit, but then I wonder, *maybe he can't relax. Maybe he's nervous around us. Maybe that's why he doesn't ever talk unless he has to.* I sit across from him and try my best to not be scary or hard to talk to.

Ander grabs his notebook from the bin and puts one foot on the chair. "Okay, Big Guy, what kind of set should we build?"

Jax shifts in his seat.

Ander tilts his head. "Come on. We want to hear your idea. What do you think?"

"You want to hear what *I* think?"

"Yeah," I say. "Why wouldn't we?"

Jax turns red. "I'm not used to people listening to me."

"How come?" Ander asks.

Jax looks down at the table. "I guess I figure since I'm quiet people don't want to hear what I have to say. But I guess maybe I don't give them the chance."

I smile as big as I can. "Well, now you have the chance to say whatever you want."

Jax lets out a breath, like he's been holding it in his whole life. "We could make a back drop like they do in theaters. The frame could be made out of metal, and we could hang fabric from the top like curtains."

"It would have to be big though," Ander replies.

"We can make it as big as we want."

I try to imagine a large, curtain-like backdrop. "That would look good, I guess. I mean it's a great idea, Jax. But is that as creative as we can get?"

"I don't know," he replies.

I feel an idea ready to burst. "What if we build a set that moves or something instead?"

"Yes!" Ander points to me. "It could spin or change shape."

"Exactly! The whole point of the play is to answer the question of where people go after they die. What if our set is the object that rotates?"

Jax looks confused. "I'm not sure I understand."

"We can use our set to show examples of where humans go after they die."

"Yeah," says Ander. "We could build a set that turns into a coffin!"

"Or the boxes the Egyptian Pharaohs used to be put in for all of eternity," I say.

"Right!" he shouts. "That could be the object that rotates. But, since none of us is exactly sure where people go after we die, we have to show where we *think* they go—or where the ghosts *think* they go."

Jax pulls the printed copy of the task out of the bin and flips through to the description page. "The task states that we need to build an object that changes three times and then goes back to its original place—in the form of a circle. I don't see how we can make the object our set."

"We already know we're going to show ghosts giving a dead person a tour of choices—where they can go after they die," I say.

"And," says Ander, "the rules don't say it has to be an actual circle. What if the ghosts use a giant object to show the different places dead people could go? Like . . . we could make a big rectangular box. The first side could show all three choices, like a gallery or something, then the next side could show the first choice, a casket that gets buried in the ground."

"And then it could rotate to the next side—a giant oven where your body gets cremated and sprinkled throughout the air," I say.

Ander walks near the sound board. The lasers are freaking out. "And then it could switch to the last side which is the third choice . . . a rocket that sends your body into space!"

"Yes! That's perfect!" I answer, walking around the room in circles, resisting the urge to jump up on Ander's bed. This is going to be so great!

Jax is finally smiling too. "But it has to go back to its original spot at the end."

"Okay," says Ander. "At the end, it can rotate back to the first side with all the picture choices. That's when the dead person-ghost makes his decision."

"'That would be awesome!" I squeal.

"What do you think, Jax? Do you like that idea?"

"Yes, and I think the judges would like it."

"I like it," says Ander.

"Me too!" I say. "None of the teams will create a rotating set and a play. I know they won't."

We high-five each other and check the clock on the wall. It's almost lunch time. The boys and I make a run for it through the halls of Piedmont Chamber to meet Mare and Jillian. When we enter the dining hall, Jillian runs over and drags us to the table.

"Okay, so Mare and I planned the materials we need to make costumes, all of them creepy and ghost-like. Jax you're the serious ghost guide. Mare is his ghostly assistant. I am the dramatic ghost. Ander you're the silly ghost, and Kia, you're the little ghost girl, new to the after-life, who must choose a way to spend eternity. What do you guys think?"

"Oh! I love it," I say. "That's perfect!"

"Awesome," says Ander. "I can be silly, weird, and strange."

"I'm fine with that too," says Jax.

"Okay, good," says Jillian. "We were hoping you'd all agree."

We reach the New York table where Mare is waiting. "We like the character ideas, and the boys and I figured out the set," I say. "It can be our rotating object that shows all the places a ghost could go to spend eternity. We were thinking a coffin, a crematory oven thingy, and a rocket ship that sends your body to space. What do you guys think?"

"I like it," says Jillian.

"Me too," says Mare. "But I want to be the one to show the ghost girl the oven thing and since I gave in on the play idea, I get my way with this."

I want to roll my eyes but I don't.

"Fine," says Ander. "I call the rocket ship!"

"Then I'll show the coffin," says Jillian, "And Jax, you can show all the choices at the end, since you're like the head ghost."

He nods and we end up all talking at the same time. I can't tell who's the most excited about their character. Through the chatter, I picture myself as a little ghost in a ragged costume. I'm twirling around, looking at my choices for the after-life. I twirl and twirl and that's when I figure out what to choose. Soon though, I snap out of my daydream and look around the room at all the other teams talking and eating their lunches too. For the first time, I don't feel so overwhelmed. *We're going to ace this task. I just know it!*

NACHO CHEESE BALL

THAT NIGHT AFTER dinner, my teammates and I, stuffed
with raviolis and garlic bread, walk out to the college square
across from the entrance to Piedmont Chamber. The white
pillars on the buildings make it look like a giant playground
from ancient Greece. Tonight, the Piedmont sports games
begin, and we've signed up for Nacho Cheese Ball. At the
filling station at the edge of the field, we pick up buckets
and plastic suits from the referees. The suits are covered
with sensors and link up to the scoreboard. Once we're
dressed, one by one, we turn a spigot and gooey cheddar
cheese balls plop into our buckets. We grab nacho-chip-
shaped scoopers, gloves, and goggles and head out to battle,
looking like astronauts.

The object of the Nacho Cheese Ball is to throw cheese

balls at the other team's target for points. The targets are bulls-eyes marked 58, 46, 34, 22, 10. You get 58 points for hitting the small circle in the center. The New York target is placed at one end of the field, and the Iowa target is placed at the other. All players begin standing in the center of the field in a section painted yellow. It's called the neutral zone—the only safe place on the field, the only place where you can't be hit with cheese balls. If you get hit while you're running anywhere else on the field, your team loses four points.

We're up against the Iowa team for the first round. We step into the neutral zone, buckets in hand, ready to whip some cheese. The referee blows the whistle and we make a run for it. A red-haired girl, who looks like she's six, winds up her scooper and whips one at me. I'm too quick though. It misses me by a few inches and I keep running for their target. When I'm a few feet away, I dig into my bucket. I scoop out a cheese ball but . . . GLOP! Goo explodes on my ankle. The six-year-old got me! Ugh. I may have just lost four points for getting hit, but I'm about to get fifty-eight. I whip a cheese ball at their target. Smash! 34. That's good. I'll take it. I dig in for another, but a scary boy is racing for me. No! I turn away from their target, and he chases me back into the neutral zone.

I have nowhere to go. I can't get past him so I come up with a new plan. If I can't get any more big points, I'll just fire away at him for lots of little ones off his score. When he steps out of the box, I chase him down. Dig, scoop, fire! Dig scoop, fire! I get him at least nine times. That's probably 36 points!

The whistle blows and we freeze. The scoreboard flashes—New York: 416, Iowa: 242. Yes!

My legs are dripping in cheese as I meet up with my teammates. Mare trudges over too, her whole body covered, even her hair. She freaks out and I don't even try not to laugh. Jillian, Ander, and Jax have escaped with just a few cheese stains. That makes Mare even madder. We jog off the field together with a win in our first round of Nacho Cheese Ball. Not bad, even if we do look like astronauts.

THE PANTRY PROWL

EARLY THE NEXT morning, I'm startled out of sleep by a bunch of loud knocks on our bedchamber door. I know it's Swissa, even though I can hardly open my eyes. I mean, who else would it be? I pretend to be asleep so Jillian will let her in. Mare sleeps like a dead person, so my only hope is Jillian.

Swissa knocks harder, shouting this time. "Get up, girls. I'm not going to knock again!"

Jillian jumps out of bed, carrying her pillow. Swissa marches in, her blonde hair pulled back in a messy bun, and places lilies on our work table. The curtains fly open and I cover my face. Why does she have to be so mean? I slowly pull the blankets away, but only because the sun feels so warm on my face.

"Come on, girls. Get up. You have a busy day planned."

"Every day is a busy day," Mare whines from under the

blankets. "When do we get a day off?"

Swissa laughs. "A day off? You get a day off when I get a day off."

"When is that?" asks Jillian.

"At the end of summer, when camp is over."

"But I'm so tired!" calls Mare.

"You're tired? Why don't you switch places with me? You can work in the chamber crew and wear this ugly white dress. I'll gladly solve that stupid task in your place."

I rub the gritty sleep from my eyes. Swissa is as miserable as ever today.

Mare climbs out of bed. "No, thanks. I'm good."

"I didn't think so. Have fun brainstorming. Don't worry about me; I'll be doing laundry." She picks up our basket of dirty clothes and slams the door on her way out.

I jump out of bed and run to the shower before Jillian can beat me to it. She always takes forever, and I don't want to be the last one ready when Swissa comes back to send us down to breakfast—not when she's in a mood like this.

I finish getting dressed and climb onto the window seat near my Golden Light Bulb. I send a message to Grandma Kitty with my phone.

> *Hi, GK! So much to tell you. We're doing a play for the judges after all. I thought Mare would never give in. It's a story about ghosts. Our set is going to move and everything. We've gone on a run every morning, played Nacho Cheese Ball and eaten scrambled apples for breakfast. Yum! Have you made any new earrings? I'm going to wear the pink cupcake ones you made for me today! XOXO Kia.*

I start to put my phone away when I think of my mom. Maybe I should message her too. I type quickly before

Mare and Jillian finish doing their hair.

Hi, Mom. You might like it here. The buildings are old and pretty, just like the college you went to. Our task is hard but we're finding ways to use all our skills, even math. The food is good. Not as good as fried macaroni, but close. Say hi to Dad and Malin and Ryne. I miss you. Love, Kia.

I wonder what Mom and Dad really think about me being here at camp. Are they counting the days until I come home? Are they secretly wishing that we don't win the competition? I hope they aren't doing that. Grandma Kitty says that negative energy can disrupt my success. I don't want anything to disrupt my success.

When we get to the dining hall, Seraphina and the boys are already at our table. "I have a surprise for you. We're taking a field trip," she says, clapping her hands. Today her purple nails are striped with light blue.

Ander grins. "Where are we going?"

"You'll find out after breakfast, so hurry up. Gregor is meeting us outside in fifteen minutes with the aero-carts."

"Aero-carts?" I ask. "I'm in!"

"Yes!" says Ander. He jumps out of his chair, and we all race for the buffet line. We take blueberry muffins to save time, and carry them back to our table.

A few minutes later, we're outside beside two large aero-carts that look like regular golf carts. Gregor sits behind the wheel of one. Ander jumps into the driver's seat of the other.

"Can I drive?" he asks to no one in particular. "Not a chance," says Seraphina. "Andora would put me on the next plane out of town if I let you do that."

"Fine," he says, and slides over to the passenger seat.

Seraphina gets behind the wheel, and I jump onto the back of her cart. Jax gets in the other cart next to Gregor, and Mare and Jillian jump on the back.

"Are you okay back there by yourself?" Seraphina asks me.

"Sure," I say. I grab the metal bar, and she turns the key. She drives us along the paved path behind Gregor's cart, then lifts off a few feet above the ground. We pick up speed and soon Piedmont Chamber fades out of site. The morning breeze sends shivers up my arms, but the cool air doesn't bother me at all. It feels good, just like it does when I ride my aero-scooter.

My hair blows all over my face. I tuck it behind my ear but it just falls back out again. Seraphina and Ander are talking about something but the wind has muffled their words. We pass over a pond that looks like the one we jog around each morning during break time. I don't want to stop at this one though. My brain feels free riding through the air like this.

Soon we pull into a parking lot in front of a warehouse. It's made of metal or aluminum and doesn't have any windows. "Is this it?" I ask as she lands the cart.

"It sure is!" Seraphina replies. She turns the key and the motor slows to a quiet hum and then to nothing at all.

"It looks scary," I say.

"It looks like a hockey rink," says Ander, walking towards it like he's been there hundreds of times.

She laughs. "I promise you both—this is neither a hockey rink nor scary. You'll love it. It's my favorite place on campus."

"What is it?"

Her smile widens to a grin. "Come inside. You'll see."

We walk to the entrance with the rest of our team, and one by one we file in. The building is several stories high, but all I see is one giant room with short dividers—separating it into about fifty tiny areas. It reminds me of a farmer's market, where people sell stuff like fruits and vegetables and crafts.

"What is this place?" Jillian asks.

"This is the Piedmont Pantry. This is where you'll gather items to use for your solution. You'll find materials for your sets and costumes and anything else you need. Think of it as your team's personal shopping mall."

"Really?" Jillian's face lights up.

I scan the room. It's like craft supply heaven with teams walking around gathering up their items. My brain jumbles. *I wonder what they're picking.*

"This is awesome!" Ander yells. "We can pick whatever we want?"

"It's yours for the taking."

"But how do we pay for all this stuff?" asks Mare.

Gregor clears his throat. "The materials don't cost you anything. They are provided by the Piedmont Organization for your use in the competition. You'll find everything you need here to fuel your creativity. There are some rules, though. You must only take items your team agrees are needed to solve your task, and you have only today to shop for your supplies. Each team is only allowed *one* trip to the Piedmont Pantry.

"How do we get all of it back to our chambers?" I ask.

Gregor takes a clipboard from a nearby table and hands it to Ander. "You will keep track of the items with these. Anything that's too big to carry back on the carts will be delivered later today."

Ander bounces up and down, like he's ready to play in a championship game or something. "Where do we start?"

"That's for your team to decide," says Seraphina.

"Let's walk around the booths first and break into small groups later if we need to," Ander replies.

"Okay," says Mare. "Let's go."

We come to a booth of mechanical parts and Jax stops to look at every table. Most are filled with metal boxes, each containing tiny pieces. They look like a big mystery to me. Next we pass several computer booths filled with circuit boards and wires. Jax examines each of those too. I want to put a motor on his feet. There are so many more booths, and we don't need any of this stuff for our solution. Jax doesn't seem to notice we're all watching him.

Finally, Ander says, "Jax, do we need this stuff to make the object rotate?"

"I'm not sure. It depends whether we use wood or metal to build it."

"Let's keep looking. We can come back to this area later."

Way in the back corner of the warehouse, we come to a booth that contains tables covered with clothes. Two women are taking shirts, pants, and dresses out of boxes and folding them on their laps. Racks along the side are filled with fabric, needles, and thread.

Ander picks up some blue fabric. "Should we all pick a color for our costumes?"

Mare grabs it from him. "I don't think this is what we're looking for, unless maybe we cut up all the pieces."

"That seems like a waste," says Jillian. "It's such nice fabric. What we really need are scraps."

"Oh," Ander replies. "To make us look more ghost-like.

Right?"

A man and woman stand nearby organizing the spools. The woman smiles at us.

"It's nice to see you kids. We never get any visitors way back in this corner. If you look behind those tables, I have some boxes filled with scraps of fabric. They may be of use for you depending on what you're doing with it."

Jillian skips to the back. We follow her and see a ton of boxes. At least twenty are filled to the brim. We search for anything we might be able to use to look spooky and ghost-like. Soon we leave with arms full of fabric and race to the next booth.

Seraphina gathers our scraps into a garbage bag so we can explore the wood booth. We find rows and rows of two-by-fours, one-by-sixes, and other sizes that Jax thinks we might be able to build with. He and Ander and Gregor walk towards the back to place the order.

"Wait up, guys!" calls Mare. "Do you even know what kind of wood to get?"

"We'll figure it out," says Ander.

"Well, make sure you don't pick hard maple. It's really tough to work with. Soft maple would be fine, but pine would be better if they have it."

"How do you know that?" I ask her.

She shrugs. "My dad works in construction. On week-ends I help him pick up materials. Sometimes I help him remodel houses too."

Ander's eyes grow big. "You do?"

"Yeah, so . . ."

"Nothing. I just didn't know, that's all."

Wow. Mare with a hammer. That's scary. But kind of cool that she helped the boys like that.

Marc helps them pick out the pieces, and soon our team has ordered enough wood to get our structure built.

We stand in the aisle, planning where to go next. The team from Alaska—three boys and two girls, all wearing brown shirts—walks up to the booth and rummages through the rows of wood. One of the boys asks, "Is this stuff any good?"

"Yeah," says Ander. "But most of the good pieces are in the back."

Mare grins at the boy.

"Really? Okay. I'll check it out."

"You guys are from Alaska?" Ander asks.

"Yup."

"Cool. Is it really freezing there like every second?"

"Not every second, but yeah, it gets pretty cold."

"Do you ride on dog sleds?"

He laughs. "Yeah, almost every day."

"We ride on aero-scooters," I say.

"We do too, but riding on dogs sleds is way more fun. You're from New York?"

"Yeah," says Ander.

"Oh no. Gotta go! My team left me. See ya."

"See ya, Alaska boy!" Mare giggles.

Jillian and I try not to laugh, but Mare doesn't even care that he probably heard her! The boys take off to find paint. The girls and I decide to look for things that might make us look like ghosts. We run back with Seraphina to the booth with the old clothes. There has to be something cool in those piles. We try on hats, vests, gloves, shoes, jackets, and scarves.

"Look at me!" says Jillian, wearing a curly gray wig. "I'm an old lady ghost. Where did I put my dentures?"

I pull a cane out of the box and hobble over to her. "My dear old friend, your teeth are still in your mouth!" I see the West Virginia team staring at us and I drop the cane. I don't want to give them any ideas!

We keep digging through the boxes. I can't get through them fast enough. Images of ghosts wearing farmer's clothes and party clothes clog up my brain. By the time we've finished, we've picked a furry vest for Ander, a top hat for Jax, long gloves and a feather boa for Jillian, a light blue mini skirt and leg warmers for Mare, and yellow overall shorts for me.

On the way back to find the boys, we pass a table filled with beads and jewelry. Grandma Kitty would devour this! Jillian finds a strand of long pearls, and Mare picks a sparkly choker necklace. I choose eight rings for my fingers and try them on. Perfect!

By the time we're finished, we've filled our bags with fabric scraps, old clothes, jewelry, scissors, duct tape, glue, needles, thread, pins, measuring tape, sketch paper, markers, paint, tools, and some mechanical stuff too. We load them into the storage containers under the carts and get ready to fly back to Piedmont Chamber.

Ander jumps onto the back of the cart. "Here KK, you can sit in the front this time."

I'm startled when he calls me that. I get in the front seat like he suggests and think about it for a second. He just called me KK. Not 718 and not even Kia. Wow. I think Ander just gave me a nickname!

GHOST STORIES

THE GIRLS AND I lug the bags into our bedchamber and drop them next to our work table. Jillian immediately pours out every scrap. "This is better than Christmas!" She picks up the pieces of fabric and holds them up to the light. "They're so pretty. Look at them all." She rearranges pieces on the carpet and crawls over to a green feathery strip. "I bet we could turn this fluffy stuff into arm bands to wrap around my gloves."

"Don't forget the pearls," I sing.

"Hmm. Where are those?"

We search through the items on the floor. There's so much it's hard to tell there's even a carpet under it all.

"Wait a second," says Mare, picking up spools of thread.

"We need to organize. I can't work with this stuff thrown everywhere. We'll need a fabric pile, and a jewelry pile, and a sewing pile, and an accessory pile."

Jillian doesn't seem to notice what Mare is doing. She's already cut up the pieces of silver fabric, sprinkled them over the pink fabric, and set the green fluffy stuff, the white gloves, the pearls, and the feather boa next to it. She stands up to get a better look. "Would this transform me into a glamorous ghost?"

I jump up from the floor. "Yes, Dah-ling, but only if you speak with an accent and walk like this." I sashay across the floor with my hand on my hip.

Mare is too busy admiring her piles to watch us. "There," she says. "Now we can get to work. Just make sure you put the tops on the glue and glitter when you're done with them and don't leave the sewing needles in the carpet. I don't want to step on those with my bare feet." She has sorted the fabric by color, the thread by shade, the glue by bottle size, and the accessories by character. *Yikes.*

"Can you guys help me make my dress?" Jillian asks.

I bite my ring nail. "I don't know how to make a dress."

"You don't have to," she replies. "I just need you to hold it up while I cut a hole for my head. Then I can drape it over you and sew up the sides."

"That would look like a Grandma dress," says Mare.

"But only if I left it like that. I'm going to add a belt."

"How?" I ask.

"I'll use some of that silver fabric if we have any left."

"There's some right there." I point to a wadded up piece under the table.

Mare lays it out. "We could cut this into a rectangular shape."

"Then how does it become a belt?" I ask.

"We twist it up, wrap it around her waist, tie it, and tuck the end under. Simple."

"That's genius," I say.

Jillian giggles. "It's just a belt."

I pick up my overall shorts. "Just wait until our families see us in these costumes."

Jillian squirts glue onto a silver piece. "Are they coming to the rehearsal at the end of the summer?"

"Yeah, my parents, my brother, my sister, and my Grandma Kitty too."

"You're lucky you have a sister," she says. "I have two brothers, Dexter and Davis. Dexter is my older brother. We fight all the time. Davis isn't so bad though."

"Are they all coming too?" Mare asks.

"Yeah. They can't wait to watch me play a dramatic ghost."

Mare rearranges the straight pins.

"What about yours, Mare?"

"My mom's coming. I'm not sure about my brother or sister. They both have jobs now so I don't know if they can."

I look down at my overalls and my brain clogs up. "I don't know how to make this look like a ghost costume."

"Really?" says Jillian. "Yours is the easiest one. Take these black and gray scraps and cut them into strips—all jagged-like. Then attach them to the overalls."

"Yeah," says Mare. "Let's make it look like you went through a dangerous tunnel or something to get to where the ghosts hang out."

"Cool idea. I like that." I sit down at the table with a mountain of fabric in front of me and snip the pieces, trying not to make the strips too straight. I imagine myself as a little ghost walking toward the structure the boys have built. I know they probably don't need my help, but I want to build the rotating object too. Maybe if I finish cutting the strips I can work with them after. I tuck my feet under the chair, spread out the pieces of gray fabric, and cut really fast.

Later, I call Ander and tell him I want to help build the rotating object. If Mare knows how to do that stuff, I know I could learn too.

"Why?" he replies. "This is man's work—we're using saws and nails. Don't you want to keep sewing?"

"I'd rather punch you in the face. How about I do that instead?"

"I'd like to see you try."

"I'm on my way!"

"Okay, okay. I'm just kidding. You can help."

Soon, Ander and Jax lead me out the back door of Piedmont Chamber to see what they've done so far. I practically skip the whole way. Ander stops short at a shed door attached to the back of the building while boys in tie-died shirts from Nevada walk by. "What are you waiting for?" asks Jax.

When the boys are out of earshot, he replies, "I don't want anyone to see where we're keeping our project."

"Why not?"

"So they don't figure out what we're building. It's a competition, remember?" Jax nods and pulls open the heavy door. I shiver as we step inside the cool, dimly-lit shed filled with ancient-looking tools with long handles. *Were they used for gardening or something?*

Back home no one has to do that stuff anymore, even with all the oaks and maple trees everywhere. Houses practically do their own yard work with the flip of a switch. Blowers are built into the siding. When too many leaves cover the ground, they blow them into the center of the yard. A small, steel mixer lifts up from under a section of fake grass. It collects the leaves, chops them up and pours them into a container. Then we get to use the leaf pieces to nourish the plants—like compost.

Jax turns on the light. A huge, rectangular box made of wood sits in the middle of the room. It looks like it could hold a giant!

"Is that the coffin?" I ask and walk around to see the other side.

"Well," says Jax. "We'll turn this side into a coffin, but when it rotates, it will become an incinerator."

"You know," Ander says, "an oven where body parts are cremated—burned to smithereens!"

"Yuck. That's gross."

"And," Jax continues, "when it rotates again, it will become a rocket ship that can catapult bodies into space."

"Oh, that's good!"

Ander jumps on top of the box. "But, there will also be the side that shows the Ghost Gallery. Remember, that's the part that shows pictures of each one—the coffin, the oven, and the spaceship, giving your character a choice of where to spend eternity."

Jax glares at Ander. "Do you have to jump on the box every five minutes?"

Ander steps down. "It's not every five minutes."

Jax raises his eyebrow. "We're lucky it hasn't broken."

I want to side with Jax, but I know Ander can't help it. His brain must think best when he jumps all over the place.

I lift up the corner to see how heavy it is. "So, how do

we make it rotate?"

"We haven't figured that part out yet," says Jax. His face is serious with a deep wrinkle between his eyes.

"I could paint the gallery side," I say. "I have some good images of ghosts that would look really creepy."

"Where did you get those?" asks Ander.

"In my head."

Ander laughs. He seems to understand. "Should we start working on that now?"

"No. I think we should wait for Jillian and Mare. I want to make sure they like this idea before we start. We all know what will happen if Mare doesn't like it."

Ander rolls his eyes. Jax picks up his computer case. "I want to figure out the mechanical stuff anyway. Do you guys mind if I go back to my bedchamber and do some research?"

"Sure," says Ander. "What can we do then, KK? Take the rest of the morning off? Play some street hockey? What do you say? Huh? Huh?" He elbows me in the arm.

That sounds like fun, actually, but I stand firm. We've already been here two weeks. Only three weeks until the rehearsal for our families. "No! I think we should start the script."

"Okay, whatever you say, but Jax is going to work in our chamber and the girls are working in yours. I'm not sure we can get into Meeting Room Twelve. Another team may be using it."

"Let's pick up a notebook from my bedchamber and work down by the pond."

"Okay. Cool. Jax, I'll meet you for lunch. Come on, KK, let's go."

I grab my backpack from my bedchamber and fill it

with pencils, my notebook, water packs, and granola bars. I know I'll have to keep Ander focused. Maybe snacks will help. We race down the path toward the pond. After a sprint, he finally slows down first. "Wow, you're faster than I thought you would be," he says, catching his breath.

I smile. I was not about to slow down first.

"But not faster than me."

"Are you sure about that?" I take off. He scrambles to start up again, but soon he's right on my heels. Just as I reach the fallen tree, he gets there too. We collapse on the ground trying to catch our breath. I smile in victory even though I'm not sure I actually won.

"I guess we share the running title for now, since you got a head start."

I shake my head and hand him one of the water packs. "We better get started. This ghost story isn't going to write itself."

"Nope, but I have a feeling you could write it all by yourself."

"Me? No, I couldn't—I need your help. We have to make it *really* good. Remember, we have to be memorable for the judges." Ander shakes the pack and watches the bubbles rise to the top. "So how should we start the script?" I ask.

He tips the pack over and examines the bottom. "Why do you want to win so badly?"

I look at him, surprised by his question. He's still watching the bubbles. I'm glad because I think my face is turning red. "What do you mean?"

"We all want to win, but for you it's different. You're super intense about the whole thing. How come?"

He's right, but I didn't think it was so obvious. "I don't

know. I just don't want to get programmed for Math or Human History or whatever."

"Are you gonna get programmed into Math or Human History?"

I laugh. "Math, yes. Human History, no way. I'm terrible at Human History."

"You can't be that bad. You won a Golden Light Bulb, remember?"

I think of my trophy sitting on the windowsill, all shiny and gold. "Yeah, I just hate thinking about being forced to study one category for all of seventh and eighth grade. That sounds like prison."

"Human History wouldn't be so bad for me. I like reading about all the people that came before we did. I wonder all the time about my ancestors and what they did when they were alive. Sometimes I look them up and try to find out."

"Hmm . . . I just imagine all of mine creepy and dead."

He shakes his head. "Not me. I imagine mine doing something cool, like my Great-Great-Grandpa Jim who played professional hockey."

"So is that why you like hockey?

"No, I just like playing it. But that's why I might want to be president. Think of all the cool stuff my great-great-grandson will say about me."

"So if you like Human History so much, and want to be President, why do you want to win this competition? If you lose you can just go back home and get programmed for Human History?"

"Because I also want to design the first house in space. If I make it all the way to the Global Championships, I can enroll at PIPS. My dad always tells me that to run fast, you have to run with the fastest runners. That will make you faster. So, if I can work with the best kids, I may be able to learn how to design a space house. I can run for President after that."

I never would have guessed any of that about Ander. "That's a good plan."

"Maybe, but I still have to get to the Global Championships. Besides, I hate losing."

"Yeah, me too. And . . . I have sixty-seven inventions waiting to be built."

"You have sixty-seven inventions?" His eyes open wider than usual. I can see the thick, black rim around his pupils. *Maybe that's why his eyes look so blue.*

"Well, sixty-seven *ideas* for inventions. I have a whole list. I just need to learn how to build them all."

"Wow. That's a lot of ideas."

I take a sip of water. "But only kids at PIPS get to build inventions. If I get programmed, the only thing I can do is *send* my ideas to them. They'll get to build my *Underwater Bubble Bike*, or my *Pants Pockets That Bake Muffins*. It's just not fair."

He nods. "Cool inventions," he says and sets his pack on the ground. "But is there another reason you want to win so badly? I think there is."

"I don't know. I just do." I draw a circle in the dirt. I can feel him staring at me, but not in a creepy way—like he really is wondering. I decide maybe it wouldn't be so bad to tell him the real reason. "Maybe it's because my Grandma won the very first Piedmont Challenge."

"The first one?"

"She's been to Camp Piedmont and everything. She says creativity runs in our family."

"Yeah, it must, since you won too."

"I guess so."

"Don't you think so?"

"I don't know. Sometimes I think I only won because she gave me tips for the competition."

"What do you mean?"

"She told me to do something crazy for Swirl and Spark Recall like sing my answer or talk in an animal voice or something."

"So?"

"So, maybe I wouldn't have thought of that by myself."

"KK, lots of our teachers have said to do stuff like that."

"Yeah, but most kids forget what their teachers say. Grandma Kitty drilled it into my head so I wouldn't forget."

"Well, that's good. You won. That's all that matters."

"Maybe." I scribble out my circle. "She's told me tons of stories about PIPS. She thinks I belong there just like her. She said you get to talk about your ideas all day long with the other kids and then make the things you talk about. The teachers teach you ways to build your inventions."

"Yeah, it sounds like a cool place."

"I bet you can even sit on the ground while you think. I bet they don't have chairs in the classrooms either."

"I hate chairs!"

"Me too!" My stomach gets all fluttery, but I'm not sure why. I open up the notebook and write big letters across the top: GHOST STORIES and underline it twice. I hope we get to go to PIPS. It would be fun to be there with Ander.

He sits up. "I guess that means we have to work on the script now?"

I hand him a granola bar. "Yup, the ghosts aren't going to write their own story."

BUILDING A GHOST TOWN

ANDER AND I jog into the dining hall where Jax, Jillian, and Mare are already eating. "Hi, guys," I say. "We wrote the script."

"All of it?" Mare asks.

"Most of it," says Ander. "And it's spectacular. Wait until you hear it."

"You didn't give me stupid or embarrassing lines did you?"

Ander grins. "Every single one."

Mare scowls and I hold in my laugh. I look over at the team from Michigan, sitting at the table next to us. Witch Girl is watching me again. What the heck? Her team is eating pizza even though all the other teams are eating ham sandwiches and Jell-O.

Ander calls over to them. "Where did you guys get the pizza?"

A skunk-haired boy pulls the stringy cheese from his slice and stuffs it into his mouth. "Our preceptor brought it in because we finished our task."

"Already?" asks Ander. "We still have three weeks to go."

"Yup, we did. And it's good. It's *really* good."

Witch Girl grins. "He's right. We have Oswald over there on our team. He's brilliant." She points to the scrawny boy barely sitting at their table—his chair pushed far away from it. He's sitting with one leg crossed over the other and staring into a small computer.

Witch Girl leans in. "The National Finals are going to be a breeze. I don't see how we won't make it to the Global Championships."

Are you kidding me? I almost say something, but Ander beats me to it. "Well, you should see our solution. It's totally original. No other teams will even think to do a play. It's really cool."

"Well, you guys better hurry up. Last minute preparation equals last place." She turns around and her braid whips around after. His eyes get huge. I want to slap her. Instead, I grab Ander's arm and pull him toward the lunch line. The rest of our team walks with us, all squished together.

"I'm going to go punch that girl!" says Mare.

"No, you're not," says Jillian. "She's just being an idiot."

"She's trying to intimidate us," says Jax.

"But did you hear her?" asks Ander. "And her stupid witch hair almost whipped me in the face again."

Mare looks disgusted. "Did you see the skunk-haired kid sitting there eating his greasy pizza and that nerdy kid on his computer. He probably made up their whole solution. I'd hate to be on that team."

Ander plops ham on his bread. "Their solution probably stinks anyway."

"Yeah," says Jillian. "They probably rushed through it."

My stomach feels sick. *What if their solution is amazing—and better than ours?* "Maybe they did, but let's eat fast so we can get back to work."

The Michigan team is gone by the time we get back. They left the empty pizza boxes, cups, and crumpled napkins all over the table. *What jerks!*

We finish eating and run out to the shed so we can show Mare and Jillian the rotating object.

"Ew, it's gross in here," says Mare. "It's so dreary."

"No, this is perfect," says Ander. "This is just the kind of place we need to get into the spirit. Get it? The ghost-spirit!"

Mare smirks. "Yeah, I get it."

We gather around the wooden box, and Jax explains his idea. "I did some research on how to make an object rotate. There are several ways. We can put together something that will make it move up and down, or we can make something that can slide back and forth, or we can build something that will make it turn."

"It sounds like we need to make it turn," I say.

"I think so too," he says. "I got some cranks and gears from the Piedmont Pantry the other day. We can attach them to the box."

"That will make it turn?" asks Jillian.

"Yes, it will."

"What if we put it up on metal legs so it's even higher," says Mare, "like the height of a real coffin when it's set up for a funeral."

"That's a good idea," I say.

"Okay then, since I came up with that idea," says Mare, "I get to take a break. I want to call someone."

"If it's break time, we're playing street hockey," says Ander.

I want to explode. "It's not break time! We have to read the script and see the costumes."

"We can't work all the time," says Mare. "We have a life outside of this camp you know—well, some of us do."

"Well some of us want to win this competition, and if we're going to win, we can't take breaks!"

"Why are you such a bummer?" asks Mare. "It's okay to have fun sometimes."

Ander puts his arms around both of us. "No need to get into a fight, girls. KK's right. We have a lot to do. Mare, we can take a break in a while, okay?"

"Whatever," she says.

"Thank you," I say. She doesn't smile but at least she doesn't yell at me.

"So Jax," says Ander. "What do we need to do to get this thing turning?"

"We have to build a metal stand to support the box's weight. Then attach the box to it and add the crank and gears."

"I'll work with you on that."

"We need to paint and decorate the box before you attach it to the stand," I say.

"Okay," says Jillian. "I love painting."

"Can we at least go back to our bedchamber first so we can show you the costumes? It's creepy in here," says Mare.

"Sure," says Ander. "Then Kia and I can show you the script."

We walk around to the front of Piedmont Chamber.

The afternoon sun feels good, especially after being cooped up in the musty shed. Teams are playing Frisbee and lying in the grass. I wish I had my aero-scooter. My brain un-jumbles when I'm riding. Somehow though, since I've been here, my brain has managed to un-jumble itself without my scooter—*strange*.

My team is now lying in the grass. *I thought we decided not to take a break. Ugh.* I guess I don't have a choice, so I lie down too, but just for a second. The blades of grass tickle my skin, and soon the sun puts my whole body in a trance. Maybe a short break would be okay.

I look up into the clouds, shielding my eyes from the direct sunlight, and think of Grandma Kitty. I wonder if she ever laid down in the grass when she was here, watching the clouds change shapes with her team. I bet she did.

Eventually, we go back to our bedchamber and Jillian and Mare get ready to give us a fashion show. First Jillian comes out in her pink dress, but it looks different than it did before. The pink pieces are tattered and torn—ripped to shreds. Her hair is messed up and falling in her face. She looks like a ghost who's been roaming the afterlife forever. "Wow!" I exclaim. "That's even better than I imagined."

She takes a bow. "Why thank you, Dah-ling!"

Ander nods his head. "Not bad. Not bad."

Mare comes out next wearing the light blue mini skirt and leg warmers. Gray lace that looks like cobwebs hangs from them both. Her hair is piled in a high pony tail, and she's wearing the choker necklace too. "That's perfect," I say. "You definitely look like a teenager ghost." I want to add that she looks like a bratty teenager ghost but I don't. Fighting with Mare will take up way too much time.

Ander says in his cool voice, "Hey Baby, how you doin'?"

She flips her pony tail around. "Too cool for you." He covers his heart and pretends his feelings are hurt. He's so weird.

Jillian calls from the bathroom, "Come on, Kia. You're next." I walk in and she hands me the yellow overalls covered in ghost-like tatters and an orange T-shirt with holes in it. "Be careful when you put this on. It's fragile."

I can see why. I carefully slip it on and admire myself in the mirror.

"You're amazing, Jillian! I love it!"

She laughs like it's no big deal. Mare helps me put my hair into two pigtails and rubs brown dirt stuff all over my face, squishing my cheeks in strange positions. She's probably doing it on purpose. I slip all my rings on and get ready for my runway debut.

"Are you guys ready?" Mare calls out to the boys.

"Yessss," Ander replies. "I get dressed in my hockey equipment faster than this."

Jillian calls out, "Introducing, Little Ghost Girl!"

I open the door and skip around in a circle.

"Doesn't she look cute?" Jillian sings.

Ander stands up. "You look like you're six years old."

"She's supposed to look six years old," says Mare.

"Then it's perfect, KK."

I don't think that was a compliment, but it's okay. I love my Ghost Girl costume.

Ander stands up. "Okay, Jillian. What about me and Jax?"

"Your costumes are in there. We'll wait out here."

"Don't forget to walk out like you're on a runway," Mare calls.

Ander grins like the Cheshire cat. "Oh, I won't." Jax

doesn't look as excited.

After a few minutes, Ander bursts through the door wearing black baseball pants and a long, furry vest with pointed shoulders. His hair is slicked back, and he's wearing green sunglasses. "Greetings, ghost friends! May I interest you in the space box option? For the low price of ninety-nine dollars your body can be rocketed into space where you'll spend the rest of eternity. *But* if you act now, we'll even throw in an extra box for your ghost cat too."

I laugh out loud. Ander will be great in front of the judges.

"Pretty good, huh? And now I'd like to introduce you to our guide for the evening . . . Master Ghost Man, the man with the top hat!"

Jax walks out stiff as an oak tree. His black cape grazes the floor as he walks. He doesn't smile. Maybe he's afraid the top hat will fall off.

"Jax, your costume is great," I say. "Jillian, where did you get all this stuff?"

She smiles. "Well, I made the black cape from a big piece of fabric. That was easy. I found the white gloves and baseball pants mixed in with our other stuff."

Jax flares out his cape. "Thanks, Jillian. I like it."

I look at all of us in our ghost costumes. "We're going to look so good for this competition! Do you guys want to hear the script now?"

"Yeah," says Mare. "I need to make sure you didn't give me too many lines."

"Don't worry," says Ander. "We didn't."

Ander and I read the script from my notebook, alternating parts. We read the whole thing through once to see if the rest of the team likes it. I'm pretty sure they do since they laugh really hard at all the funny parts. When we've finished, we go through it more slowly, line by line, to see if each person likes what we've written for them. By the end of the afternoon, Mare is happy she only has ten lines. Jax is fine with his fifteen, and Jillian is happy with her seventeen. Ander and I are tied at twenty. I'm not sure how we both got so many, but no one else seems to mind that we have the most.

I lean against my star bed. My whole team is almost sleeping on the floor. The filter revs up and floating sparkles slowly fill the room. I close my eyes. I can't believe that one of the teams created these to purify the air. What a cool invention.

I hope we can make our rotating set just as good. Jax is the only one who knows anything about mechanics. I bet it would help if we could see some objects move and get some ideas. Maybe Seraphina and Gregor can point us in the right direction.

After dinner, they suggest we go to the mechanics room on the fifth floor. We're mixed in with the teams from Hawaii, Georgia, and New Mexico, but with so many instructors and materials, we get our questions answered. We play with the metal gears for a while and eventually figure out a way to make our box open and close, and rotate in both directions.

While we're cleaning up our materials, a girl from Hawaii walks over to our table. Her eyes are very brown, and her smile is friendly. "Hi, guys! I'm Kolleane."

Jillian looks up. "Hi, I'm Jillian. You're from Hawaii!"

Kolleane laughs. "Yes, I am."

"You're so lucky," says Ander. "Do you surf and climb volcanoes and stuff?"

"Well, I do surf—sometimes. And I have hiked up a volcano before, but only once."

"I want to visit there so badly!" says Jillian. "And wear grass skirts!"

"Me too," I say. "And go to a luau!"

"Well, I want to visit New York City," she replies. "Do any of you live there?"

"No, we all live about six hours away," says Mare. "It *is* amazing though. If you like shopping."

"Oh, I like shopping!"

"There are other things to do there besides shop," says Ander.

"That's why I want to go," says Kolleane. "I want to be an artist. I'd love to see all the museums."

Jax clears his throat. "It's kind of cold in the winter."

"I wouldn't mind. I've never even seen snow!"

"We have lots of it in New York," I say.

"Hmm—maybe someday . . . Well, I better catch up with my team now; we have a lot of work to do tonight." She walks out of the mechanics room, waving. "See ya later!"

"See ya!" calls Jillian.

"She was so nice," I say.

"Yeah, she was," says Ander. "*Really* nice."

I punch him on his shoulder.

"What? I was just admiring the beauty of Hawaiian culture, wasn't I, Jax?"

Jax shrugs. "I guess so."

"Well her team is going to be working hard tonight. She said it herself. Maybe we should too."

"I'll pretend I didn't hear that," says Mare. "Besides, I heard they're delivering special snacks to our bedchambers tonight. I don't want to miss it."

THE PERFECT PLAN

WHEN THE GIRLS and I get back to our bedchamber after lunch the next day, I stare at the calendar. How can we finish so many things in three weeks? We haven't even started the original language yet. I bite on my poor pinky nail but quickly tuck it into my fist. That's not helping me figure this out.

I think back to the weeks before the Piedmont Challenge. How did I get ready for so many tasks all at once? I know—Grandma Kitty and I made a schedule. I worked on one hundred practice problems in each category during the months of April and May, and I think that's what it took for me to win. That's it. I need to make a plan. But Grandma Kitty isn't here. Who can help me this time?

Jillian is sprawled on the floor adding more cobwebs to Mare's costume. She's in her own world, like she always is when she's creating something. She hums some song, and her head tips from side to side. I don't think she realizes she's doing it.

Mare is sitting inside the closet organizing her clothes cubby. She has arranged her shirts and shorts into separate piles. Then she organizes them by color. She uses a ruler to measure her T-shirts after she folds them. By the time she finishes, her piles are perfect.

Mare. That's it. She's perfect. She's organized, and she doesn't want to look like an idiot in front of everyone. But . . . she's Mare. I don't want to ask her for help. *Ugh!* I let out a huge breath and pick up a pencil. "Mare, can you come here?"

"Huh?"

"I need help."

She crawls out of the cubby and sits down next to me. "What?"

"Okay, so we have twenty-one days until we do our play for the judges."

"So?"

"And we have a lot of things left to do, like draw and paint and learn our lines and make up our new language—"

"Why are you panicking? We have three weeks."

"I don't want to make a fool of myself in front of the judges."

Her eyes narrow. "Me neither."

"Well, we can't start rehearsing until all these things are done, and don't you want to have enough time to rehearse?"

"We better have enough time. That's the only way I agreed to do a play in the first place. All of you promised me."

"That's why I need your help."

"What do you need?"

"I need someone to make a schedule for the next twenty-one days. We have to get everything done so we have enough time left to practice. You're so organized; you can help all of us stay on track. Ander wants to take a break every five minutes; Jax wants to work on the movable set or research stuff on his computer; and Jillian is off in her own world with our costumes. See? Look at her."

Jillian is still singing to herself and stuffing more padding into Ander's vest.

"Will you help me make a schedule so we have enough time to rehearse?"

"I guess. I don't want to make a fool of myself, so sure, I'll help you."

"Yes! Thank you. Here's the calendar. What should we do?"

"Let me see that." She turns the calendar her way. "I think we should work backwards. Which day is the competition?"

How does she not know that? "It's a two-day competition. July 28th and July 29th."

"How many days do you think we need to rehearse?"

"At least a week."

"You said we have twenty-one days left, but look. One of those days is today and one is the first day of the competition, so we actually only have nineteen days."

I tap my pencil on the table. "That's worse than I thought."

"We'll make it work." She twists her hair into a ponytail. "Let's start rehearsals on July 19th. That gives us a full week and a few extra days right before the competition starts— just in case."

"Just in case what?"

"In case we need extra practice time. We are not going to make fools of ourselves up on that stage, remember?" She smiles and I do too. She doesn't look so mean for once.

"That means we have all these other days to finish the work."

My stomach churns. "That's nine days."

"Yes. Nine."

"That's not a lot." I turn to a new page in my notebook. "Okay, let's make a list. You write. I'll dictate."

When we're done, this is our list:

-Finish script
-Sketch pictures onto box
-Paint box.
-Build mechanical pieces for box.
-Attach box to mechanical pieces.
-Finish costumes.
-Make up language.
-Add language to script.
-Decide how each category is used in our solution.
-Create document that shows how we used each category.
Learn lines.
-Rehearse.

Gulp. This list is *really* long.

We divide up the jobs and close the notebook.

"Thanks, Mare. At least we have a plan."

"We just have to work hard for the next nine days."

"Work hard? I can definitely do that."

AT 7:00 p.m. the next night, we meet up with the team from Nevada for Round Two of Nacho Cheese Ball. Several other teams have gathered on the sidelines to watch. Five boys stand across from us in the neutral zone. This is not good. *What chance do we have against them?* A boy with black hair crosses his arms in front of him. "Ready to get smashed with cheese?" His grin is huge. His teeth are crooked. I consider grabbing my teammates and making a run for it. We could sprint back to our bedchambers and work on our solution. Instead, I look Crooked Teeth straight in the eye. I'm not a quitter. I clutch my bucket and plant my feet.

The whistle blows and I run. These boys won't expect me to be fast. Ander has the same idea. We dodge them, and as we get within throwing range, we scoop up cheese balls and fire off shot after shot. 58, 22, 22, 46, 10 points! The scoreboard lights up. 222 points from just Ander and me. But my victory is short lived. Splat! Cheese smacks me in the neck and oozes down my back. Gross! Crooked teeth runs for our target but not before I whip him in the foot. But I must have a target on my back. One, two, three globs hit me and I wipe out on the slippery grass.

By the time the cheese war is over, I'm covered in orange goo, and I'm sure we've gotten creamed. My team gathers underneath the scoreboard but I see I was wrong. We've beaten team Nevada by fourteen points and advanced to Round Three—the Semi-Finals!

NINE DAYS

MARE AND I sketch pictures on each side of the wooden box while Ander and Jax connect the pieces to hold it up. Jillian has just finished our costumes when Seraphina brings us five clear bags with our names written on them. Mare folds the costumes perfectly and tucks them inside. We find a safe spot—in an old cabinet in the back of the shed—and hide them away.

On day two, Jillian begins inventing the new language. She has a plan so we leave her alone. Mare and I paint the pictures on the box, and we actually make a good team. She's careful when she paints and even though we don't talk a lot, I get the feeling that she doesn't mind working with me too much.

On day three, all but one of the sides are painted. The five of us lift the box and turn it so we can paint the last side—the Ghost Gallery.

"I want to paint today—can I?" Ander asks. "I haven't gotten to paint at all."

"Well, if Ander's going to paint, can Mare help me with the language? I need someone else to practice it with," Jillian says.

"I'm sick of painting anyway," says Mare. "No offense, Kia."

I shrug. As long as we stay on schedule, I don't care where she works. I turn to Jax. He's winding a crank on the base machine.

"Jax, do you need help?"

"Nah, I'm fine. I'll start working on the platform."

So Ander and I paint while Jax goes to the corner of the shed, and Mare and Jillian leave to work outside.

"So, KK, what should I paint first?"

"Why don't you paint the letters to Ghost Gallery, and I'll paint the pictures?"

"Cool. Does it matter what colors I paint them? Wait. I got it. They need to be gray and black, but not painted perfectly. They should be smeared and then dripping in red—red blood."

"That's great!"

"Yes! I like when that happens."

"When what happens?"

"Have you ever had a lot of stuff going on in your head? You know, like an awesome idea?"

"Yeah."

"No, I mean a really awesome idea, like you just can't wait to get it out of your head. The only trouble is, sometimes it's small and you don't know how to turn it into something bigger."

I laugh. "Yeah, I get that—all the time. Only sometimes

I have so many ideas at once that they get jumbled. It's like they want to swirl around free until they can get bigger but they can't until I can find a way to untangle them. It's really frustrating when I can't. I'm happier when they can just swirl in my head."

Ander stares at me.

Great. I've done it again. He's definitely going to think I'm weird, if he doesn't already.

"Wow."

"Wow, what?"

"I've never heard anyone explain it like that before. I totally get what you're talking about."

I stare back. "You do?"

He walks in a circle around the box. I'm not sure where he's going. "So your ideas just get in the way of each other sometimes?"

"Yes."

"You must have a lot of ideas." I feel my face turn red.

"Yeah."

"And they swirl around?"

Now I'm sure he can see my face burning. "Pretty much."

"Well, I don't have too many ideas—and they definitely don't swirl. I usually have one idea at a time and it's like torture waiting for it to make sense. But when it does, when it turns into a full blown amazing idea, I feel this thing— this spark."

"A spark?"

"Yeah, like kaboom! It explodes in my head, and I suddenly figure out what it means. I feel a spark."

"That's pretty cool."

"Yeah—like the letters. I knew we had to find a way

to make the letters seem ghostlike, and so I felt that spark when I thought of the dripping blood idea."

I shake my head. "I get it now."

"So where's the red paint? I'll start with the drips."

We paint and I realize that it's easy talking to Ander. I don't have to hide what I'm thinking. "Do you like going to school at Crimson?" I ask him.

"That's a random question."

"Well, do you?"

"I don't know. I never thought about it before. It's not like we have another choice for school."

"Yeah, I know."

"Don't you like it there?"

"It's okay."

"I don't remember seeing you around at school. Who are some of your other friends?"

"My other friends?"

"Yeah, like who do you hang out with?"

"Oh, a bunch of kids. You probably don't know them."

"Oh."

"I mean I have friends. Well, I *had* a best friend, but she doesn't like listening to my invention ideas anymore, and she told me to be best friends with someone who does. I just haven't found anyone yet."

"Oh."

"Plus, it's so big at Crimson. I hate that everyone calls each other by their number instead of their name."

"I hate that too. I like nicknames better."

"Do you give all your friends nicknames?"

"Nope. You're the first one."

I don't know what to say to that. My stomach feels all flippy inside again. "Um, thanks."

"Yup."

"I don't actually think I've ever had a real friend before."

He looks up from his red drips. I'm such an idiot. Why did I tell him that?

He laughs. Not at me, but like I said something funny. "Well, now you do, KK. Real friend at your service."

At about two o'clock, Jillian and Mare come back to the shed, and Ander announces it's time for all of us to take a break.

"Why now?" asks Jillian. "Seraphina and Gregor will be here to check in with us in ten minutes."

"Exactly. I need a break before Gregor comes. He's always watching me, and staring at every crank I attach and hole I drill. I need to mentally prepare myself for his check in."

We lean against paint cans where the cement floor is so cold it chills my bare legs. Jax pulls his computer out of his backpack. This doesn't surprise me though. He does this during break time.

Mare watches him. "What are you doing on that thing all the time anyway?"

"Research."

"For what?"

"App stuff."

"What do you mean, app stuff?"

"I've been researching how to make computer apps."

"Why?" asks Jillian.

"I want to make one."

"That's cool," says Ander. "But don't you want to relax for a minute?"

He doesn't have a chance to answer. Gregor barges into

the shed, looking stern as ever. We jump to our feet. "Break time? You must feel very confident in your solution if you're allowing yourselves to slow down."

Uh oh.

Seraphina strolls in behind him. "Oh, hush, Mr. Serious. Everyone deserves a break, especially with cupcakes. There's one for each of you in all of your favorite colors." She holds out a box of multi-colored cupcakes. We attack them like vultures. I take yellow, Jillian takes pink, Mare takes light blue, Ander takes midnight blue, and Jax takes green.

"How did you know these were our favorite colors?" Jillian asks.

Seraphina smiles. "You're my team. Of course I know important things like that. And Gregor, you should take notes. Not only do children need fresh air to be creative, they need snacks."

"Very well, then while you eat, tell me the status of your solution."

We look at each other but no one says anything. They're such wimps. One time I won't answer and they'll have to.

"Well," I say, "our rotating object is almost painted. Then all we have to do is attach it to the platform over in that corner. That's the mechanical part that'll make it move."

Gregor doesn't say anything.

"Um, and we finished our script. We just have to add the language."

"I see."

"And our costumes are done too!" Jillian says.

"And have you incorporated all six categories into your solution?"

"No," I say, "But we have five days until we have to

rehearse. And we have a schedule that we're following, so we'll definitely get it done."

He doesn't look convinced.

"So what do you think?" I ask.

"It looks great," says Seraphina. "I can tell you've been working really hard."

"We have," says Mare. "Very hard."

Gregor walks around our wooden box. "So, your team is sure that this Ghost Gallery is the best way to solve this problem?"

"Yup," Ander responds. "Did you notice the dripping blood? Nice touch, huh?"

"I see that. Dripping blood. Yes."

Ander grins at me like this is a proud moment for him. I grin back. Gregor doesn't grin at all.

"So you have no thoughts to alter your presentation?"

Is he crazy? "Why would we do that?"

"I would like you to be certain that this is the solution that will get you to the Global Championships."

What is he trying to do, make us nervous?

Mare takes a step towards him. "We're doing a play. No other teams will do that. The judges will love it. We're *sure* this will get us to the Global Championships."

Wow. You go, Mare!

"Very well. I would like to see how your platform mechanism works."

Jax and Ander take him over to the platform and explain the details. Jillian and Mare show the language to Seraphina and me. "So the language is a bunch of moves to go with the words we say?" I ask.

"Yes!" Jillian replies. "What do you think?"

Seraphina grins. "I love it!"

"Me too!" I say. Mare's right. No one else will have a solution like this. It'll definitely get us to the Global Championships. I watch Gregor staring at the Ghost Gallery. Who cares what he thinks anyway?

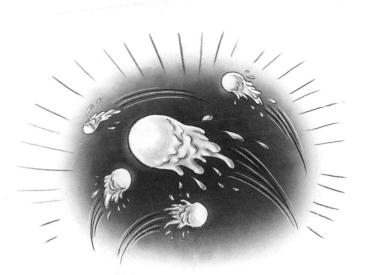

HUMAN PRETZEL

ONLY SEVEN DAYS left, but my team is on fire. The paint is dry on the box and Marc has made herself in charge of attaching it to the platform. With all the moving parts, she's going to make sure nothing falls apart. She's got a checklist and everything. The boys attach a lever, she checks to see if they put it on the right way. She's bossy, but they don't mind and at least she's not complaining anymore.

Jillian and I walk outside. Tons of teams are spread out on campus. It looks like one big carnival but without any games or rides. I guess they're working on the last minute parts of their solutions too. We search for a quiet place away from everyone and find a shady spot underneath a tree where I lean up against the crooked trunk. We flip through the script and examine every single line. Are Ander's funny enough? Are Jax's serious enough? Does Mare sound like a teenager? Should Jillian act more dramatic? Do I sound like a little kid?

When we're sure the script is perfect, we work on the language. We add the moves to the script, making them really big. We try to imagine people sitting way back in the auditorium; will they be able to see what we're acting out? If our motions are big—then no one will miss a thing.

Later on, Mare, Ander, and Jax find us under the tree. Mare collapses on the grass. "I'm so tired and that shed is so creepy. I feel like real ghosts could be watching us."

Jillian laughs. "Wait until you see how we added the language to the play. We call it Ghost Garble! It's the way ghosts communicate with each other—a dance move to go with each word. All the new ghosts must learn the garble once they're welcomed into Ghost Town, and then use it to choose where to go for all of eternity."

Jillian and I jump up to demonstrate. "See ghosts don't just talk, they garble."

Ander jumps in line with us. "Show me! How do you do it? Like this?" He spins on his heel, and says, "Let's go tango in the grave yard!"

"Sort of," I say, and show it to him again. Before long, all of us are garbling, even Jax. His moves look like Frankenstein's monster, but for the serious ghost director, I guess that's good. Before too long, we've invented something else to go with our ghost garble lines—a finale song and dance. We twist, we dance, we jump—making up lines as we go.

"Dancing Ghosts in the Gallery!" Ander exclaims. "We are so going to win this competition."

Over the next few days, we spend our time under the tree memorizing our lines and putting together the packet for the judges, that includes our team's question, our original language, our rotating object, and a list telling how we used all six categories in our solution:

Art Forms: Creation of costumes, designs on the movable object, and the original language.

Earth and Space: Model of a rocket and explanation of how it works.

New Technology: Computer research for the movable object and script ideas.

Communications: Creation of original language and play.

Human History: Script and character histories.

Math: Measurements for costumes and set.

By the afternoon of the ninth day, we meet with Seraphina and Gregor in the shed, where they've come to preview our movable object before our first practice in the morning. First, we sit in a circle, each of us reading a copy of the competition task.

Our home, the Earth, is shaped like a circle.

Your task is to create an object that transforms three times into something else, and then transforms back to its original position . . . creating a circle effect. The object you create must answer a question that is universally asked, but has not yet been answered by mankind. Your solution must include elements from each of the six academic categories and one original language. Your presentation to the judges may not exceed twelve minutes.

Seraphina flips the page. "So?"

"That's it. We're done," says Ander.

"Have you forgotten anything?"

I flip through the pages of my booklet. "I don't think so. We made a document describing our team's universal question."

"And we included skills from each category in our solution," says Mare.

"And we created an original language," adds Jillian.

"Ghost Garble!" says Ander.

"And our object rotates three times and ends up again in its original position," says Jax. "You can see for yourself."

"Very well," Gregor says, not looking impressed. "I would like to see this movable object."

"Me too!" Seraphina jumps up from the circle, her platform sandals clomping on the concrete floor. "Let's see how it turned out."

Ander jumps up too. "We'll demonstrate." He and Jax pull the plastic tarp off the Ghost Gallery. From the front, it looks like a rectangular box held up by metal brackets and cranks. The words *Ghost Gallery* are painted across the top in shades of black and gray. Oozing from each letter are creepy red drips.

Below the letters are pictures of the three designs: a brown coffin with the top propped open, a crimson-red oven cremator, and a silver-blue rocket ship.

Ander steps in front of the gallery. "Here we have our Ghost Gallery. Kia is playing a little girl who just died. She wonders where she'll go now. That's our universally asked question: Where do humans go after they die? Kia will figure out that humans go to Ghost Town after they die."

"But they don't stay long," I add. "And neither will I. I'll have to choose where to go for all of eternity once I leave

Ghost Town." I look at Jax and nod toward the crank.

"Um yes, I'm playing the Ghost Guide who points out all three choices to Kia. Then I push this button and wind this crank. The box lifts up and turns over." Jax's voice shakes, but his face only turns dark pink.

"See? The gallery sign has changed into the coffin," says Jillian. "The top opens and everything! I'll say the reasons to choose it."

"When she's done, Jax will push the button and wind the crank again. The box will flip again to show the oven cremator." I wave my arm for dramatic effect.

"I'll show the reasons to pick that one," Mare says quickly. "Then, Jax will wind it again and the object will flip, this time to show the rocket ship."

"I," Ander straightens up and pounds a hand to his chest, "*of course,* will demonstrate the rocket choice." His voice fills with certainty. "Who wouldn't want to ride in this luxury capsule for all of eternity?"

Seraphina beams. Her purple lips are bright as ever. Gregor looks stone faced. I'm not sure his lips even know how to make a smile.

"Then I'll push the button and wind it one more time," Jax continues. "The object will transform back to its original side, the Ghost Gallery, with the pictures of each choice."

I twirl around. "That's when I get to pick which way I want to spend all of eternity!"

"That's so clever!" says Seraphina, her voice bursting with praise. "So cute! I love it. I like the way the object transforms. It creates that circle effect the judges will be looking for."

"Yeah," says Ander. It turns like a circle even though it isn't shaped like a circle. We thought we'd get extra points for that."

"You just might," Seraphina laughs.

"Gregor," asks Mare. "Do you like it?"

"It doesn't matter if I like it. It matters if it follows the rules. It matters if the judges deem this solution to be superior to the other teams' in the competition."

"So you don't like it," Ander replies.

"I didn't say that. I would ask you though, if this is as original and technologically advanced as you can make it. If history is any indication, teams that have moved on to the Global Championships have created the most scientifically sound and technically advanced solutions to the tasks they've been given."

My stomach flips. "It's even better with the script. Wait until you see the whole thing put together, with costumes and everything. Maybe the judges want to see something different this year."

Seraphina pats me on the shoulder. "You may be right, Kia. I think your solution is highly creative. I haven't seen anything like this in the years I've been a preceptor here at Piedmont."

"See?" Ander gives Gregor an I-told-you-so look.

Gregor doesn't seem to notice.

"Okay, my creative Crimson Kids, let's get all of this put away for tomorrow. I'm anxious to see how it works in the play."

We cover the Ghost Gallery with the tarp and store our paperwork inside the cabinet next to our costumes. While we do, Seraphina drags Gregor to the door. I pretend to check on the tarp so I can hear what they're saying.

"Why are you so mean to them?"

"I am not mean to them."

"Oh, yes you are. They are so proud of their solution. They've done a great job, but you can't even give them one compliment."

His face looks like stone. "Compliments don't win competitions."

"They can't hurt."

"Sometimes they can."

"What do you mean?"

"My father has never complimented me. Not once. Not when I won my Golden Light Bulb and not when I became a preceptor. He always said people who need compliments are weak."

"Well, didn't you hate when he said that?"

"We don't need to continue this conversation about my father."

"Well, it would be okay if you patted them on the back once or twice, especially now that they've achieved so much."

"I'll pat them on the back when they win the National Finals."

She shakes her head and I quickly walk away from the Ghost Gallery. So that's why Gregor is so mean. His father *made* him that way.

We lock the shed door with our project inside but bring our scripts with us so we can practice our lines before lights out. Seraphina leads us to the team building room. "I have one last thing for you to do before you go to dinner. I know you're tired, but this is important."

The Team Building room looks the same as it did the first day we met here—the same day we bombed the team building exercises.

Mare scans the room. "Where's Gregor?"

"He needed to stop at the Chamber office but we could wait for him."

"We don't have to." Ander's tone projects what we're all feeling by now.

Seraphina gives him a knowing look. "You're right. We don't actually need him for this. I want you to give the Human Pretzel another try."

"But we stunk at it the first time." Leave it to Mare to focus on the bad stuff.

"I told you I would give you another chance, and this is it. Now please arrange yourselves in a circle and hold out your right hands."

We step into a circle. This time no one seems to care who they're standing next to. I end up in between Ander and Jax.

"Now, clasp the right hand of someone who's not next to you."

I grab hold of Jillian's hand.

"Now reach in toward the center with your left hand and clasp the hand of a person who is not next to you, and who's other hand you are not already holding."

I grab hold of Mare's hand.

"Now, as you can see, you're all tangled up. You've essentially formed a human pretzel. Please do not let go of each other's hands. When I say, 'Begin,' try to untangle yourselves so that both of your hands are at your sides."

We work at our pretzel for seconds. Arms lift over heads. Legs step over arms. We turn. We twist. We instruct each other. We laugh, and in forty-five seconds flat, we're not a human pretzel anymore!

Seraphina grins. "I knew you'd be better at it this time. In the last five weeks you've gone from strangers to teammates who can work together to solve a task. If you can do the human pretzel, you can do anything—and that includes winning some Nacho Cheese Ball!"

Wow.

"Now, let's go get dinner. You have round three of the tournament tonight, and then your rehearsals begin in the shed at eight o'clock in the morning tomorrow. I, for one, cannot wait to see how you do at both."

I smile inside. She's not the only one.

At fifteen minutes to seven o'clock in the evening, we head over to the field. Ander's in competition mode walking backwards as he talks to us. "We have an advantage in this round. We've seen this Michigan team, so we should be able to make a strategy that will put us in the finals."

"I call the nerdy computer kid," says Mare.

"Okay," Ander says. "I get Witch Girl."

"Then who do we get?" asks Jillian. "I'm not taking the skunk-haired kid with cheese hanging out of his mouth."

"Me neither," I say.

Jax shakes his head. "Okay, I guess I'll take him." That leaves the other two boys for Jillian and me.

The sidelines are filled with teams from all over. We head to the neutral zone and the referees meet us in the middle. "Hey, kids. Nice job reaching the semifinal game. Please keep this game fair but fun. The winner will play either Florida or Rhode Island in the Finals. Good luck."

I size up my blond boy. He's taller than me but preoccupied with swinging his bucket. I got this. My team stands ready to run. Witch Girl yells out, "Hey, New York, don't feel bad when we smear this stuff all over your faces. We know any team who spends their time making costumes can't be any good at Nacho Cheese Ball."

Skunk Boy snickers, sticks his finger into his bucket, and licks a glop of cheese.

Gross!

The whistle blows. I fire a cheese ball at Tall Boy before I take off, and another as I run for the target. Witch Girl yells to Ander, "Hey skinny kid, did you build sets for your play too? I bet your teammate over there had to do all the building. You couldn't even lift a hammer with those scrawny chicken arms!"

Oh no! Ander makes a run for her and chases her down. He lifts his whole bucket over his head. "No!" I shout. "You'll get disqualified!"

He lowers the bucket and scoops out four cheese balls. He catapults them at her as she runs for our target. Splat! All four explode on her black witch braid. "Ha! That was with my chicken arm!" He turns around and sprints for her target. We're down but we still have a chance. Jax comes from behind me and fires a shot. It hits the target immediately after Ander's. The buzzer sounds. New York 322 and Michigan 310. Take that, Michigan!

Witch Girl glares at us as we peel out of our suits. We say, "Good game," to her team anyway and all head back to our bedchambers. On the way, Mare and Jillian argue about who gets the shower first. They take off laughing, but I take my time walking down the hallway.

I open the door to the stairwell and hear a familiar voice. I get to the landing and see that it's Swissa talking on the phone. I start climbing the steps and she suddenly yells. "What do you mean they gave the part to Clare? Rehearsals don't start until September. Miss Piper told me I could try out for the lead."

Her face is red, like she might cry.

"It's all because I'm stuck working at this stupid camp this summer!"

We lock eyes as I pass by. She lowers her voice and turns her shoulder away, so I quickly open the door to my floor and race for my room. Swissa sure doesn't like being here at Camp Piedmont. Maybe that's why. She's missing her big chance to be the lead in a play.

150 POINTS

THE BELLS RING and Andora's voice crackles into our bedchamber. "Good evening, boys and girls. We have a special bulletin for this evening's announcements. All teams must report to Appelonia Dining Hall tomorrow morning at precisely 8:00 a.m. Thank you. Sleep well. Dream big."

"What's that about?" asks Mare.

"I don't know," says Jillian.

"Great," I say. "We have our first rehearsal at eight o'clock so now we'll have to start late."

"It's fine, Kia," Jillian replies. "It might not take that long."

But I don't feel reassured, and I'm not sure why. When Mare turns off the light, I pull my blankets close to my chin and stare out the window. My eyelids feel too heavy for thinking, and soon I drift off to sleep.

I wake the next morning to knocking at our

bedchamber door. I'm the first to move. Ugh. Now I have to be the one to open the door. I roll out of bed and drag myself across the room. Swissa walks in wheeling a cart—with daisies this time. Their pretty petal faces are so cheery compared to her grouchy one.

"Cool, you're up," she says with droopy eyes, and unloads the flowers onto the table. Her cart is full of neatly folded pink towels and our team shirts.

"Do you need help?" I ask, looking for a sign that she still hates this camp for ruining her life.

"No. It's my job. I can do it."

"But you don't have to wait on me." I help her anyway, taking the piles from the cart. "Thanks for all this," I say giving her the best smile I can. "I like your headband."

She tilts her head. "This thing? It's part of my uniform."

"I like it."

She smiles a little and looks at me with a weird expression. Maybe she's not used to the kids here being nice to her. "Thanks," she says and carries yesterday's carnations out the door.

I stare at the daisies. It's weird. I'm used to getting flowers every day now. I'm used to scrambled apples and floating sparkles over my bed. The competition is seven days away, and as soon as the Piedmont National Finals are over, I might have to go back to Crimson. If we don't finish in the top five, then we won't advance to the Global Championships. I won't get to enroll at PIPS. I'll get sent home to be programmed for math.

I shove the thought out of my head. No room for that right now. We have to get to the bottom of the staircase. Ander and Jax are probably waiting for us.

"What do you think's going on?" Ander asks, as we

walk into the dining hall. "Andora's message last night was strange."

I feel a pang in my stomach. "I don't know."

"Maybe they want to pump us up. We only have a week left."

"Yeah, that's probably it."

Seraphina and Gregor slip into their seats as Master Freeman steps up to the microphone. I'm expecting more balloons, confetti, or a laser show. The bells chime in a quiet rhythm, but that's all we get.

"Good morning, State Champions. I address you this way as a reminder that you have come here as the brightest and most creative sixth graders in your states. Over the past five weeks, you've worked together to solve a task using skills from each of our six categories. You have seven days to put the finishing touches on your solutions. Just one week from tomorrow, you will present to the judges at our Piedmont Rehearsal. Parents and family members have received their invitations, and I'm sure they are as anxious as we are to see the solutions you've created."

We glance at each other. I don't think any of us can believe we'll see our families and show everyone our play in one week!

"This year, the Piedmont Organization has made a change to the rules of the Piedmont National Finals."

The bells ring again louder this time. Still, nothing can mask the sounds of two-hundred and fifty kids and their preceptors shuffling in their seats.

"In previous Piedmont National Finals, all fifty teams have competed for a chance to advance to the Global Championships. This year, however, the Piedmont Rehearsal will not be just a practice. All fifty teams will be judged. The teams who receive at least one-hundred and fifty points out of a possible two hundred at Rehearsal Judging will be allowed to compete in The Piedmont National Finals."

What?

"We believe the amendment to the rules will encourage our teams to push themselves even harder during the final week of camp. Good luck with your final preparations. Preceptors, you will receive your Rehearsal Judging times later today."

"That's not fair!" I exclaim, way louder than I should.

Ander's mouth hangs open. "They can't do that! Can they, Seraphina?"

Seraphina looks as shocked as the rest of us. "I can't believe they changed the rules with just seven days to go! They've never done anything like this before."

"So there's a chance we might not get to compete at the Finals?" asks Jax.

"Yes," Gregor replies. "There's a very real possibility that you will not receive enough points to compete."

Mare shakes her head. "This is *not* right."

"No!" I cry. "We have to compete!"

Ander jumps up from his chair. His eyebrows are practically touching. "We have to get to the National Finals!"

"We can still do it," says Jillian. "We can get the one-hundred and fifty points."

"No problem," says Mare. "We're doing a play, remember?"

"That's the spirit," says Seraphina.

I don't get it! "Why did they have to change the rules?"

Witch Girl is watching me, and leans over close to us. "What's the big deal? Any team who can't get at least one-hundred and fifty points doesn't deserve to compete at the finals anyway. You'd have to present the judges a pile of junk not to get that."

I don't answer her. None of us do.

Seraphina stands up. "Come on. Let's get some scrambled apples and head over to the shed. We have some practicing to do."

Who cares about scrambled apples? They don't even sound good anymore.

PILES

MY TEAM HEADS outside to the shed where the air gets hotter and stickier the closer we get. I take an elastic band off my wrist and pull my hair back into a ponytail. Gregor reaches inside his pocket for the keys. There's a small part of me that doesn't want him to open the door. I'm not sure I want to go inside. I want to jump on an aero-cart and drive as fast as I can, to let the breeze un-jumble my brain, the part that doesn't get why Master Freeman changed the rules. But I know I can't. He *did* change the rules, so I have to walk inside the shed and begin rehearsing. If we're going to have a chance to compete at the National Finals, we have to get those points at Rehearsal Judging first.

I look at my teammates' discouraged faces. This is not a good way to begin practicing. "Hold on guys. Wait a second. I hate this new rule too, but let's not get mad. Maybe Witch Girl is right. What's the big deal? Our solution is good. We just have to practice really hard."

"Yeah," says Ander. "She's right. We can do this."

The keys jingle in the lock until it clicks. Gregor pushes the door open and turns on the light. I look to the center of the room at the Ghost Gallery. The tarp we've been using to cover it is crumpled on the floor like a puddle. I don't understand at first. It takes me a second to realize what's happened. But then it hits me and I catch my breath.

Our Ghost Gallery is smashed into a million pieces.

Ander screams. "What the—"

"What happened?" shouts Mare.

I stand frozen, not able to believe what I'm seeing. A letter G with a red drip lies near my foot next to a letter Y and a letter L. Our Ghost Gallery box, the whole thing— the coffin, the oven, the rocket, the gallery . . . it's all destroyed. My hopes for making it to the National Finals crash to the ground.

Seraphina runs to the pile. Jax sifts through the mess, picking up pieces of metal and wood. There are a ton of them, cracked and smashed and mixed together with nails and pieces of paint.

Gregor clears his throat. "It appears as though your object may not have been as strong as you thought."

Why doesn't he just punch us in our stomachs?

"Yes, it was!" Ander screams. "It didn't just crash to the floor!"

"How else would you explain this pile of junk?"

Jax swings around. His face is flaming red. "It's not a pile of junk! We worked hard on this."

Seraphina glares at Gregor. "I know you did, Jax—all of

you did."

I finally find my voice. "What happened? It couldn't have just fallen apart."

Jax crouches near the remains of the Ghost Gallery and tries to put a metal crank back together. "I know it didn't collapse. It was secure last night when we covered it up."

Mare and Ander kneel down next to him. "I checked and double checked the whole structure," says Mare. "It was built like a tank."

"Really?" Gregor crosses his arms across his chest. "Well, it's not like a tank anymore. I would suggest you decide what your next course of action will be."

Seraphina takes out her phone. "I'll call the maintenance crew and ask them to take all of this to the dumpsters."

"No!" I scream, running to the desecrated pile. "You can't throw it away. It's our solution!"

Jillian blinks back tears. "Kia, it's in a million pieces. We'll never be able to put it all back together."

"Then I'll do it myself!" I brush the small pieces into their own pile. "That's what got me to this competition in the first place. I know I worked harder than any of you to get here, and I can work harder on this too. You can't stop me! Seraphina, please don't throw it away!"

My team looks at me wide-eyed. Ander adds a piece to my pile. "We'll ride over to Piedmont Pantry and get some more paint and wood and nails and cranks—"

"No, unfortunately that's against camp rules," says Gregor. "Only one trip per team is allowed."

"But they'll make an exception for us," says Jillian, her eyes now filled with tears. "Won't they?"

"No, they won't. That rule has been challenged many

times. Teams have run out of materials before and needed more. Their petitions have never been approved. Part of the challenge in this competition is managing your supplies."

"Well, part of problem solving is perseverance," says Ander. "I'll call Master Freeman myself."

Seraphina steps in. "You don't have to Ander. I will petition the committee on your behalf. Gregor, please round up containers for the team. If their petition gets denied, they may need to reuse some of these parts. Kia's right. We can't throw away all their hard work."

"Very well, but I think they must start working on another solution since their petition will probably get denied."

"Another solution?" asks Ander. "You mean start over?"

"I am not starting all over!" says Mare.

Seraphina lets out a big breath. "No need to panic. Let's find out about the petition first. I'll know today if you'll be allowed to make another trip to the Pantry."

Jillian wipes her eyes. "I hope so. I loved our Ghost Gallery."

I look at the mess, and then at my team. "I'll stay up all night to make another one. It won't take as long as the first time since we already know how to build it."

"We all will," says Ander.

"Yeah," says Mare. "Who needs sleep?"

"Well then, I'll submit our petition."

"And I will retrieve the containers," says Gregor. "The sooner this pile of junk is cleaned up the better."

Ander makes a nasty face at him. Too bad he doesn't notice before he walks out the door. No one says anything for a few minutes, but I can't stand the silence. "I can't believe it's destroyed."

"We were completely done," says Mare. "All we had to do was practice. Now we have to rebuild this whole thing."

"We'll never have enough time," says Jillian. "Even if we can get more supplies."

"Yes, we will. Mare will make us another schedule," I say. "It worked before. It can work now too. Right, Mare?"

"Right," she says. "I'll make another schedule, but first let's sort this stuff into piles. One for wood, one for nails and one for metal pieces. Then when we're done, I'll write out a schedule for the next seven days."

Seven days. It's fine. We *were* going to use this time to practice. Another small setback. So what if our whole object is destroyed? We'll just have to work even harder than we planned, just like Master Freeman said this morning. We must push ourselves this last week. We can do it. Seven days to rebuild, rehearse, and be ready. It's okay. It's going to be *fine*.

BLAME GAMES

GREGOR SETS THE plastic bins down with a thud near the pile that used to be our Ghost Gallery. "Seraphina and I are meeting with Master Freeman in twenty minutes. We'll return with his response shortly." He exits the shed, and we begin filling the bins with scraps of wood and metal.

"Jax is right," says Ander. "I don't think the Ghost Gallery fell apart by itself. And even if it did, it wouldn't crash into so many pieces."

"I was thinking the same thing," I say, examining a piece of my mangled artwork. If the wooden box fell off the bracket, it would crash to the ground. The sides might break apart, but they wouldn't split into tiny slivers."

Jax peers into the crevices of a metal crank. "And why would these metal pieces be smashed? If the cranks broke apart, they might have cracked in a couple places, not been crushed. Look at this one. It looks like it's been flattened by a steam roller."

"Let me see that," says Ander, grabbing the piece out of his hand. "You're right. Even if the box fell on this piece, it wouldn't end up this flat."

"So how did it get like that?" asks Jillian.

Jax closes the shed door. "I think someone did it."

"On purpose?" asks Jillian. "Like who?"

"I don't know," says Jax.

"But why would someone do that?" she asks. "All of the kids here know how much work this is—no one would do this to another team."

"Are you sure about that?" I ask. "What if another team thought our solution was better than theirs?"

"So?" asks Jillian.

Mare nods. "Maybe they would try to eliminate their competition."

"But we don't know where the other teams have been storing their materials. How could any of them know about our stuff?" asks Jillian.

"They could if they've been spying on us!" says Mare.

"Or if someone's big mouth told them," says Ander. "It's all my fault! I told Witch Girl from Michigan we were doing a play. It must have been them. They did it and it's all because of me!" He storms off to the back corner and sits down with his head buried in his knees. I'm sure he must be crying.

"Ander, come on," says Jillian. "It's not your fault."

He doesn't look up.

I feel sick to my stomach. "The Michigan team probably was spying on us. When they found out we were doing a play, I bet they wanted to wreck our sets so we wouldn't beat them. That's why they destroyed our Ghost Gallery!"

"That's so mean," says Jillian.

"I knew Witch Girl was evil," says Mare. "I'm going to find her and—

"And what?" asks Jax. "Yell at her? Fight her? You can't prove her team did this."

Jillian kneels next to Ander. He looks up and explodes. "You all hate me. I know you do! Well, that's okay because I hate me too. I'm so stupid. We were going to win this competition, and now we don't even have anything to show the judges."

"We don't hate you," says Mare. "They smashed all this. You didn't."

"But they wouldn't have known we even had sets for a play if it weren't for me."

"Maybe they would have destroyed whatever object we created," says Jax.

"He's right," says Jillian. "It's not your fault."

I know I should agree with Jillian. I should tell Ander that I'm not mad at him. But I can't. It probably is his fault, and now we have *nothing*.

We kneel on the floor trying to organize the mess. Ander eventually walks over but I don't look at him.

"Hopefully Seraphina and Gregor will come back and say we can go to the Piedmont Pantry and grab more supplies," says Mare.

"And then we can rebuild," says Jax.

"We can rehearse during our breaks," says Jillian. "We know our lines. It will be easy. At least our costumes are okay."

"Are they?" I ask.

Mare beats me to the cupboard. She pulls out five zippered bags, perfectly intact. "Here's our paperwork too.

At least they didn't wreck any of this."

"See?" says Jillian. "It's not so bad."

I stare at the floor and I think maybe Mare's right. We'll just work hard. It was fun building the Ghost Gallery the first time. We can do it again. I'm almost ready to forgive Ander, to say that I don't blame him when Seraphina and Gregor march in.

Ander scrambles to his feet. "What did they say?"

Gregor speaks with no expression on his face at all. "Your petition has been denied."

"No!" Ander screams. "Why?"

"I'm so sorry," says Seraphina. "We did our best to plead your case. Master Freeman wouldn't budge."

I bite my ring finger nail. "Why not?"

"He told us what we already knew. No exceptions can be made to the rules. They were established decades ago by Lexland and Andora Appelonia and he would not go against them," says Gregor.

"But what about the rule he changed yesterday, the one about the Rehearsal Judging?" I ask.

"Yeah," says Ander. "He changed that one."

"I challenged that point too," says Seraphina. "Master Freeman believes that rule was changed to further challenge the teams."

"So—" says Mare.

"He feels that by denying your request for more supplies, we are further challenging you. He said you are The New York team—the Crimson Five—and you'll find a way to come back stronger."

Ander throws up his arms. "I knew they were going to judge us harder. It isn't fair!"

I fall back down on the floor. Ander's right. This isn't

fair—and it's all his fault. If he hadn't told Witch Girl that we were doing a play, then her team never would have worried that our solution was better than theirs. They never would have spied on us to see where our set was. They never would have found it, and they never would have wrecked it. Why did he have to have such a big mouth?

THE STAIRWELL

TEN CONTAINERS ARE stacked up near the shed door. Nine are filled with metal and wood parts and one is filled with our costumes and paperwork. I can hardly breathe looking at all the broken pieces shoved in there like that. It's like parts of me are shoved in there too.

Gregor has left to have the containers moved to our bedchamber. Seraphina pulls us into a huddle. "Alright, my Crimson Kids. I know your chances don't look very promising right now, but we have no time to look backward. Rehearsal Judging is in seven days. I believe you can salvage your solution somehow. Remember what we've said all summer: Be curious, be creative, be collaborative, be colorful, and be courageous. That's you—the Crimson Five. Only now you must stay cool too. Go back to your bedchamber and fix this thing. I know you can."

Mare claps her hands. "Okay, Seraphina. I got this. Let's go see how much glue and duct tape we have. We'll need a lot to reconstruct."

"Can we ask Swissa for some too?" asks Jillian. "Or is that against the rules?"

"No, that's fine" says Seraphina. "The rules say you can't go back to Piedmont Pantry. As long as you don't steal anything, you can get your materials from wherever you like."

Mare nods. "We're on it!"

"Wait," says Jax. "Is it okay if I go back to my bedchamber while you guys do that? I have an idea to work on."

"Can I go with you?" Ander asks.

"Sure. I need your help anyway."

"Then it looks like you have a plan," says Seraphina. "I'll have boxed lunches sent up to your chambers. If you need anything else, let me know."

"Will you meet us for dinner?" I ask.

"Of course. I'll want to hear how you're doing." She holds out her fist and we touch knuckles, our wristbands shining under the shed light bulb. This seems to motivate the rest of my team, but it doesn't make me feel any better at all.

The girls and I run around to the front of Piedmont Chamber. The Ohio team is gathered under an awning and they turn to look as we run by. Their whole team is made up of girls, wearing yellow shirts and matching headbands. I wonder what it would be like to be on a team of all girls. Probably not as much fun as having Ander around. I smile to myself for a second until I remember—I'm still mad at him.

When we reach our bedchamber, the containers are waiting by the work table. We open them and take inventory of our supplies. We have a jug of super glue, leftover paint, and seven rolls of duct tape. I guess that's a start.

Jillian turns on the music. "What should we do first?"

"Let's each take a container and put together whatever pieces we can," says Mare.

I open one up and dig through it. Most of the pieces are the ones I painted myself, so sad and crumbled. I do my best to match them up with random scraps, gluing small pieces at a time. The glue welds my fingers together though. I look for a place to lay the pieces and realize that I need a large cloth or something. I check the cupboard under the windowsill and find Mabel curled up in a ball. I pull her out and open up the pocket of her dress to turn her on. Her eyelids blink open and she stretches.

"Hi, Mabel," I say.

She blinks.

"Will you do a job for me?"

She blinks again.

"Can you find Swissa and ask her if we can have an old bed sheet?"

She blinks a third time. I check inside her control panel to be sure she has recorded the question. She has, so I open the door. She scurries out and down the hall. A little while later, Swissa knocks. Mare opens the door and Mabel rolls in too. She pops open her dress pocket and inside is a pink bed sheet folded into a small square.

"Thanks, Mabel. Good girl."

She blinks and wheels herself back into the cupboard, but I leave the door open so she's not lonely this time.

"Hi, Swissa," I say. "Thanks for the sheet. I need some place to lay these pieces while they dry."

She sets three boxes onto our table. "Anything for the team."

"Are those our lunches?" asks Jillian.

"Yup, Seraphina said you'd be working through lunch."

"Yeah, that's because most of our solution got destroyed last night," I say.

"Oh my gosh! That's awful." She looks at all the pieces on the ground before she heads out the door. "I'm sorry," she says like she might actually mean it.

Jillian and Mare take their lunches over to the floor near our bed, but the thought of eating anything when our project is in pieces makes my stomach ache. Our glued pieces look nothing like they're supposed to and the drawings look like a dinosaur drew them. My brain tangles up so bad my head hurts. "I'm going."

"Where?" asks Mare.

"I don't know, but the gallery pieces look terrible!"

"I think they look cool in a weird sort of way," says Jillian.

"But that's not how they're supposed to look!" I run out the door past purple shirts from Iowa and gray from Illinois. I run and run and don't stop until I get to the end of the hall and down the giant stair case. I land at the bottom and practically smash into Jax.

"Wait, where are you going?" he asks.

"I don't know. Our project is awful!"

"But we have an idea," Ander calls. "We were just coming up to show you."

"You can show Mare and Jillian." I break away and find a side exit door. But I don't want to exit. I want to hide. I crawl under the staircase and start to cry. My body shakes as I think about all of our hard work. Gone. My chance to get to PIPS. Gone. All because of one mean girl and Ander's stupid mouth. We'll never get to the finals now. We'll all be sent home. We'll all get programmed. Everything will go back to the way it was. My best friend will be best friends with someone else. The kids at school will call me by my number, and Ander and I won't even talk. I thought we were friends, but how can I ever forgive him? It's his fault my dream won't come true. There's no way we can fix our solution now.

I reach into my pocket for a tissue. Instead, I pull out a slip of paper. It's the message I got the first night here—a faded, wrinkled string of words:

Don't be afraid of change. Have the courage to believe in what you can achieve.

Change? Change what? Our whole solution? It's too late now. I don't even know where to start. Why can't Grandma Kitty be here? She'd know what to do.

The exit door opens so I slide into the corner. I can't let anyone see me crying. I peer through the steps at a pair of white boots. I quick turn back around.

Swissa peeks under the stairs. "What are you doing in there?"

I don't look up. "Nothing."

"Really? It looks like you're hiding."

"Please go away."

She crawls in next to me and I squish myself against the wall. *Why can't she just leave me alone?*

"Do I have to? This looks like a great hiding spot."

I don't say anything.

"I wish I had found this place earlier in the summer."

I look at her out of the corner of my eye. She's a lot prettier when she's not scowling. "Why would you need a hiding place?"

"Me? Lots of reasons. To get away from the drill sergeant in the laundry room who teaches us how to fold towels perfectly, or the bottle robot—"

"What's the *bottle robot*?"

"It's the machine that fills the shampoo bottles for all the bathrooms in the building. One of us has to watch it to be sure it doesn't malfunction. The team from Nebraska invented it one year. The Piedmont Committee wants to be sure we can use it."

"So what do you have to do?"

"When you're on bottle duty you can't look away for a second. A laser monitors your eyes. It reports you if you do."

"How long do you have to watch it?"

"Thirty minutes every day."

I picture myself forcing my eyes to stare at a shampoo filling robot for thirty minutes in a row. "That's almost as bad as getting programmed."

"It's worse. I liked getting programmed."

"You did?"

"Yes, I was programmed for Art Forms. That's what I'm good at, not watching bottles."

"Then why are you here, working as a chambermaid?"

"It's a summer job. I go to a high school for performing arts in New York City during the school year."

I hadn't pictured Swissa doing anything other than wheeling her cart into our room and snapping sarcastic comments at us. "Wow. Do you sing?"

"Yes! And I dance and act too. I love it there. I wish I

could have stayed all summer."

"Why didn't you?"

"Well, anyone who competes at the National Finals can come back to work here for a summer while they're in high school. I didn't want to, but my parents made me."

"How come?"

"They wanted me to give back to the Piedmont Organization. But I was afraid."

"Why?"

"I was upset when my team didn't make it to the Global Championships and I had to leave. It took me a long time to stop being sad. I was convinced that PIPS was the school for me."

"I'm sorry you didn't make it."

"That's okay. I'm not sorry anymore. Not long after I was programmed for Art Forms, I realized how much I love performing. I also realized PIPS wasn't the school for me. The School of Performing Arts is where I belong."

"But why didn't you want to work here?"

"I thought if I came back I would wish I went to PIPS again."

"Did you?"

"At first I did. I saw all of you girls so excited to be here. There's great energy in this place. Everyone is filled with such great ideas."

"So what happened?"

"I was miserable at the beginning of the summer, but then I realized that my school is full of great energy and great ideas too. We just use our ideas in a different way."

"So you're not miserable anymore?"

She laughs. "No, not really, except when I have to watch bottles. Besides, summer's almost over and soon I can go back to my own school with all my new friends."

"I'm glad you're not sad. Your school sounds fun."

"It is. So . . . why are you hiding?"

"I didn't know where else to go."

"Oh?"

"My team won't even make it to the Finals."

"Is that because your stuff got wrecked?"

"Yes, and without our rotating object, our play won't make any sense."

"Why don't you make a new object?"

"Our other one was really good though."

"Your other one is gone."

That feels like a punch in the stomach. "Yeah, but I don't know where to start."

"Don't you have teammates?"

I huff. "Yes."

"You have another week don't you?"

"But what if we can't think of something else as good?"

"So you're afraid to try?"

"I'm not afraid."

"It sounds like you are."

I bite my pinky nail. "What if we can't think up something good enough to earn one-hundred and fifty points? All the other teams and judges and parents will think we stink."

"So you'd rather tell the judges that your object got destroyed so you had to withdraw from the competition. You'll never get to the finals that way."

I cross my arms. "I guess I am afraid."

"Why?"

"What if we work hard all week to come up with another amazing solution and we don't get enough points anyway? All the hard work will be for nothing."

"So you're afraid of hard work?"

"No! But we did work hard and look what happened."

"Yeah, but what's the worst that can happen if you work hard again and come up with a new solution? You won't make it into the National Finals and you'll be sent home for programming like I was."

"But you like artistic stuff. I'll probably get programmed for math, and I don't even like it. I'll have to go to the School of Math for high school. I have all these ideas swirling around in my head all the time. I want to be someplace where I can use them."

"If you have so many ideas swirling in your head, why aren't you with your team right now, creating a new solution?"

I look down at the message in my hand.

"Kia, I wasn't meant to go to PIPS, but if you are then I bet you can pull something amazing together."

I bite on my thumb nail.

"You know I'm right."

"Yeah, I know." *I don't want to give up. I want our team to have a chance.* "Okay. I'll go back."

"Good, and I will too. At least my bottle shift is over for today."

"Thanks, Swissa."

"You're welcome."

We crawl out of the stairwell, and I run down the hall to the giant staircase. I better hurry. We have so much work to do if we're ever going to get to the finals.

GHOST-LIKE

I CRACK OPEN the door to my bedchamber. My teammates are huddled around our work table. None of them
hear me come in so I stand in the doorway for a second,
wondering what they're working on.

"Hey," I finally say.

Jillian looks up. "Where were you?"

I suddenly feel like an idiot for leaving. "I went for a
walk."

"Oh." She turns back around. No one else seems to care
that I was gone or that I was upset.

I walk over to the table and peek over Mare's shoulder.
"What are you guys doing?"

"We're trying to think up a new object that can go along
with our play," says Mare. "We can't get the Ghost Gallery
to look like it was. Jillian and I have been trying for an
hour."

The random pieces, scattered on the floor, make my head hurt again. "I'm sorry I ran out before. I was frustrated."

"Like we're not?" Jillian demands, shuffling papers on the table.

Now I feel worse. "I should have stayed to figure it out with you."

"We're teammates, right?" says Mare. "We need to stick together."

"I know."

She looks over at the boys. "Right guys?"

Jax looks up. "Yeah."

"I promise I won't run away again."

Mare pulls me over to the computer. "Ander and Jax have an idea."

"We're trying to design a new Ghost Gallery—a digital version of what we already built," says Jax.

I'm not sure what to think about a digital object. But I try to be positive because I don't have a better idea yet. "So you think we should use a computer object instead of the box object?"

"Yeah," says Jillian. "We could design our image that way this time."

"Hmm." I kneel down at the table and try to picture what they're talking about.

"We could still use our costumes and script," says Mare.

"Yes, that's the idea," says Jax, scratching his head.

We spend the next hour trying to design something worth one-hundred and fifty points. Jax doesn't leave the computer, but eventually Mare lays down on the floor while Jillian spins in the sparkles. "Is it dinner time yet?" she asks.

"The dining hall opened ten minutes ago," says Mare.

"Let's go."

"I'm not hungry," I say. "I'm going to keep working."

"I'll stay too then," says Ander.

"Okay," says Mare. "We'll bring you dessert."

Jax, Jillian, and Mare leave, and I sit down at the table across from Ander.

"I don't blame you for what happened, you know."

He looks me straight in the eye. "Yes, you do."

I struggle to keep my nails out of my mouth. "No, not anymore. I did at first, but it's Witch Girl's fault. She was sure we were going to have a better solution than hers so she convinced her teammates to help her wreck ours."

"We don't know they did it."

"Who else would have done it?"

"I don't know, but I'd rather know for sure before we blame them."

"Okay, Mr. Detective, let's find proof then. We'll spy on them like they spied on us. Or let's go confront them. I'll bet they'll squirm when they know we're on to them."

"Do you even hear yourself?"

"What?"

"First you blame me for telling them we're doing a play, and then you blame her team for wrecking our object—"

"So?"

"You've wasted all this time trying to blame someone and running off when you could have been working with us."

"I'm sorry."

"I get that you're mad. I want to blame the person who smashed it too. All our hard work was destroyed, just like that, but that's not what's bugging me. Even if the Michigan team did do it and got the idea because I have a big mouth, you shouldn't have been such a jerk to me. I didn't do it on purpose. I said I was sorry and you didn't say anything to me."

I mangle my ring nail. "I know. I was upset."

He leans back in his chair. "Well, I was upset too, and you made me feel worse."

"You're right. I'm a jerk."

"I thought we were friends."

"We are friends!"

"Friends don't ditch each other when one of them makes a mistake. They stick by each other. No matter what."

"I didn't mean to ditch you."

"Well, you did."

Great. Now he hates me. "I'm sorry! I'm just not used to having a friend who sticks by me. I told you that before, and now I've wrecked everything! I'm the worst friend ever."

He looks me right in the eyes. "You're not the worst friend ever."

"Yes, I am and now you hate me."

He punches me in the arm. "KK, cut it out. I don't hate you."

"Well, you should."

"Why, because you need to take remedial friendship classes? Maybe they have them here at Piedmont."

I punch him back.

He shakes his head and smiles. "So what do we do about this computer thing? The idea is *okay*, but I don't think it will get us one-hundred and fifty points. Everyone knows how to make a computer program."

"There has to be something cool we can think of. Maybe we should just scrap our question and start over. Think of one that can be answered using our same costumes and same script."

Ander walks around the table. "Wait a minute. I might have an idea."

"Really?"

"Maybe. Hold on. I'm thinking." He walks to the door and back again. Then he takes a random pencil eraser out of his pocket and tosses it in the air. "You know how we were talking about our ancestors—that day by the pond?"

"Yeah, I remember."

"How I said that sometimes I wonder what mine were like, and I try to find stuff out about them, especially my great, great grandpa Jim?"

"Yeah."

"Okay, so one night after Evening Announcements, I couldn't sleep. So, I started thinking about hockey, and it got me thinking about him again. So I started playing on the air screen."

"The what?"

He walks over to the white board where Swissa posts our daily itinerary, and pushes a button.

"What are you doing?"

"Accessing your air screen."

"My what?"

"Didn't Seraphina show you this? It's so cool." He waves his hand out in front of him. I hear a flutter and a glass-like monitor appears in front of him floating in mid-air!

"What is that?"

"It's like a computer but smarter."

He pushes buttons that I don't even see. It must understand him because images and words appear and disappear with each click.

"I found out some cool stuff. I already knew he was a

great hockey player when he was young."

"Right."

"But I wanted to know more so I looked him up. I found his basic information, so I created a document where I listed as many facts about him as I could, like his full name, his birthday, where he lived, where he worked, his hobbies, hair color, eye color . . . all that kind of stuff."

"That's cool."

"Well, it gets cooler. I was just messing around and found even more information—all his private records. I guess there are records stored permanently for each person in our country. They've been put into a database."

"Really? What kinds of things?"

"Like, if the person was ever interviewed, then the database would have it in his file. If that person ever sent a message to another person with their phone or computer, then that would be in there too."

"You mean if I sent you a message or talked to you on the phone, our conversation would be saved."

"Yup."

"Forever?"

"I think so."

"But that's invasion of privacy."

"Anyway, I wondered if since my great-great-grandpa was into sports, if any of his conversations about that would be saved and I guess they are because I found some. Watch."

He types his great, great grandfather's name, along with the facts on his list, with buttons in mid-air. When he's certain he's found the right person, he clicks on his name, somehow floating in the air screen. Then he types a question using the air buttons: *Did you like to go to school?*

A written response appears on the screen:

I didn't mind going to school that much. I was competitive, probably too competitive, and that's how I treated my class work. As long as I did well on my tests, I figured I'd beaten the questions. I've been competitive my whole life and that's what led me to sports.

"Oh my gosh. He answered you!"

"Kind of, yeah."

"So we can ask our ancestors questions and their answers will appear?"

"As long as the information has been stored in the database. I guess if the person was ever recorded giving that answer, then it will work."

"That's awesome!"

"It's like my great-great-grandpa is right here communicating with me."

I think about that for a second and an idea swirls free. "What if we could see him at the same time?"

"Do you mean have his picture appear too?"

"Sort of. If each person has facts and conversations on file in the database, maybe there are pictures and videos as well. What if we could find a way to get a video of the person talking while their answer appears on the screen or comes out of their mouth? If their lips were moving from one video, even if they were saying something else, we could match it up with the audio recording of an answer they gave another time."

"That's it, KK! There has to be recordings of the person's voice on that database somewhere. What if we could put it all together? Video images. Voice recordings. Facts. Everything!"

I grin when Ander calls me by my nickname again. "That would be amazing. Can you imagine being able to really talk to and see our ancestors?"

Ander jumps up on the chair. "That can be our object—our invention! That's what we can make!"

"But how?"

"We'll need help. We need the rest of our team."

I narrow my eyes. "You mean we need Jax."

When Jax and the girls come back, we bombard them with our idea.

"What do you think, Jax?" Ander asks. "Can you build a computer app that could put all of this together? Do you know how to do that?"

Jax stares at the air screen and then at his own computer. "I'll try. I think I can interface the information you found on the database with any videos and pictures and social media posts. Then I'll program the app to splice it all together to produce an image with a voice."

We take turns reading the information we found on Jax's computer, as he types it into the air screen. Then we watch him program it all together. After a long while of him typing and us watching, a tornado looking image swirls on the screen.

"Hey, KK, that's your brain!"

I roll my eyes and watch the swirl. Before long, it morphs into a picture of a man—Ander's great-great-grandfather! Jax pushes another air button and the picture morphs into a live version of the picture. Ander's great-great-grandpa is surrounded by a smoky haze but appears to be alive—like a video or a ghost back from the dead! He scratches his nose and blinks his eyes. The image looks like he's walking down the street.

"How did it do that?" asks Jillian, her eyes wide open.

"Just wait," says Jax. "Ander, ask him a question."

Ander types the same question as before, "Did you like to go to school?"

The image of the man moves his head and leans against the side of a building. A voice recording plays along with the image. "I didn't mind going to school that much. I was competitive, probably too competitive, and that's how I treated my classes. As long as I did well on my tests, I figured I beat the questions! I've been competitive my whole life. That's what made me successful when I got into sports."

"Oh my gosh!" I say. "It worked!"

"Computer apps can do anything," says Jax. "You just have to have an idea. All I did was mix the town records, which includes all the facts found on the database, with any pictures they had on file and also the social media posts. I merged them together. Then I instructed the app to make the pictures move. If the database had any voice recordings, then the image will sound like the person really did. If they don't have a voice recording on file, then the app will assign a voice to them."

"So you don't know if that's the voice Ander's great, great grandpa really had?"

"Not for sure, but since he did interviews, it probably sounds close."

"Do you think it would work for relatives that are still alive too?" I ask.

"Probably."

"Can I try? I know everything about my Grandma Kitty."

"Okay. Ander will type—you talk."

"Her name is Katharin Riley. She was born October 25th, 2009. She grew up in Rochester, NY. She played soccer and won the very first Piedmont Challenge."

Ander types in the information. The tornado swirls and we wait. Finally, it morphs into a picture of Grandma Kitty. Her hair is sparkly, and she's wearing dangly earrings! The side of the screen list facts about her, like the names of my grandpa and their children—including my mom! It tells where she went to school and what her job was, but it doesn't say anything about her winning the Piedmont Challenge.

"That's her!"

"Ask her a question," says Mare.

"Okay. What did you want to be when you were twelve years old?"

The image wiggles and morphs into a little girl. Her clothes are bright, but her boots are brown and ugly. "I'm twelve-years-old and in the sixth grade. I want to be an astronaut when I grow up. I'm going to build my own rocket ship and be a taxi driver for people visiting other planets."

"Aw, she's so cute! I didn't know she liked science and space. This must have been before she won the Piedmont Challenge."

"Let's try another age," says Ander.

"Okay, let's try fourteen. She was probably at PIPS then."

Ander types again. The image morphs slightly. Her clothes aren't as bright but she's wearing dangly pineapple earrings!

"I'm in eighth grade, my second year at the School of New Technology. I love it here, but the classes are hard. I'm working on an idea for powering an inexpensive rocket ship. I want to test it out but my teachers won't let me. I have to send my research to PIPS. The kids who won the Piedmont Challenge get to do all that fun stuff. It's not fair. I want to test my own ideas."

"Oh my gosh," I say, covering my mouth. My knees almost buckle under me.

"What's wrong?"

I take a deep breath. "Is the stuff she's saying true?"

"I guess so," says Jax. "She must have said the same thing to one of her friends while talking on the phone sometime. The app had to have gotten the information from somewhere, why?"

"But the image said she didn't win the Piedmont Challenge. She told me she did."

"Maybe there's a mistake."

"Yeah, there has to be. I've seen her Golden Light Bulb. Maybe some of her information got mixed up."

"Maybe."

"I mean there must be a glitch somewhere. We'll have to find it." I shove the Piedmont Challenge thought out of my head and look at Grandma Kitty's face practically floating in front of me. "I can't believe how real it looks. It feels like my Grandma Kitty is really in this room with me!"

My teammates and I stare at each other smiling. This idea could be the thing that helps us win. It's just as good as floating sparkles and robotic monkeys. Maybe it's even better!

THE GOLDEN LIGHT BULB

THE NEXT MORNING before breakfast, my phone lights up. I click on my mom's face, flashing on the screen. "Hi, Mom."

"Hi, Honey. I'm glad you're awake. I heard about what happened to your project! Grandma Kitty told me."

"It was awful."

"I'm really sorry."

"It's okay."

"I know you're disappointed and it's terrible how it happened. You just have to realize that things don't always turn out the way you hope they will. You and your teammates did your best. I'm very proud of you for that."

"But Mom, we're still working on our solution."

"What do you mean?"

"We're creating a new one!"

"A new one? You don't have time to start over, do you?"

"Well, we are. There's no way we can win without a solution."

"Oh, Kia—it's a little late for that. Don't you think?"

"We know, but we're going to try anyway."

"Well, Honey, I hope it all comes together."

I pick at the emblem on my shirt. "I thought you would be proud of me for not giving up."

"I am. It's just that I'd hate for you to go to all the trouble and then—"

"What, Mom—not win? You don't think we can do it, do you?"

"I didn't say that, Kia."

I think about erasing her face from my phone. "I'm not stupid."

"I never said you were stupid."

"You don't think we can win," I say as mean as I can.

"Of course I do. But at this point, your chances aren't good."

"I have to go now, Mom. We have a lot of stuff to do."

"Kia, I'm sorry. I'm not trying to upset you. I know you'll come up with another solution. You can do anything you put your mind to. You always have. It's just—I miss you terribly."

Maybe she does miss me, but she still just doesn't understand me at all. "I miss you too."

"You've been gone all summer, and I don't have anyone to make mint chocolate ice cream pie for."

"Ryne would eat it." I try not to spit the words out.

"Yes, but Ryne isn't you."

I don't want to fight with her, but ice cream pie doesn't always fix everything. "I guess not."

"I'll see you soon, okay, Honey? I love you."

"Bye, Mom. I love you too." I hang up and pretend she thinks we can win. I'll just have to show her we can.

After breakfast, my teammates and I meet in our bedchamber. Pieces of our Ghost Gallery and supplies are scattered everywhere, even on our star bed, but we ignore them for now. We have to find a way to use our new invention in our play.

Jillian gets this far off look on her face. "I've been thinking about our Ghost Gallery, and I have the best idea." She flips open to a clean page and doodles a giant circle. "I think we should use as many circles in our solution as we can." She scans the room like she's looking for something.

"Why?" asks Mare.

"Because that must be the secret theme of this year's task."

"What do you mean *secret theme*?"

"Think about it. Our problem begins by stating, 'The earth is shaped like a circle.'"

"Yeah . . ."

"There are other clues I've found too," she says. "Look around this room."

"The walls are covered in circles," I say.

"Keep looking. There's more," says Jillian. She stands up with a know-it-all smile on her face.

"Look at our closet," Mare says. "Our clothes cubbies are circle shapes."

"Wait a second," says Ander. "Remember that place on the aero-bus where we drank blueberry milkshakes?"

"I don't remember that," says Jax.

"KK, you remember—it was called the Circle Café."

"It was!"

"I noticed something else," says Mare. "What about the flower thing on our tables at dinner that first night. The one that spun around in a circle?"

"Oh, yeah!" says Ander. "The one that spit our food out."

"This whole place is set up like the shape of the Earth," Jax adds. "I bet the Piedmont Organization is trying to see how many teams notice it."

Ander walks around the table. "So we should probably add as many circle shaped things as we can."

"That might get us more points," says Jax.

Jillian sits back down. "So, do you want to hear my idea or not?"

"Yes," I say. "What is it?"

"What if we change our universal question to: *What will I be like when I grow up?* We can change our script around so that instead of Kia wondering where she'll go after she dies, she can wonder what she'll be like when she grows up. We can be characters who help her figure it out—using the computer app you guys are working on."

"That could work," says Ander.

"I can change the script around," I offer.

"We could turn our Ghost Gallery mess into a giant circle object, and divide it into five sections—the phrases in our team mantra: The Five C's."

"But why should we add the Five C's to the giant circle," asks Mare.

Jax turns to her to explain. "The circle represents all of us."

I'm starting to see how this can work. "This is what Andora was talking about, and Seraphina and Gregor too."

"What do you mean?" asks Ander.

"Remember on the first day of camp, when we registered inside that giant atrium of Piedmont Chamber?"

"Andora was sitting at that fancy table," he recalls.

"And you almost started yelling at her," Jillian remembers with a giggle.

Ander jumps out of his chair. "She said she'd expect more from our team since we came from the same school!"

"That's what I mean," I say. "I think the judges are hoping that we can create a solution that shows how special we each are, but how much stronger we are as a team."

"And we can make a mural thing to show how well we fit together as a team," says Mare.

"Good idea!" I say. We crowd around the table and our pencils can hardly keep up with what we're saying. We sort out how we're going to build and decorate the mural first. Then we spend the rest of the day super gluing and duct taping the broken wooden pieces into one giant flat circle shaped object. We turn the pieces backward so that the plain wood is showing. That way we can decorate it all over again.

We realize we have a lot more to do if we're going to morph our old solution into our new one. Mare comes to the rescue and helps us organize. She assigns us each something to be in charge of. Jax has already planned a way to put the metal stand back together and make the wooden circle spin. We've named it the Circle Spinner.

Ander takes charge of the new computer program that we've named the Ancestor App. His job is to input all the facts we've researched about our relatives or ancestors. We have to be sure the ghost-like images of the people who lived long before we did will come to life in front of the judges. We also challenge him to find a good way to show it up on the stage.

I'm in charge of the script—again. I need to find a way to re-write this play using the Circle Spinner. We're going to have to make it start in one position and then make it change at least three times before it goes back to its original position. I'm not sure yet how to do that.

Jillian updates our costumes. We work side by side so that she knows how our characters are changing and how to dress them. Mare takes care of the paperwork. Now that our solution has changed, she'll have to rewrite how we used skills from all six categories to solve the task. I ask her to work with Jillian and me. We need her to help us put these ideas all together.

Mabel has been working overtime. We have no time to go to the dining hall so we've programmed her to bring our lunch and dinner boxes. Cold sandwiches aren't our first choice, but it doesn't matter. My teammates want to win this competition as much as I do now!

By the time we've packed up our dinner boxes and stored them inside Mabel's dress pocket for the trash, the glue has dried on our Circle Spinner. We divide it into five sections from the middle with strips of red duct tape. Red is the color of Crimson Elementary so that's our unanimous choice. Now that our circle looks like a pie chart, we each pick a section to decorate, using our favorite colors and our team mantra: Be Curious, Be Creative, Be Collaborative, Be Colorful, and Be Courageous.

We use the materials left over from our smashed Ghost Gallery to decorate around the words. When we've finished all the gluing, Jillian stands up to get a better look. "It's like a piece of artwork."

I unstick my fingers. She's right, but something's missing. I'm just not sure what it is. I can feel something forming in my brain, but it doesn't turn into an idea. I take a breath and try to be patient. It takes a few seconds of staring but then I realize. We need something in the center, something that pulls each of us together as a team.

"But what?" Mare asks when I tell them my idea. "We could write Crimson Five in the center since everyone is obsessed with calling us that but besides that, what else do we all have in common?"

"This competition," says Jax.

I snap my fingers. "That's it."

"What could we use to show that?" asks Jillian.

"What if we display the Ancestor App in the center somehow? We used all the skills in our team mantra to create it." Jax explains.

"That's perfect!" I say. "But how do we display it?"

Ander walks around the table twirling a pencil. "I have to think about that."

WE SPEND the next few days working out the details of our new solution. Eventually, the metal bracket gets put back together, and we attach our Circle Spinner to it. Jax is a genius. The circle spins and everything. With Jillian and Mare's help, I change the lines in our script. Our play is now about a little girl who wonders what she'll be like when she grows up. She stumbles upon a magical place where the townspeople tell her how they figured out what they would be like when they were younger.

That's where our Circle Spinner comes in. The spinner starts in the upright position, at "Be Curious," the place where all children begin as they ask themselves this question. Then as each character helps the little girl, they rotate the spinner and explain to her how important it is to understand her past, using one of the words on our spinner, before she can move on to her future. Then they show an image of one of their ancestors who have similar personality traits to them. They explain to the little girl that by using the circle spinner, she can get a glimpse into her past so that she might get a glimpse into her future too. At the very end, the Circle Spinner returns to its original position at "Be Curious," just like the rules require.

Jillian fixes the original language by changing the lines but keeping the motions the same. I try to rewrite the finale song, but it's really hard, and I get stuck. I need the rest of my teammates too. They help me change it, and then we all try to help Ander with the Ancestor App. But all he can do is throw his arms back behind his head. "I just can't find a way to display the Ancestor App on the center of the Circle Spinner. Every time I try to, the paint and duct tape block the images. It's not a good back drop."

"But we have to project those images onto the spinner. That's the key to our rotating object," I say. "Otherwise, all we have is a spinning circle with words and pieces of wood glued all over it.

"What if we cover the center with something, like maybe the fabric scraps over there," Jax suggests.

"We can try it," says Ander.

Jillian throws Jax a pile of pink fabric and he holds some of it in front of the spinner.

Ander directs the app to project onto it by pushing the invisible buttons. Nothing appears, and he huffs out a breath.

"See? I don't know what else to do!"

Jax walks closer to the spinner. "How do you think the

app transmits the image?"

My teammates look at each other. I know this. I'm sure we learned this in math. "It's digital," I explain. "You must have to program it to find some sort of binary code."

"What's binary code?" asks Mare.

"It's a series of zeros and ones. They can be transmitted through the airwaves. That's how our cell phones work."

"Then why can't they transmit onto the paint or fabric?" asks Ander.

"That's because those aren't transmitters for digital code," I explain. "You need something like, let me think. Metal!"

"We have a lot of that left over," says Jax. "Let's use some of the cranks and brackets. We could attach those to the center and then transmit the images right on it."

"I'll try it," says Ander. Jillian and Mare hold a few pieces up as a test. Ander enters in the information for Jillian's great aunt. The image is blurry, but it's there.

"That's better but it's not bright enough," says Ander. "I don't know how to make it clearer."

My head starts to hurt. We are so close. This new solution is way better than I imagined, but not like this. If the judges and people in the audience can't see the ancestor images, they won't understand what we're looking at. Our play won't make any sense. There has to be something that will conduct zeros and ones better than regular metal. But what's a better conductor than metal? My brain swirls. I start to bite my nails but then I stop. Gold. Gold is a better conductor than metal.

"I've got it, you guys! I know what to do. We can attach a Golden Light Bulb to the spinner. The app needs gold!"

WE WALK onto the field in silence. I think my team-mates are imagining the Ancestor App with my Golden Light Bulb glued to the center. We have to change our focus though. It's time for the Nacho Cheese Ball Finals! We watch Team Rhode Island march out in matching uniforms. They look like a professional sports team—two boys and three girls. I catch Ander's eye. He doesn't seem to have a plan—and neither do I. Other teams from all over the country are holding up signs. Some for Rhode Island. Some for New York. Seraphina walks across the grass and stands near the scoreboard.

The whistle blows. I guess we're going to wing it. A girl with big muscles in her legs plows by me. It takes me a second to react. By the time I do, her whole team has beaten us out of the neutral zone. They fire shots at our target, and before we can even get to them, the score is two hundred fifty one to zero. We fire back, bringing their score down to two hundred and seven, and force them back to the neutral zone.

My team sprints toward their target and get some points up on the board. One hundred eighty to be exact. They clobber us with glob after glob, and we have no choice but to retreat. The crowd cheers as we bounce back and forth from their target to ours and back again. I run by Ander. His face is covered in cheese, except for two holes for his eyes, but I don't see the usual fire in them. I don't feel it in myself either.

The whistle blows after the longest game of the summer, and we are not the winners. Rhode Island is crowned Nacho Cheese Ball Champions. We walk over to them looking more orange than ever, shake their hands, and accept our runner-up medals—a bucket with a scoop in it. We walk off the field together looking like astronauts thrown off the moon.

"The best team won," Ander shrugs. "I guess they wanted it more than we did."

"At least we made it to the finals," says Jax.

"Yeah," I say, skipping off the field. "And in two more days, we're going to make it to the finals again. The one that really matters."

QUARTER 'TIL TOMORROW

THE GIRLS AND I stayed up way past lights out last night. We knew it was against the rules, but we *had* to learn our new lines and practice our dance. Time was practically up. It wasn't so easy trying to whisper and dance silently in the dark, but we did it. Who needs sleep anyway? We could sleep when the competition was over.

This morning, I step through the Meeting Room Twelve doorway, and I remember how I felt the first time I walked into this room—like I couldn't wait to start solving our task, but I worried we wouldn't ever agree or work well together. Today, I can't wait to practice our amazing solution as a united team. I guess we have come a long way.

We'll have until dinner time tonight, when our families finally get here, to practice. Seraphina has planned a big party! Gregor didn't want her to because he said we needed our rest for Rehearsal Judging, but she convinced him that after all our hard work this summer, we deserve a celebration no matter how the judges score us tomorrow.

He has arranged to have our costumes, sets, and props transported here. He said he wants to keep our stuff safe, especially after what happened in the shed. And that's a relief. We can't have another disaster happen.

We grab our costume bags and scatter to the hallway bathrooms. I slip into my yellow overalls, minus the ragged pieces, and brush my hair into pigtails. After removing some of the tattered pieces of fabric on her own costume, and adding more sparkly pink fabric to her dress, Jillian has turned herself into Madam Sparkles, the dramatic townsperson who chats with all newcomers to the magical land of Crimson Catroplis. Mare has changed too and is now a mystical teenager, snapping her gum and staring at her reflection in the Circle Spinner's metal bracket.

We meet up with the boys in the hallway. Ander puts on his funky hat and bows to us, now looking like a court jester—like one of those clowns who could entertain the whole town. Jax, the Gate Keeper, flares his cape and smiles a little bit. His face doesn't even get pink.

Back in Meeting Room Twelve, Seraphina gasps. "You guys look spectacular!"

"Thanks Seraphina!" I squeal, skipping around the room. "We do, don't we?" My teammates skip behind me until Gregor clears his throat. Loud.

"It's quite early to celebrate—don't you agree?"

I know he's right so I stop skipping.

Seraphina ignores him and grabs a small box. "I have my timer ready. I'm going to sit in those seats with Gregor. We'll pretend we're the judges. Tomorrow the audience will be seated behind them. When I say, 'New York team, time begins now,' you'll quickly carry your spinner and other props to the judging area and begin."

We scurry to our assigned spots. Mare and Jillian go to each side of our team sign. We've decorated it with the word, *New York,* a picture of the statue of Liberty made out of torn up newspapers, a picture of our school, Crimson Elementary, drawn out of duct tape, and in the center we've painted out our question, *What will I be like when I grow up?* Jax and Ander grab onto either side of the metal base on the Circle Spinner, and I grab hold of the wooden circle to keep it steady.

Out of nowhere, Ander starts dancing around the spinner. "Look at me in my fancy pants. I'm ready to do my crazy dance!"

I try not to laugh, but I can't help it. Gregor clears his throat. Again. Seraphina raises her timer. "Okay very funny, Ander. Let's focus now. Team, are you ready?"

Ander yells out to her in one of his many random voices, "Yup dee dup dup dup. We're ready to show you our Team Circle!" The rest of us burst out laughing.

Gregor stands up. "Ander, I thought you were going to focus."

Gregor seriously has no sense of humor.

"Sorry," he says.

"Wait!" says Seraphina. "Don't be sorry. That was great. If the judges ask your team if you're ready, I want you to sing that altogether."

"Are you sure?" Mare asks.

"Yes, I'm sure. They won't be expecting that."

"That's good," says Jillian. "Then that will make us memorable!"

We stand very still and wait for her signal. When she

asks if we're ready, we chant, "Yup dee dup dup dup, we're ready to show you our Team Circle!"

Seraphina puts her finger on the timer. "New York Team . . . begin."

We sing a short version of our finale song as we wheel out our Circle Spinner and Team Sign. Once they're set up in the right spots, we scurry behind the Circle Spinner so we can't be seen. Then, I skip out first, inside the pretend taped off area and look at Seraphina and Gregor as if I've just stumbled upon a strange place.

"Where am I?" I say in a slow, loud voice. "This doesn't look at all like Crimson Elementary, but where could I be?"

Ander jumps out from the other side of the spinner. "Where could you be? Well, Small Person, I will tell you where you could be! You have entered the magical, mystical land of Crimson Catropolis and I am Freddie Dinkleweed."

"Freddie Dinkleweed?" I repeat.

He spins on his heel. "At your service."

I open my arms in confusion. "I think I'm lost. One minute I'm at school trying to find the answer to a question and then—poof, I'm very far away from home."

"Welcome!" calls Jax, creeping out from behind the spinner. "I am the Gate Keeper. Freddie forgets that it's my job to welcome visitors."

Ander dances a short jig and slaps Jax on the back. "The Gate Keeper has control issues."

Jax ignores him. "Hello, Small Person. I am certain I know what question you were asking."

I place my hands on my hips. "How would you know that?"

Jillian twirls out from behind the spinner and places her hands on my shoulders. "Oh, Dahling, we all know what your question is. It's the question all children ask. I wanted to know the answer when I was small like you too."

Mare struts out from the other side and leans against the corner of the spinner. "Me, too. I always asked, 'What will I be like when I grow up?'"

"Yes!" I jump up and down. "That's my question. That's my question! I want to know what I'll be like when I grow up!"

"Of course, you do," says Jax. "That's where we come in."

"That's right," Ander sings. "We're here to help. Yes, we are. Yes, we are. We're here to help . . . aren't we Madam Sparkles?" He slides over to her, his face two inches from her face.

She crinkles her nose and waves him away. "Get away, Freddie. Please get away."

He sulks back to the spinner.

"What do you mean when you say, 'You're here to help me?'" I ask.

Jax flares his cape. "We mean this magical place is here to help you. Crimson Catropolis is the place all children come to find the answer to that question."

"But how did I get here?" I ask.

"You knew the way the whole time. Now follow me."

Ander jumps out from behind the spinner. "It's spinner time! It's spinner time!"

Teenager Mare waves her arm as if to introduce the giant spinning wheel. Madam Sparkles throws her feather boa over her shoulder and spins it. Ander slides over to me. "Pay close attention, Small Person. This is where it gets fun. It's time for the Great Golden Light Bulb Spin."

My eyes grow big. "Will this tell me what I'll be like when I grow up?"

Ander motions so that he can whisper in my ear. "More," he says. "It will tell you even more."

We say the rest of our lines, all while Seraphina times us. When we say our last one, she jumps to her feet. "Oh my gosh! That was awesome, awesome, awesome! You even used a Golden Light Bulb. Guys! That app thing is genius! How did you ever think of that?"

Gregor claps real slow.

I should have known he wouldn't like it, but then his serious face turns into a *sort of* grin. "Bravo, Crimson Five. Bravo. Now that is a solution worthy of your team."

"You liked it?" I ask. "Really?" *It's a miracle!*

Ander takes off his hat. "Do you really think it was good? I messed up one of my lines."

"Me too," I admit.

"And I was late spinning the spinner," says Jillian.

Gregor waves his arms. "I knew you had the ability to create something special—I just knew it! And don't worry about those small details—we can fix them. We have the rest of the day. We will practice until it's right. Just focus. You *will* get it right."

Wow. This is a first from Gregor. And now he's going to make us perfect.

"What was our time?" asks Mare.

Seraphina checks the timer. "It was twelve minutes and twenty-eight seconds."

"That's bad!" I say. "We'll get a penalty if we go over twelve minutes."

"That's right—you will. But that was only your first time through. Some of your lines came slowly, which is to be expected. You'll get faster each time you practice."

So that's what we do. We run through it again. Our

time is 12:18. And again. 12:14. And then 12:20. Ugh. And again. 12:11. We break for lunch and come back ready to try again. 11:58. Yes! Still too close though, so we shorten some of our lines.

It takes us four more tries but each time we run through it, our time is around 11:40. "Perfect!" Seraphina exclaims.

"Finally!" says Mare, and we all collapse on the floor. I feel like I could sleep until tomorrow. Somehow, we drag ourselves back up though and pack up our sets. And that's when it hits me—*we're competing tomorrow!*

"Okay," says Seraphina. "We'll meet at Piedmont Coliseum, the building across the square in the morning where all of your sets and costumes will be waiting. You'll practice one more time before the actual Rehearsal Judging Competition. Our report time is 1:20 p.m."

My butterflies wake up as she gives us our instructions. "But in just a little while, we have our celebration with your families, so go back to your bedchambers and change. That will give me just enough time to work my magic in this room. Your parents will arrive at 6:30 p.m. Make sure you're back here by then. They'll be anxious to see you and I'll be anxious to celebrate!"

At 6:25 p.m. I yell to Mare and Jillian, who are *still* getting ready in the bathroom. "Come on! That spray stuff is hurting my head." Finally, after four more squirts we run down the hall, grab the boys at the bottom of the stairs, and keep running. We round the corner and there they all are, standing outside Meeting Room Twelve—my whole family and everyone else's too. I see Grandma Kitty first. Her hair sparkles are different somehow. They're blue! She runs to me and pulls me into a hug. She's strong like I remember, but shorter than me now!

"Oh my goodness, my Smartie Girl, you have grown. You're taller than me!"

I feel like singing. Grandma Kitty can finally see this place again and we can share our stories about Camp Piedmont. My Dad and brother and sister wrap me up like a burrito. Their smiles are huge. From the cramps in my cheeks, I bet mine are too.

They finally loosen their grip and that's when I see my mom. Tears are running down her face. She squeezes through the people in the hallway to get to me. "Oh, Baby Girl, I'm so happy to see you." She hugs me and I squeeze her tight. I hadn't realized how much I missed her. "Hi, Mom!"

"So how is it here?" Malin looks around the crowded hallway. "Are there any cute guys? How about the ones from California?"

"I guess so. I never noticed really, but wait until you see our bedchamber."

"Your bedchamber?" says my dad. "That sounds fancy."

"It is. It has sparkles and Mabel and, oh, never mind. I'll show you." Before I can though, lights and lasers pour out from Meeting Room Twelve. Music blasts and my teammates and I run for it. Seraphina has transformed the room into a concert and game room!

Tables are scattered everywhere with spinning food flowers on each one. A ping pong table that floats, a foosball table with hologram players, a pool table with light saber sticks, and an air hockey table with 3D pucks are set up in the corners. Even in the last week of camp, we're still seeing new inventions! I wonder what team made all this.

Ander runs to the center of the dance floor dragging his older sister Daphne with him. Ryne runs after them, making up dance moves on the spot. Ander has a few moves of his own, and they start a dance-off. Daphne looks like she's about to run away, but Seraphina grabs her arm and motions for me, Jillian, and Mare to start dancing. We do, and so does Jax. Soon the dance floor is packed, with Grandma Kitty too. Her sparkles fit right in!

We play games, sing, dance, and eat with our all our families. It feels like we've been friends forever. Seraphina chats with everyone. Gregor talks to no one. I guess he's not the party type.

When the celebration is over, we bring our families up to our bedchambers. We show them the floating sparkles, the star bed, Mable, the air screen, the rotating bunk beds, and the laser board. My family is amazed. Even my mom looks impressed by it all.

"Time to clear out," Ander suddenly announces. "It's quarter till tomorrow and you know what tomorrow is!"

My dad laughs and I wonder for the hundredth time how he comes up with this stuff. We say goodbye to our families, and when they leave for their hotel, I start to miss them. But not for long. I don't want to go with them. Not yet. I have to get into my bed and go to sleep. Rehearsal Judging is just eleven hours away!

Be Curious
Be Creative

Be Collaborative
Be Colorful
Be Courageous

Be Curious · Be C...

WRIST BANDS

THE KNOCKING AT the door won't stop. The pounding hurts my brain, and I can't figure out why someone would be coming to my house so early. My mom will be really mad. Don't people have any manners at all?

"Girls, wake up! Open the door!" Boom. Boom. Boom!

My brain un-fogs and I realize who it is and where I am. Swissa! I fly out of our bed. What time is it? Jillian beats me to the door. What's happening?

She sets red roses down on the table. "You guys are awesome. On the day of Rehearsal Judging you decide to sleep in?" She gives us a worried look.

"What time is it?" I ask.

"It's 7:00 a.m. You have to be at breakfast in thirty minutes. Don't worry. You have time to get ready, just get moving—okay?"

Swissa leaves and we fly around the room. We have exactly five minutes each to take a shower. I run in before the bathroom hogs can beat me to it and turn on the hot water with my heart still racing. This was not a good way to wake up—especially today.

I press four buttons and let the steamy water run down my face. I feel so lucky to be in this fairy tale bathroom. Today could be my last day here. *How did I let this summer go by so fast?* I promised myself I would remember every single day here at Camp Piedmont. Did I do that? I'm not ready to leave, but what if something happens during our performance? What if the spinner gets stuck? What if one of us forgets our lines? What if the computer crashes and the app doesn't appear on the golden light bulb? If we don't get one-hundred and fifty points, we're done. And we'll all go home tomorrow. No. We cannot go home tomorrow. I make myself take a deep breath as I rinse the shampoo from my hair. We have to get those points.

I finish up and get dressed as fast as I can. I don't know why I'm hurrying. Mare and Jillian will take forever anyway. I guess I want time to think about the big day ahead of us, picture our performance, and say my lines in my head. I move onto the window seat and stare at the magnolia tree by my window. The vanilla ice cream cups are just as pretty as the ones I saw on registration day.

That day I wanted to get started. I wanted to know what our task would be and what category it would be in. I wanted to get to know my teammates and figure out how we were going to solve it. That day I hardly knew anyone. Today, Ander, Jillian, Jax, and Mare are my best friends each in their own way, and I'm their friend too. I always knew I could make it to Camp Piedmont. Grandma Kitty knew it too. I guess amazing ideas really do run in our family. Now all I have to do is show the judges.

I wonder who's knocking now. I open the door and Grandma Kitty is standing there with rainbow sparkles in her hair. She pulls me into a giant hug. "Oh, Little Miss Muffet, I just had to see you before Rehearsal Judging and wish you luck."

I smile so wide. "Hi, Grandma!"

"So are you ready for today? I cannot wait to see your team's solution."

"I'm nervous but I'm excited too. Our solution is the most amazing thing ever!"

"What's it about? Or do you want me to be surprised?"

"You'll be surprised even if I tell you about it because it's even better in person."

"I bet it is!"

"Grandma, I'm not kidding. We made a solution that could be used by people all over the world."

She adjusts her dangly earring. "That sounds important."

"We created a computer app that practically brings people back from the dead."

"You did what?"

"Well, their images anyway."

"What do you mean?"

"We found a way to bring the image of a person to life on a monitor and animate them like you see on TV."

"Really?"

"Yes, but that part's no big deal. We were also able to take information about their old schools or jobs—the stuff that has been kept on file with the town, and download it into the app. Then we found a way to show the person moving and talking about events that really happened to them long ago in practically their own voice!"

Grandma Kitty's eyes open wide. "The app can really do that?"

"Yes! We can see for ourselves the people who came before us and listen to their stories first hand."

"That's incredible! Where did you say the information comes from?"

"Lots of places. For example, if a person told a story years ago to a friend on a phone, the recording of that conversation was saved. So the image of that person will retell the story again—to all of us."

Grandma has a strange look on her face. "You are amazing."

"I got it from you, Grandma. That's what we always said, right? I wouldn't be here at Camp Piedmont if I didn't get all my swirly brain genes from you."

She picks at a blue sparkle in her hair. "You are amazing anyway."

"Thanks, Grandma. So anyway, when we were testing out the app, we each picked a relative who lived a long time ago. Except me."

"Who did you pick?"

"I picked you!"

She pulls the sparkle right out. "Me?"

"Yes, you. But the weirdest thing happened. When I asked your image about Camp Piedmont, it didn't give any information at all. It was like you were never here."

She doesn't say anything at first. "That's very strange."

"That's what I thought too, but I'm sure we just have a glitch with the app. If we make it to the National Finals, maybe we'll have time to fix that part."

"Yes, of course," she says. "Well, Lovey Girl. I better let

you prepare for the competition. I'll see you in a few hours."

"Okay, Grandma. Thanks for coming to see me."

"You'll be great today. I know you will." She gives me a thumbs up and after she leaves, the girls and I race down to breakfast with the boys.

After shoveling down cheese omelets and scrambled apples, we head for the Prep Room at Piedmont Coliseum, a building even grander than Piedmont Chamber, with stone archways and stained glass windows. Our voices and footsteps echo as we walk down the halls.

"This place is like a medieval castle," says Ander. "I need a suit of armor."

We arrive at the Prep Room and Seraphina and Gregor are waiting with our costumes and sets. My butterflies start dancing. *Why did I eat so many apples?*

Gregor is standing with his hands on his hips. "Hello, Team."

"Hi," we say all awkwardly. Even after all this time, he's still so stiff—like a teacher you can't wait to not have the next year.

Seraphina is sitting on a windowsill, swinging her long legs. Her purple platform sandals are about five inches high. "Hi, guys. Let me see you. Okay. Do you have your wrist bands on? You can't compete today without them. You have to have them. You might need the inspiration or maybe I'm just superstitious."

I've never heard her talk so fast. "Yes, we all have them," I say.

"Yeah," says Ander. "Crimson Powers Activate! Now hold out your wrist bands and make them touch. That will activate our special powers."

Mare rolls her eyes. Seraphina jumps off the window

ledge. "Before you change I have something to say to you so listen up. Your team has a great deal to show those judges today. When it's time for you to go out there, I simply want you to show them what you've got—because you've got a lot, and it's time for them to see what I see: A team that's curious, creative, collaborative, colorful, and courageous. You are the Crimson Five from New York. Now do it. Show 'em what you've got!"

"Yes!" says Ander. "That's it—our team chant. We'll say, 'Crimson Five: Be Curious. Be Creative. Be Collaborative. Be Colorful. Be Courageous. And then we'll shout, 'Show 'em what you've got!'"

We place our arms into the center of our team huddle and shout the chant. It definitely feels like we're ready. Seraphina thinks so too. I can tell by the look on her face.

"Here's what we're going to do next," she says. "I want you to run through your solution one more time in this room before any of the other teams get here to set up. I know we're early, but I'd rather you do it without anyone else watching. When you're done, you can change into your costumes. Then we'll wheel your sets down the hall and around the corner to the Rehearsal Judging room. We need to report at 1:20 p.m. with your paperwork."

So we run through our solution one more time. We say our lines, rotate our set, sing, and dance. The whole thing runs fine. Our voices sound a little shaky, but Seraphina says that's okay. The adrenaline will kick in when we're in front of the judges. I sure hope she's right. We have time to spare so Ander pulls a tennis ball out of nowhere. It's like he always has something to play with. We bounce it back and forth. Gregor watches our every move. Seraphina tells him to relax.

"They are going to damage their sets."

"No, they won't," she says.

"They will ruin the app."

"The app is fine."

"They will trip and fall."

"They need to unwind. Everyone knows that a relaxed person competes better than an uptight person."

She's right. I feel better getting the jitters out. Soon, the other teams pour into the Prep Room, and my stomach drops to my knees. The team from Pennsylvania is carrying a metal box with long bars hanging off the sides. They're dressed in matching green cat suits. The team from Maine comes in next. They wheel in a small star with wires wrapped around it. They're dressed in white lab coats.

"Cool star," Ander calls as they set up in the far corner of the room.

"Thanks," says one of the girls. She looks at our sets and then at us. "Awesome costumes. Are you guys putting on a play?"

I look at Ander. I think he's afraid to answer. At this point it doesn't really matter so I say, "Yeah, we are."

"That sounds fun. I wish we'd thought of that. Well, good luck!"

"Thanks! You too."

It's kind of strange. As badly as I want to win, I also want to know what the other teams have created. I bet they've made really cool stuff too.

SMARTIE GIRL

I WALK OUTSIDE the room to get a drink of water from the fountain, but it's not like our fountains back home. I push the button and a cup rolls down a shoot. The water pours into the cup as it flies down and by the time I catch it, it's full. I chug the entire thing before I see Grandma Kitty watching me.

"Grandma, what are you doing here?"

"What is that, Cupcake?"

"It's a drinking fountain. Cool, isn't it? One of the past teams probably made it."

"My goodness."

"Do you want to see where we've set up?"

She folds her hands. "Well, I want to talk to you."

"Okay, but first, come see the Prep Room. She follows me and peeks in at all the teams and their creations. "Is this the same room you waited in when you were here?"

"What?"

"Did you wait in this room before you competed? You know, when you came to Camp Piedmont."

She looks confused. "What do you do in here?"

Now I'm confused. "We wait until the judges call us, when it's our team's turn to compete."

"I see."

"Don't you remember, Grandma?"

"I—I . . . yes, of course."

Why is she acting so weird? "So where are Mom and Dad?"

She pulls one of her earrings out of her ear. "They're outside sitting on a bench under a tree. A Magnolia Tree."

"Aren't those pretty? I bet they were baby trees when you were here."

She puts the earring back in. "Yes. Well, I better get back to them."

"But I thought you wanted to talk to me."

She turns away. "Oh, it can wait." She walks very fast down the hallway.

I call after her. "Grandma!"

She stops quick but turns around slowly. Her face is serious. Something's wrong.

"Oh, Peanut Butter Cup. This can't wait. It can't wait one more second."

"Grandma, what? What's wrong?" My stomach feels jumpy.

"Let's walk down this hallway."

I nod and she leads me to a bench under a window. I'm scared. I don't know what she's going to say.

"I'm just going to tell it to you straight, Peanut Butter Cup. Your app for the competition didn't have a glitch.

There's a reason when you typed me in and searched for my information it couldn't tell you about the time I spent at Camp Piedmont."

"I don't know what you mean."

"The app couldn't tell you about that event because I've never been here."

I don't understand. "What?"

"I have never been here before."

"Do you mean that Camp Piedmont was held someplace else?"

"No. Camp Piedmont has always been held here at Piedmont University. I've never been to Camp Piedmont."

My brain clogs up. "But you won the Piedmont Challenge."

She purses her lips together and lets a big breath out of her nose. "I didn't win the Piedmont Challenge."

"What are you talking about, Grandma? Yes, you did. You won a Golden Light Bulb!"

A tear runs down her cheek. "I did win a Golden Light Bulb . . . for being an alternate."

My stomach drops like a brick. "An alternate?"

"Yes. Back then, they awarded a trophy to the person in sixth place too, the student who would go to camp in the event that something happened to one of the other five kids, like if they should get sick or have a family emergency. I was that person, but no one got sick. No one had an emergency. I *never* got to go."

I think I'm going to be sick. "But you told me all about it. You told me everything." I feel tears floating in my eyes. "How would you know all this stuff if you were never here?"

She tightens her lips again. "My best friend won. She was the one who came to Camp Piedmont."

I choke back a sob. "Your friend?"

She takes hold of my hand. "Her name was Annabella, and that's how I knew everything about this camp."

I don't understand.

"I was crushed when I didn't win and she did. It was my dream to come to this camp. Annabella felt really bad for me. She promised to write me letters and tell me everything about this place. But she did more than that. She kept a journal and gave it to me when she came home. She wanted me to be a part of Camp Piedmont just like she was."

"But I've read that journal. I thought—"

"—I know. You thought I wrote it."

"But why did you tell me that you did? Why did you lie to me?"

"I'm sorry. I should have told you the truth."

Grandma Kitty is a stranger. "You made me think you were the best. You made me think you went to this awesome school for really smart and creative kids. But you didn't."

"No, I didn't."

"You told me *I* was so smart. You told me *I* was the most inventive child you had ever known. You told me I could be just like you!"

"I did tell you that."

"And I believed you. And I thought I *was* those things because you were. But you weren't!"

She leans in to hug me, but I pull my hand away from hers. "I better go, Grandma. I have to go back to my team."

She stands up slowly. "I was wrong to mislead you, Smartie Girl."

"My name is Kia."

As soon as I hear my own words I wish I could take

them back. But I don't.

"I'm sorry I brought this up now. I never should have told you right before Rehearsal Judging. You're going to be amazing. You're meant to go to the Finals. Mark my words."

What does she know? She's never even been here.

She leaves, but I don't get up from the bench. Why should I? I can't go back to the Prep Room. Everyone will see me crying. All those teams will stare at me. All those smart kids. All those kids with awesome ideas. *Why am I even here?* Grandma Kitty said I belonged because creativity runs in our family, but she's a liar. It doesn't, and maybe I'm not that creative anyway. I'll probably crash and burn in front of the judges like she did. *I don't think I can do this.*

Seraphina comes running down the hall in her clunky heels and finds me on the bench, hugging my knees.

"Kia, what's wrong?"

"I can't go back in there."

"In where?"

"The Prep Room—I don't belong here."

"Of course you do. What are you talking about? You're about to compete!"

"No, I'm not. I can't do it. I'm not as good as all those other kids!" I bury my head in my arm and cry and cry for a long time.

I don't know how long I've been sitting here, but at some point I feel her rub my back and push the hair out of my face. "I thought I was really smart and I thought I had great ideas. Grandma Kitty told me I did. But she was wrong!"

Seraphina doesn't say anything. I look up at her, but instead, it's Mom—kneeling down next to me. She looks back at Seraphina and Seraphina leaves us alone.

"Kia, your Grandma was wrong to lie to you about attending this camp, but she wasn't wrong about the other things. You are extremely smart. Why else would I wish so much for you to be programmed for math?"

I don't want to hear about programming—not now.

"You could be an amazing mathematician with the mind you have."

I want to hide under the bench.

"But Kia, that would be a waste."

I look up to see her green eyes staring into mine. "What?"

"Your Grandma *was* right. You have bigger and better ideas than anyone I know."

Why is she saying this?

"I was wrong to keep you from challenging yourself in ways other than math. This camp is where you belong."

"I don't think so."

"Why? Because Grandma didn't belong here?"

"Why did she do it, Mom? Why did she lie to me about all this?"

She rubs her hands together. "Kia. She didn't lie to you. I did."

"What?"

"You were a very little girl when you first found Grandma's Golden Light Bulb trophy in the bottom drawer of her bed side table."

"That's where she keeps it, wrapped up in a yellow towel."

"And you pulled it out of her drawer every time you visited her. She told you that she won it in the Piedmont Challenge and that part was true. But one day, you found a journal telling details and stories of a girl's time at Camp

Piedmont. By then you were probably seven years old."

"Grandma and I walked in on you that day. You were snuggled under the blankets on her bed, holding her Golden Light Bulb and reading every page. By the time we realized what you were reading, you had read halfway through the journal. You looked up at Grandma, with those big, beautiful eyes of yours and said, 'Oh, Grandma. You are the smartest and best inventor lady in the whole world.'

"I knew how hurt she had been over being an alternate. We had talked about it many times while I was growing up. I knew she questioned her abilities, always wondered how much more creative she could have been if she had made it to this camp. So when you spoke to her with such admiration in your little voice, I couldn't help myself. I blurted out, 'Yes. Yes she is.'

"Your Grandma looked at me in confusion, but I wanted her to have that gift—the gift of knowing that someone else thinks you're the greatest person on the planet. Because to me, she was that.

"So as the years passed, whenever you both talked about the competition, she embellished a little. Anabella's stories became her stories."

"That's sad."

"But it became something positive for your Grandma, Kia. It seemed like the right thing to do at the time. After that day, your Grandma became the person she always thought she could be. She wasn't living a lie. She was living the life she always dreamed for herself."

"But then why were you always so mad at her? Every time we talked about the Piedmont Challenge, you tried to discourage me."

"Yes, I did. Your Grandma eventually took it too far.

She made it her life's goal to get you to Camp Piedmont. I saw how she was filling your head with ideas and making you believe that you could win. I always knew you had the ability to win. I just didn't want you to be disappointed the way she was for all those years."

"Really?"

"Of course. You know how small the chances of winning are. I didn't want you to lose faith in your abilities if you lost."

My brain is completely tangled. My mom did all this for Grandma Kitty? I didn't even think they liked each other.

"But I was wrong, Kia. I was wrong not to encourage you all this time. You are an amazing student, and an amazing person. You are similar to your Grandma, but you're so much more too. You're both extremely smart and creative. That part is obvious. You, however, are very determined to succeed, like no one else I know. Nothing she has said changes that."

I lean over and hug her tight for a long time. I was really, really mad at her before. All this time I thought she thought I was only smart in math. I thought she thought the Piedmont Challenge was stupid. But she didn't think any of that. She does think I'm good at a lot of things.

"So you really think I belong here at this camp?"

She looks at me and smiles. "More than any other place."

I don't know what to say.

Footsteps pound on the floor like a stampede. My team is running at us like a herd of elephants. They stop, out of breath and stare at me.

My mom smiles. "Maybe we should ask your team that question too. Kia is wondering if she really belongs here in this competition."

Ander pulls me off the bench. "Nah, actually I don't think she belongs here."

"What?"

"You belong in the Prep Room with us, KK. We need you to play four square." He tosses the tennis ball to me and I catch it in one hand.

"Uh, no," says Mare. "We need you in the bathroom. It's time to change into our costumes!"

I wipe my eyes. "What time is it?"

"It's time to get ready," says Jax.

"Good luck, Baby Girl. You go do your thing—all of you, and have fun. We'll be out there cheering for you!"

"Thanks, Mom. I love you. But wait. I have to talk to Grandma Kitty first."

"We don't have time, Kia," says Jillian. "We have to do your hair."

"But I can't compete like this. Not after what I said to her."

"I will tell her how you feel right now and then you can tell her yourself after Rehearsal Judging is over."

That doesn't feel good enough, but I can't let down my team. I can't forget about my dream. This is our one chance. I hug my mom and run off to get my costume bag. I look at all the kids in the Prep Room waiting and talking. I know they're smart. I know they have great ideas, but I do too, and so does my team.

Before I run to the hallway bathroom, I ask Seraphina for a sheet of paper. I try to write a note to Grandma Kitty, but I don't know exactly what to say. I hope she can forgive me for the mean things I said to her. Finally, I write in my best handwriting:

Grandma,

You are the smartest and best inventor lady in the whole world.

Love, Smartie Girl

I hand the note to Seraphina. "Can you please take this to my Grandma while we change? I can't do this without her knowing that I'm sorry. Please, Seraphina?"

She looks at the clock on the wall and then down at her platform heels. "I guess these shoes weren't the best choice for today, but . . . I am a fast runner."

I smile and sprint down the hall with my costume bag.

REHEARSAL JUDGING

OUR WALK THROUGH the halls takes forever. There are no voices, only the echoes of our footsteps bouncing off the walls. An usher with a floppy hat leads the way, as my teammates and I follow him, pushing our circle spinner, team sign, paperwork, and the computer to control the Ancestor App. Gregor trails behind but his footsteps are on my heels. I'm sure he's watching every move we make, hoping we don't do anything stupid, like tip over the spinner.

We stop at a closed set of doors and a man with a sunny smile greets us. He's wearing a red shirt that says JUDGE in white letters. He checks something on his clipboard, looks at each of us, and then at our materials.

"Hello there, kids. I can see from your sign and from my schedule that you are the team from New York."

"Yes, we are," says Jax. His face looks serious but doesn't

turn red.

"Look at those costumes! I'd name you winner for most elaborate clothing right now if that was a category." We laugh our nervous laughs and he smiles bigger than ever. "Don't tell me you're nervous?"

"A little," I say.

"Well, no need for that. It looks like you have prepared something special. I'm sure the table judges will be happy to see what you've put together."

"I hope so," says Ander. He's now bouncing on his toes.

"When I open this door, I'd like you to bring your items inside. The head judge will tell you when to begin. Do you understand?"

"Yes!" I say. I need to get inside that door.

"Before we do," Mare says, "can we have a second, please?"

"Of course," he says. "You have a minute or two."

I look at Mare. What is she doing?

"What?" she says. "I thought we were going to do that chant thing."

"Oh yeah!" says Ander still bouncing. "I got this. Crimson Five?"

Together we shout, "Activate! Be Curious. Be Creative. Be Collaborative. Be Colorful! Be Courageous!"

"1—2—3."

"Let's show 'em what we've got!"

We smile at each other, not with our nervous smiles but with our we-got-this smiles. This is it.

The Judge opens the door. There's no stage—just a giant room with desks lined up in rows. Hundreds of people are sitting in them, including our families. All here to watch us. I'd bite my nails off right now if I wasn't so afraid to tip the spinner. The judging table stretches in front of the desks and like on the day I gave my mermaid performance, the table judges are wearing matching shirts. Today they're yellow.

We pour into the room and put down our sets. I bite my ring finger nail. I can't help it. Besides, biting my nails worked at the Piedmont Challenge. Why wouldn't it work now? My parents are near the front with my brother and sister. I search for Grandma Kitty but I don't see her. I look at the back doorway. Swissa is leaning against the wall. Our eyes lock and she smiles. Grandma Kitty walks through the door. She's holding something. A piece of paper, I think. It must be my note. She unfolds the paper and holds it up to me like a sign. It says, MARK MY WORDS! She smiles her Grandma Kitty smile, and I know she's not mad at me. I suddenly let out a breath I didn't know I was holding in.

The head judge walks over to us. "Good afternoon, Team from New York. Do you have your paperwork?"

Jillian hands him the packet. "Thank you," he says. "When I get back to my seat, I will read the task that you and all the teams were given to solve six weeks ago. Then I will ring this bell. That's your signal to present your team's solution. You will have twelve minutes to carry your materials out into the taped off area and give your presentation. Use any space up to the judging table that you like. Do you understand?"

We answer together. "Yes, sir."

"Very well, then. Good luck." He walks to his seat and my brain flutters the same way it does when I'm home on my aero-scooter.

He turns on his microphone and powers up a screen displaying our task. "New York Team, you have been given the following task to solve:

Our home, the Earth, is shaped like a circle.

Your task is to create an object that transforms three times into something else, and then transforms back to its original position . . . creating a circle effect. The object you create must answer a question that is universally asked, but has not yet been answered by mankind. Your solution must include elements from each of the six academic categories and one original language. Your presentation to the judges may not exceed twelve minutes.

When he has finished reading, he says, "Team, are you ready?"

We quick glance at each other and shout. "Yup dee dup dup dup. We're ready to show you our team's circle!"

Ding!

We sing our song as we carry out our materials and when we've finished setting up, we begin. I skip out, saying the first line. My voice sounds loud in the silent room. Everyone's eyes are on me but it doesn't make me feel nervous. I feel special, like a star. I can't hear anything at all, but the voices of my teammates and the magnified sounds of our spinner.

Some of the judges are writing. Some are watching. They laugh hard at the funny lines, especially the judge all the way on the left. She cracks up almost every time Ander speaks. When the image of his Great-Great-Grandpa Jim shines on the Golden Light Bulb like a friendly ghost, one of the judges gasps. The app is clear—and loud too, I think. I hope the people in the back row can hear what the image is saying.

We continue performing, rotating the spinner like the

rules require. The magical characters use it to show me how my question will be answered. Every single member of the audience is leaning forward in their seats. I wish I could stay in this room and act out this play forever.

In the last scene, the characters sing a farewell song to me. I join in and we dance the finale together. I can't help but smile through every step. By the time we've finished, the crowd has jumped to their feet, just like the Day of Brightness all over again. It's amazing to hear their applause and I feel like we should take a bow, but we don't, because like Mare said weeks ago, this is a competition, not a Broadway play. The crowd gets quiet, and we stand stiff like soldiers next to our spinner.

The Head Judge stands up. Some of the other judges keep writing. Some keep typing on their computers. "Thank you, Team from New York, for your thoughtful solution and hard work. You are dismissed. Please carry your materials out this door to your right. Your preceptors may pick up your scores at precisely 6:07 p.m.. One hundred fifty points out of a possible two hundred are required to compete at the National Finals. If you do not receive that score you will be dismissed from Camp Piedmont tomorrow morning after breakfast.

We carry our materials out to the hallway where Seraphina and Gregor meet us. I can't believe it's over! Our families hug and fire questions at us about our costumes, play, and spinner—especially about the spinner. It's a crazy scene in the hallway and I've never felt so proud of something I've done before.

Seraphina hugs us, one after the other. "That was incredible. You guys were awesome! Even better than in practice. The judges were definitely impressed you did a play. I can tell."

"I agree," says Gregor. "That was certainly unexpected."

"Do you think they liked the Ancestor App on the spinner?" I ask.

"Are you kidding?" asks Seraphina. "They were in awe."

We spend the next half hour taking pictures with our sets. I'm sure every team is doing the same thing today, but our parents are going overboard. We pose in a straight line. We pose in a clump. We pose around the spinner. We pose with our preceptors. The boys pose with Gregor. The girls pose with Seraphina. We pose with our wrist bands. We pose with our own families. By the time we're done, I decide to invent a camera that takes faster pictures—I mentally add it to my list of inventions.

We change out of our costumes and pack them away, just in case we need them for the Finals. Gregor arranges for our sets to be sent back to the Team Storage area, and then we all head back to Meeting Room Twelve at Piedmont Chamber to pass the time until we can pick up our scores. Seraphina has ordered pizza and scrambled apples for everyone. I hope she ordered a lot, because I can probably eat most of it myself.

The room has not been transformed. It's just the way it looked on the very first day we met here—plain tables and plain chairs. That's okay, though. We don't need anything fancy today. All the crazy brothers and sisters will be enough.

We devour the pizza and scrambled apples and find a corner in the back of the room to crash. Ander tells jokes. Jillian's little brother Davis laughs. Daphne paints Mare's nails. Ryne teaches Jax's sister Micha dance moves. Mare's brother Ace and my sister Malin talk in the other corner.

Jillian's brother Dexter pretends he's a news reporter. The rest of us are so tired. We just sit and watch.

Meanwhile, the parents talk like they've known each other forever. After a while, Ander whispers in my ear. "Come on. Let's go follow Gregor."

"Why?" I ask.

"Because I'm bored and he's creepy. Besides, he's been acting weird—weirder than usual, ever since we got back here. He keeps checking his phone and looking around to see if anyone's watching him. He just left. Let's go see what he's doing."

We grab Jillian, Mare, and Jax and tell the brothers and sisters to hang out until we get back. Seraphina yells as we race down the hall. "Don't go too far. Our scores will be ready in thirty minutes!"

I force myself not to freak out. "Okay, we'll be right back."

"Where are we going?" asks Jax.

"Just taking a walk," says Ander. "You know, team bonding."

"I think we've bonded enough," says Mare.

"Let's just go," says Jillian. "My brothers are getting annoying already."

"How do you guys think we did?" I ask.

"I think we did well," says Jax.

"Me too," says Mare. "And I didn't even mind being in front of all those people."

"And the spinner didn't get stuck or anything," says Jillian. "Even when my feather boa got in the way."

"We were *awesome*," says Ander. "The judges loved us."

"Our families loved us. We don't know what the judges thought," I remind him.

"I'd rather think like Ander," says Jillian. "No other team is dressed like us. No one else did a play, I bet, either."

"And no other team built a spinner that can bring people back from the dead," says Jax. We laugh because he's right. Maybe the judges did love our solution.

We turn the corner. Gregor is at the end of the hall with his back to us. He's talking on his phone. Ander motions for us to be quiet. We realize he wants us to spy on him so we scoot into a nearby closet. It's hot inside and gets hotter as we squish together. Mare groans and we shush her. With the door cracked open we can still hear what he's saying.

"Yes," he says in his stiff Gregor voice. "I do think my team was able to pull it off . . .Yes. They had a very well put together presentation today . . . They will certainly score high for creativity . . . That's not the portion I was concerned with . . . It was the task solving portion . . . I agree. Their original solution was amateur at best . . . Of course I'm happy I got rid of it . . . Their revised solution was a great improvement . . . Yes, the scores should be ready soon. I hope the judges think their solution was as good as I think it was . . . You'll be hearing from me soon."

He's happy he got rid of it? What? Gregor did it?

My teammates and I stand frozen.

His footsteps pound the floor. They head back in the direction of Meeting Room Twelve. Soon, they're just a patter. When I can't hear them anymore, I peek my head out to be sure he's gone and when he is, I push open the door.

"Oh my gosh!" Mare squeals and we pile out of the closet.

Ander screams at the top of his lungs, "I. Hate. Him. So. Much."

Jax shakes his head. "I can't believe it was him."

"How could he do that to us?" Jillian asks.

I can't believe this is happening. "Why would Gregor, our own preceptor, destroy our solution, with just one week to go before the competition?"

"It makes no sense," says Jillian.

Ander waves his arms like a mad scientist. "But you heard him. He did it! I knew he wasn't a good guy. I knew it!"

"I'm going to find him!" says Mare, charging down the hall.

"Mare, wait! You can't!"

She turns around. "Why not? I'll slap him right across his mean face, and then I'll tell Seraphina!"

I take a deep breath. "I don't think we should tell her."

"Why not?" asks Jillian.

"What if she doesn't believe us?" I ask.

"Why wouldn't she believe us? She doesn't like him either. I can tell by the way she looks at him whenever he talks to us," says Jillian.

"But that doesn't mean she'll take our side. It's our word against his. Besides, our scores are almost ready. Let's see how many points we get, and then we can decide."

"Fine," says Mare. "But after that, we wipe that stupid smirk off his face."

The rest of my team reluctantly agrees, and we race back to Meeting Room Twelve. We're out of breath when we reach Seraphina and Gregor, both of them leaning against the door. I can hardly look at Gregor. All I want to do is pull his legs out from under him and watch him crash to the floor like our Ghost Gallery did.

"There you are," Seraphina says. "Our scores are almost

ready. Come on."

Once outside, we follow the same cobblestone path we walked along on registration day. I try to find the speakers in the ground, but I can't see anything beneath the bumpy cobblestones.

We enter a side door to the Coliseum. It doesn't take us long to find the Judge's Room. Gregor and Seraphina slip inside, and my teammates and I sit on the floor in a circle. We hold hands until we realize they're too sweaty. Instead we say, "Please be 150, please be 150 . . ."

Seraphina and Gregor stay in that room forever. *Come on! How long does it take to hand someone a score sheet?*

REUNION

GREGOR WALKS OUT of the Judging Room. Seraphina follows, carrying a silver paper and a white envelope. Her expression is normal. What does that mean? "I have your score," she says and sits down in the circle with us. "The judge wanted me to give you something first though."

I groan. "Oh my gosh! Just tell us!"

She ignores me and pulls a set of pictures out of the envelope. I have a picture for each of you, taken on the day of registration—your first day as a team. This is a small reminder of just how far you've come together this summer."

I lean over to see it. "Who took that?"

Seraphina laughs. "It was taken automatically by the magnolia tree, the one at the entrance to Piedmont Chamber."

Ha! I knew something was up with that tree!

"How did it do that?" asks Jax.

"The team from Massachusetts invented tiny, white cameras that sit on the branches. They added timers and a release system to give the petals an authentic scent."

Wow.

"Anyway," she continues. "The head judge told us that he had heard all about the Crimson Five from New York. He knew you had come from the same school, but was warned to judge you fairly, not to expect anything more or anything less than the other teams. He said he vowed that he would do that and he did. So based on your solution to the task, your score out of 200 points is . . . 174.25!"

We explode from the circle screaming—and hugging and jumping! Ander dances and his voice thunders over all the rest of ours, "We're going to the Finals! We're going to the Finals!"

Seraphina explodes. "I knew you could do it!"

Gregor stands outside our circle. "Yes, congratulations, team. Job well done."

"Thanks," I say, swallowing the urge to spit in his face.

Seraphina smiles. "Wow, not bad, Gregor. Did I just hear you give them a compliment?"

"They have earned the one-hundred and fifty points. That's worth mentioning."

"Oh wow, thanks," Ander mutters.

"Gregor and I have been instructed to pick up an information packet for the National Finals. It won't take long, and then we'll join you and your families back in Meeting Room Twelve."

Seraphina and Gregor walk the other way and I scream, "We did it!"

"No thanks to our evil preceptor," Mare whispers.

"What should we do about *him*?" asks Jillian.

"I don't know," I say. "What do you guys think?"

"Maybe he was just trying to help us," says Jax.

I think about that for a second. "That was a rotten way to help us."

"Yeah," says Jillian. "It was. Maybe Jax's right though. He did force us to come up with a better solution. Maybe our other one wouldn't have gotten us enough points. So in a way, he might have done us a favor."

"So you don't think we should tell anyone?" I ask.

"I don't know," she says.

"I don't think we should do anything yet," says Jax. "We have the National Finals to get ready for."

"But I don't trust him," says Mare. "I can't even look at him."

"I think," says Ander, "that we pretend we don't know the truth—for now. We'll get ready for the competition, but really, all the while we'll act like Russian Spies."

"What are you talking about?" asks Mare.

"We figure out a way to prove he did it."

"But we need to focus on the Finals," I say. "We only have a few days until we compete again. Besides, after that, we may never see him again."

"So you want to let him get away with it?" asks Ander.

"No. I just don't want this to mess up our performance for the Finals."

"Can't we just go back to Meeting Room Twelve and tell our parents what our score is?" asks Jax.

"And then we can think up a secret plan," says Ander.

"Can we take a nap afterwards?" asks Mare.

"Seriously? That's what you guys want to do?" asks Jillian. "Sleep and play detective?"

"What do you want to do?" I ask.

Jillian shrugs. "I don't care, as long as we hang out together. Part of me doesn't want the National Finals to come yet. I'm going to miss being here with all of you when it's over. This has been fun, even the Gregor part."

"Aw," says Ander. I bet you're going to miss me the most."

Jillian scrunches her face. He pretends to cry.

"You know what?" I say. "I have a way that we won't have to say goodbye to each other after the Finals."

"How?" asks Ander. "We glue ourselves to each other?"

"No. We don't need glue. We make it to the Global Championships and then enroll at PIPS. That way we'll get to spend the next two years together."

"It's a deal," says Ander. "But this week when we're not rehearsing, I'm going to get proof that Gregor is a bad guy."

We get to Meeting Room Twelve and our families explode like we did, but with so many people it's more like fireworks. My mom hugs me and smooths out one of my pigtails. "Kia, I'm thrilled for you! I knew you'd get those points."

"You did?"

"Well, I read through the details of the task last night after we settled into the hotel. Seraphina gave all of us a copy to look at. I must say, I was worried at first. There was a lot of skill that needed to go into solving this problem. I would have had trouble coming up with something good enough."

"Really?"

"Yes, of course! I only have a science brain, remember?"

I laugh. "Yeah, I know."

"But you're good at so many things, Kia. I'm glad you

were able to show everyone here today, especially me."

"Thanks, Mom."

"And I never knew you could perform like that, in front of all those people!"

"Me either, but we had to make them remember us."

"Well, I certainly won't ever forget any of this. I'm so proud of you." She leans close. "I bet your Grandma would like to talk to you too."

Grandma Kitty is talking to my dad. I break away from my mom and walk over to them. Dad pulls me into a giant hug. "Great job, Little Bear! That was amazing stuff out there. I knew you'd find a way to use all the ideas swirling in your head."

"Thanks, Dad. Can you stay until this weekend and watch us in the National Finals?"

"Are you kidding? Of course. I need to see my little girl use that Ancestor App again. That was really something."

I look at Grandma Kitty. Her face looks sad. I've never felt strange around her before, but I hug her anyway. "Grandma, I'm really sorry about what I said before. I didn't mean it."

"Oh, Sugar Dumpling. Yes, you did. But that's okay. Can we walk for a bit?"

I look for Seraphina. She and my mom are talking. So is everyone else in Meeting Room Twelve. I'm sure I can sneak out for a few minutes, especially for Grandma Kitty.

We walk in silence out the door where Swissa found me crying all those days ago. Pretty soon camp will be over, and she can go back to her own school where she belongs. That will make her happy. I didn't think I'd ever want to leave here, but maybe it would be easier if I wanted to go back to Crimson—if I wanted to be programmed.

As we step out into the late summer afternoon, the sun, even though I can't see it, blinds me for a few seconds until my eyes adjust to the light. The clouds over Piedmont University are swirling in slow motion. I see one arrange itself into the shape of the sun—one of the brightest stars. I want to drag my friends out here with me. We could lie in the grass and call out the shapes we see.

Grandma Kitty finds a bench near the cobblestone path and we sit down. "This is an amazing place, Smartie Girl. I knew it would be."

Now I feel sad for Grandma Kitty. "But you never got to come here."

"No, I didn't. But I dreamed and dreamed about it for more years than I can count. It's everything I hoped it would be—all because of you."

"What do you mean?"

"I think what happened to me in the Piedmont Challenge was exactly the right thing because it eventually brought you here to this camp. You were meant to come here, not me. This is where you belong, and I am so very happy to share it with you."

"Really, Grandma? Then you're not sad anymore?"

"Sad? Heavens no! You just earned your spot at the Piedmont National Finals, and I get to hang around all this creative energy for the next few days. Maybe I'll even set up a blanket under one of those trees and make you and your friends some earrings."

"Jillian and Mare would love some. But wait, what about the boys? They don't wear earrings."

"Well, now let's see. I'll just have to let some of my creative ideas come back to me and think up something else to make for them."

I lean back and look up at the clouds. It feels good to talk to Grandma Kitty again. I had missed her so much. But now I want to get back to my friends. I know they'll be looking for me, and we need to talk about Gregor.

"Girl, you just got a very strange look on your face. What is it?"

I think about Gregor's phone call. I picture the pile of junk he smashed our Ghost Gallery into. Grandma Kitty would know what to say to him. She'd probably hunt him down and slug him, even harder than Mare. I can't tell her about this though. We promised not to tell anyone, and that includes Grandma Kitty. "Oh nothing," I say.

"I think we should head back inside. Don't you, Butter Cup?"

I smile and hug her tight. Grandma Kitty always knows what I'm thinking.

BRAIN SWIRLS

EVENING ANNOUNCEMENTS HAPPENED hours ago, but none of us can sleep. We can't stop thinking about what Gregor did, and we're not going to let him get away with it. Even if he did help us get to the National Finals.

Ander and Jax must have looked like criminals sneaking out of their bedchamber and into ours, and now we're huddled under a blanket with just the glow of the flashlight to see each other's faces.

"I don't know how we can convince Seraphina that we're telling the truth," says Jillian.

"She might think we're making it up because we don't like him," Mare replies.

"I told you guys, we have to find proof," says Ander.

"But what?" asks Jax. "There aren't any video cameras in the shed."

"How do you know that?" I ask.

"I checked while we were working in there one day."

"Why?" asks Ander.

"I was curious."

"This is so frustrating," says Mare. "Why can't we think of a way to get proof? I want to see him cry and run away when we tell him we know what he did to us."

"You know, I was just thinking," says Jax.

"What?" asks Jillian.

"After we tell Seraphina and confront Gregor, what happens after that? Will he still be our preceptor?"

"I guess that's up to Seraphina," says Jillian. "Or Master Freeman."

I'm listening to my friends talk and all the while my brain is pounding my skull. I know there's an idea in there. I can feel it. *Why can't I figure this out?*

"It really stinks that there weren't any video cameras in that shed," says Ander. "Everything he did to our Ghost Gallery would have been recorded. That could have been the proof we needed."

Jillian sighs. "We're supposed to be so smart. Here we are at Camp Piedmont and none of us can think of a way to prove he did it."

"What if we trick him into confessing?" suggests Ander. "We can say it was actually a good thing that someone smashed our Ghost Gallery. Then maybe he'll admit it. You know, take credit for it."

Jillian raises an eyebrow. "He might even brag about it."

"I don't know," says Mare. "I don't think he'll fall for it."

The pressure in my head gets worse. Video cameras

weren't watching Gregor but someone had to see him. My head thumps. *Recordings . . . Gregor bragging . . . Talking on the phone about recordings . . . Wait a second. That's it. He was talking to someone about this on the phone!* "Wait! I got it."

"Shhh," says Jillian, pulling the blanket tighter around us.

"What?" says Ander.

"The Ancestor App!"

"What about it?" asks Ander.

"We can get proof from the Ancestor App!"

Jax nods his head.

"How?" asks Jillian.

"You mean his phone recordings?" asks Mare.

"KK, that's it. The Ancestor App is even better than a Russian Spy!"

"We have to get a recording of his phone conversation from earlier today," says Jax. "That will be the proof we need."

"Grab the air screen," says Mare.

Ander is already out from under the blanket and pulling it away from the wall. He moves it towards us and bumps into the table. "I'm okay!"

"Shh," says Jillian.

Ander mouths the words, "I'm sorry," and motions for us to gather around the screen. He types in *Gregor Axel, New York.* Two Gregors appear on the screen. One is very old. The other is the Gregor we're looking for. "There he is," whispers Mare, "with that stupid smirk on his face."

"What do we type in?" I ask.

"Try *phone records*," says Jax.

Ander types the words and the Ancestor App searches for the calls. A swirl covers the screen, but then fades. A list of dates and times appear in its place.

"The one at the top is from twenty-three minutes ago," I say.

"Yeah, it looks like the creep is still awake, talking on his phone," says Mare.

"Let's check that call," says Adam.

"No," says Jax. "That's not the call we heard."

"So?"

"We can't listen to all his calls. They're private," says Jillian.

I move closer to the screen. "We need to find the call he made right before we picked up our scores."

"When was that?" asks Mare.

"Our scores were ready at 6:07 p.m.," says Jax. "Check the call before that."

"There's a call at 5:35 p.m. Let's try that one," I say.

Ander taps the air and a document appears on the screen. "This is it. It's the whole conversation."

We squish together and read the whole thing.

224-271-2805:

Hello, this is Gregor.

585-809-4532:

How do you think they did? Do you think they were good?

224-271-2805:

Yes.

585-809-4532:

Do you think they made it? Were they able to pull it off?

224-271-2805:

I do think my team was able to pull it off.

585-809-4532:

Did they look professional? Did they look like winners?

224-271-2805:

Yes. They had a very well put together presentation today.

585-809-4532:

Do you think the judges will score them high for their play?

224-271-2805:

They will certainly score high for creativity.

585-809-4532:

Was it creative enough?

224-271-2805:

That's not the portion I was concerned with.

585-809-4532:

Yes, I know. You made that clear right before you destroyed the first project.

224-271-2805:

It was the task solving portion.

585-809-4532:

The ghost boxes weren't good enough.

224-271-2805:

I agree. Their original solution was amateur at best.

585-809-4532:

Well, I hope you're happy you got rid of it.

224-271-2805:

Of course I'm happy I got rid of it. Their revised solution was a great improvement.

585-809-4532:

Well, I hope it worked. We have a whole town here thinking I'm the greatest principal the town has ever seen. Will you find out tonight if they make it to the Finals?

224-271-2805:

Yes, the scores should be ready soon. I hope the judges think their solution was as good as I think it was.

585-809-4532:

Call back when you find out.

224-271-2805:

You'll be hearing from me soon.

Jillian's mouth hangs open. "That was Principal Bermuda!"

"Are you kidding me?" says Ander. "He was in on it too!"

"But why?" I ask. "That makes no sense."

"I don't know, but we could look up more phone records and listen to all the things they said to each other," says Ander.

"Yeah," says Mare. "Let's do it."

"No," I say. "We're going to ask him ourselves and give him a chance to explain. Sometimes people do bad things for a good reason."

"I don't care what reason he has," says Mare. "He's awful."

"KK, you have a good point," says Ander.

"No way," says Mare. "We should just report him to Andora or Master Freeman or at least Seraphina."

We all stare at Mare. I feel like we're back in Meeting Room Twelve trying to convince her to do a play.

She stares back but then shakes her head. "Fine. I'll give him a chance to explain, but just because we're a team, and I want to get this crap over with."

I smile at Mare. On second thought, this doesn't feel anything like that day in Meeting Room Twelve. This feels like my team has solved another task, just like the human pretzel.

SPARKS

IT'S EARLY IN the morning when my teammates and I leave for Piedmont Coliseum. We've barely reached the college square when Ander starts bouncing on his toes. "Does everyone know what they're doing?"

"Yes," says Mare. "We're going to walk into the practice room, and when we see Gregor, we're going to jump on top of him, grab his legs, and twist them over his head."

"Mare!" Jillian scolds.

"Oh, sorry. I forgot that's not the real plan—just my plan."

"Mare," I say.

"I'm just kidding."

We march into the building and down the hallway. Ander's talking even faster than we're walking. "We're going to go in there and act normal. When Seraphina tells us to rehearse, we're going to run through our performance like we always do. Got it?"

"Got it," I say. "Then, when it comes time to play the videos on the Ancestor App, we'll play the recording of Gregor's phone conversation instead."

"That's when I'm going to ask Gregor to come up for a closer look," says Mare. "I'll say, 'Gregor, do you recognize that voice? Well, you should. It's you and Principal Bermuda talking, isn't it? Isn't it?' I'll point my finger at him too."

"He won't be able to deny it," says Ander.

"No," says Jax. "It's clearly his voice and his phone number."

"And then we watch the fireworks," says Mare. "Seraphina will get all fired up at what he did and tell him that she's reporting him or whatever. It's going to be great."

"Well, let's hurry up," I say. "I want to get this over with."

The hallways are crowded with kids from other teams walking to their own rehearsals. My stomach flutters as we approach our practice room, 1026.

Seraphina stands in the doorway. "Hi, guys, come on in. I have more information about the competition this weekend."

Our Circle Spinner, costumes, and other props are piled against the back wall. The other side of the room looks like a mini theater with a bunch of theater seats. Gregor is sitting in the front row. His spiky hair is flattened down. "Hello, everyone."

"Hi," we say, but none of us looks him in the eye.

"So," says Seraphina, "We found out yesterday that thirty-two teams scored enough points to get into the Finals."

"That's better than all fifty," I say.

Ander nods. "Not bad odds."

Seraphina laughs. "Not as bad as they could have been."

"What about Witch Girl's team? Did Michigan make it?" Ander asks.

Seraphina looks on her list. "Yes, they did. I don't know their score but they're in."

"Ick," says Mare. "Figures."

"What about Pennsylvania?" I ask. "They're the ones with the green cat suits. We saw them in the Prep Room."

"Yes, they're in too, but don't worry about the other teams. You'll have your hands full practicing your own solution for the Finals and finishing up some details. We also know there will be an Opening Ceremony to kick off the competition. It will include a procession of each team. You'll walk in, along with all the other teams, dressed in costumes or shirts that represent your state."

"Where we do we get the costumes?" asks Jillian.

"We still need to work on that."

I bite my pinky nail. Then I remember I don't bite my nails anymore.

"Should we set up our Circle Spinner now?" asks Jax.

"Sure," says Seraphina. "Let's get to work."

Ander looks at me, and we head to the back wall so we can put the Circle Spinner in place. My heart beats into my throat. I don't know if I can do this. I've never accused anyone of anything before—especially not a grown up.

"Wait just one moment," says Gregor. "Please come back over here. I'd like to say something first." He motions for us to sit down. I'm not sure what's going on, but we do as he asks and sit cross legged on the carpet. Gregor presses his hands together standing before us like a giant. He's probably going to squash us like bugs. Right here on the floor. *Splat.* That'll be the end of us and Seraphina will never know what he did.

"Jax, Ander, Kia, Mare, Jillian, I would like to speak to you before we make final preparations for the National Finals." He's talking so slowly, my heart thumps with his every word. "It is important for me to tell you something." He looks down at his shoes and then back at us. "I was the person who destroyed your Ghost Gallery."

Ander and I look at each other. Seraphina's hand flies up to her mouth.

"I apologize for my actions. I am not proud of what I've done."

Seraphina makes a strange face. "What are you talking about?"

"It was me. I did it."

Seraphina's eyes are wild. "It was you?" She covers her face with her hands, but then takes them away. "Why? Why would you do that to them?"

"I am ashamed of my actions."

"Ashamed of your actions? You should be ashamed of your actions! What is wrong with you?"

Gregor doesn't look up. "I wanted them to win."

None of us says a word—not even Mare.

"That's unbelievable. Unbelievable! Winning is not the most important thing! These kids worked so hard for so many weeks. How could you wreck their whole project? What did you do, sneak out to the shed in the middle of the night and take a hammer to it?"

Gregor cringes at her words.

Mare stands up and glares at him. "We already figured it out, you know."

Seraphina turns around. "What? You knew?"

"We figured it out last night," says Ander. "With the Ancestor App. But we don't know why you did it."

Gregor sits down next to Seraphina.

"Well," she says. "We're waiting."

"I didn't mean for it to happen exactly."

"So it was an accident?" Mare asks.

Gregor runs his hands through his hair and walks over to the Circle Spinner. "Ander, could you please set up the Ancestor App? You should see this first hand."

Ander slowly pulls the Circle Spinner away from the wall. The rest of us shift in our places. He presses the air buttons on the screen. The swirl spins against the Golden Light Bulb, and then the screen turns into a blank canvas of blue.

"Can you find the phone call I received around 9:00 p.m. on July 21st?"

Ander pushes more buttons, his fingers bending and poking into the air.

A link appears as the swirl disappears. Ander presses it and a transcript of the phone call pops onto the screen.

"You should be able to find a video attached to this call."

"Where?" Ander asks. "Oh, there." He selects a square box marked "Visual."

"I imagine this will be a video I took and the recording of the call I received from your principal."

"Their principal? Why were you talking to him?" Seraphina asks.

"That's who he was talking to when he admitted to destroying our Ghost Gallery. That's how we knew," Mare says with a smirk.

"Principal Bermuda had been calling me throughout the summer, insisting that I provide him with progress reports of the team."

"Why?"

"According to Principal Bermuda, our New York team is a very big deal in the town of Crimson Heights."

"Yes, of course," she says. "That's their home."

"He demanded to know how the team's solution was coming along. He ordered me to take videos to show him their progress."

"What does that have to do with you destroying their Ghost Gallery?"

Gregor takes a deep breath. "May I?" he asks Ander.

Ander steps aside and Gregor pushes start on the video. Our Ghost Gallery appears as Gregor's voice speaks:

"Principal Bermuda, I present to you, my team's Ghost Gallery."

Silence follows as the video shows our Ghost Gallery at all angles. It looks so good—and sturdy. I feel sick looking at it like that, knowing what happened to it.

"This is the team's main prop for their play about where people go after they die. It also acts as the movable object required in their task. It will start in the first position, turn three times and ultimately end up at the original position. You can see the gallery of choices, the coffin, the cremator oven, and the spaceship as well." The video shows all sides of the Ghost Gallery as Gregor turns the crank.

Principal Bermuda shouts on the recording. "That's what these smarty pants kids have created?"

"Yes, sir."

"There must be something more."

"Yes, there are costumes, a script, and an original language."

"You promised me these kids would invent something

incredible. You promised me you'd get these kids to the Global Championships. This isn't good enough to get them to the county fair competition. Crimson will be the joke of the country."

"Principal Bermuda, we don't know what the other teams have prepared. It doesn't matter what we think of their solution. It matters what the judges deem to be the best and most creative solutions."

"And you think this could be the best? Don't be ridiculous! I will be the laughing stock of Crimson Heights. We have not one kid but five in this competition. We have been all over the news. This town, this whole state is expecting great things from them!"

"Sir, this is their solution, not—"

"You haven't delivered what you promised. What kind of preceptor are you?"

"What would you have me do? I cannot influence their solution in any way."

"Then you will find a way to make them rethink their solution."

"I don't understand."

"You will make them see this solution is a piece of junk."

"I don't know if I can—"

"You will do it. In fact, you will turn their solution into a piece of junk."

"Principal Bermuda, I can't do anything to their solution."

"You can and you will. I want you to break it apart. Smash it into a million tiny pieces—force them to start over."

"Start over? The competition is a week and a half away!"

"Then you better work quickly."

"I won't do it."

"You don't have a choice."

"What do you mean?"

"You're in your final year as preceptor, right?"

"Yes."

"Well, you haven't had a team reach the Global Championships yet have you?"

"No, I have not."

"Well, what happens to you if this team doesn't make it either?"

"I'll go back to my home to live with my father and look for a job."

"And your father will be disappointed in you?"

"Success is very important to my father."

"I see. What if your team does get to the Global Championships?"

"I'll have my choice of positions here at Piedmont University in the Piedmont Inventors Prep School. I could be a Teacher or a Researcher or a Developer."

"And which would you choose?"

"I would choose to be a Researcher or maybe a Developer, a person who assists the children in the development of their inventions."

"Ah, so it seems to me that you would rather stay there at Piedmont University?"

"Yes, of course."

"Well, Gregor, that's not going to happen if you don't do something to ensure that your team makes it to the Global Championships."

"But I can't destroy their set."

"Then I will see to it that your father is aware that you are failing miserably as a preceptor. Keep in mind that I am on the Board of Educators. You know how important education is to our citizens. I have a lot of influence over who gets jobs throughout the state."

"So if I don't destroy their set, I may never get a good job?"

"You catch on fast. Now place the camera where I can see what's in the room . . . Do it! Okay, slower. Zoom in on that spot in the corner. What are those long poles against that back wall?"

"Those are old shovels and rakes."

"Perfect! Now take those and get to work."

"I can't take a shovel to their set and—"

"Do it now or I call your father. I'm sure he'd like a progress report too."

"No! Please don't call my father. I'll do it—just let me hang up the phone."

"No. I want you to record the whole thing. I'm not sure I trust you to do as I say."

The video stays focused on the Ghost Gallery. Gregor walks into the picture carrying a giant shovel.

"Stop it!" I scream. "Turn it off! I don't want to see this!"

Seraphina stands up. "Stop the video. Stop it right now!"

Ander jumps up and stops the video.

I wipe away the tears from my face. Jillian is crying too. Neither of us can watch our hard work get destroyed.

Gregor turns away from the Circle Spinner and sits down in the theater seat with his head in his hands.

Seraphina sits next to him. "I don't know what to say."

We don't say anything either. Principal Bermuda is an evil man.

"You don't have to say anything. Please just know that I am sorry for what I did." He stands up and walks to the door. "I will leave your team alone to rehearse. I don't know if Andora will assign you another preceptor, Seraphina. I'm sorry to leave you with all the work. Good luck to all of you at the National Finals."

Seraphina looks at our team.

"Wait!" I say.

"Gregor, hold on," says Ander. "Don't go."

"You don't have much time to practice. You should get to work."

"Gregor, I don't know if you should tell Andora," he says.

Mare stands up. "Are you kidding me? If he doesn't tell her, I will. She needs to know what Principal Bermuda did. He forced Gregor to do it!"

Gregor shoves his hands into his pockets. "Marc, I should have stood up to him. I was a coward."

"I would have been afraid of him too," she says.

"Me too," says Ander.

"Gregor," says Jax. "I think what you did was awful."

Gregor swallows hard and the Adam's apple in his neck moves.

"But I don't blame you anymore. I don't know if I could have stood up to him either. He's a principal, and a principal *should* be a good man. A good man would never force you to do that to us."

Seraphina puts her arm around Jax.

"I don't blame you either," says Jillian.

"None of us do," I say.

"This competition is supposed to be a celebration of intelligence and creativity, the ability to solve problems and to make situations brighter. You have made this situation brighter for me by giving me your forgiveness. You have risen to the challenge of this camp given an obstacle that you never should have faced. I'm sorry more than I can say for putting that obstacle in your way, but this competition is a celebration of character as well. I did not display good character when I gave in to Principal Bermuda's threats. If there's one last thing I can teach you at camp, it's that we must always stand up for what's right. I will go to Andora and tell her what has happened.

"If I am not back for rehearsals tomorrow morning, you'll know that I have been removed as your preceptor. In the event that happens, please work hard for Seraphina. She has many details to attend to in the next few days. But also remember to have fun. I had forgotten the importance of it. That's when you will do your best in the National Finals."

THE EMPIRE STATE

IT'S LUNCHTIME AND Gregor still hasn't arrived.

Seraphina checks her phone again. Nothing. "I'm surprised the Piedmont Committee hasn't sent us a substitute preceptor. According to the rules, each team must have two."

"I don't want another preceptor," says Jillian.

"Me either," says Ander. "It'll be weird with someone else."

"Yeah," I say. "No one else will fit in with our team."

Mare leans forward in her seat. "I feel bad for him now, especially because we know Principal Bermuda forced him to wreck our set."

"Is there any chance he could still come?" I ask.

"It's already twelve-thirty," says Jax. "Didn't he say he'd be here in the morning if he was allowed to be our preceptor still?'

"He did," says Seraphina. "It doesn't seem likely that he's coming back."

My stomach rolls. "What's going to happen to him?"

"I don't know what the Piedmont Committee will decide—about him or your principal. But Gregor has worked so hard to get here, and he's so smart. It'll be a waste of his talent if he's sent home."

Mare stands up. "What's Andora's number? I'm going to call her and tell her that Principal Bermuda has to go to jail and Gregor—"

Seraphina snaps, "No, you're not."

"But what if Gregor gets in trouble but nothing happens to Principal Bermuda?" she asks.

"I have a feeling the Piedmont Committee will be very tough on your principal. They value goodness and creativity and teamwork, not winning at all costs. I can't say for sure what will happen to Gregor though."

"They have to let Gregor stay!" says Jillian.

"I think he's going to come," I say.

Jax nods. "There's still time."

"I don't want you to get your hopes up. I want him to come back too. His coaching style may be rough, but he is a great preceptor. We have to accept the fact that it might be just us from now on though. Besides, he would want you to focus on your work, don't you think?"

"Yeah," says Ander. "He'd be yelling at us right now for taking a break."

"Exactly. He'd want us to keep going, and that's what we're going to do."

I bite my thumb nail, but then sit on my hands. "So what's next?"

Seraphina pushes a button behind the theater seats. Mabel rolls around the corner. She drags a bag, a roll of canvas, and a metal bar. "We're going to decorate our team banner for the Opening Ceremony tomorrow. We've been given this blank canvas. We can draw on it or paint it, whatever we want. We must include the name of our state, but we can add pictures too, if we like."

"Can you help us?" asks Jillian.

"I can! This is the one project preceptors are allowed to participate in."

Jillian smiles. "This'll be fun."

"What's the metal bar for?" asks Ander.

"It slides through the opening of the canvas so it can be carried."

"Who gets to carry it?" asks Mare.

"You all do. You'll walk in a procession with all the other teams."

Ander spins around his baseball hat. "So what should we put on it?"

Mare grabs onto one end of the canvas, and I help her roll it out flat. "What if we draw pictures of places from all over the state, like the Statue of Liberty?"

"Good idea," says Ander. He picks up the metal bar. "What else?"

"How about the Adirondack Mountains?" Jax suggests.

"And maybe all the Finger Lakes, with houses nearby or something," says Jillian.

"We need more from New York City too," I say. "That's the part most people know about."

"What if we draw the Empire State building with some stores and delis all in a row, oh and Broadway," says Mare.

"That's fantastic," says Seraphina. "Is that everything?"

Ander pushes the bar over his head like a warrior. "No! We forgot Niagara Falls, the largest waterfall in North America."

"Oh yeah. We can't forget that one," I say.

"But can I draw it?" he asks. "I want to see if I can make it look like the water is crashing over the rocks. 3,160 tons of water flows over the falls every second."

"That's scary," says Jillian.

"Yeah, I wouldn't want to slip on one of those rocks," says Ander.

"It's beautiful though, too," says Seraphina. "And it's all yours, Ander."

"Yes!" He sets the bar down and searches through Seraphina's bag for a pencil.

"Can I work on the Statue of Liberty?" I ask.

"And can I do the New York City scene? I'll make lots of stores," says Mare.

"Okay, then I call the Finger Lakes," says Jillian.

"Good, then I get the Adirondacks," says Jax. "I like it there."

"Then what should I work on?" asks Seraphina.

"You can hand us the markers," says Ander.

"Hand you the markers? No!"

Ander laughs. "Just kidding. Do you want to paint the words, NEW YORK?"

Seraphina claps her hands together. "Sure! I'll make them really fancy."

"But use a ruler," says Mare. "And make sure it doesn't slant downhill."

"Don't worry, Mare," says Seraphina. "I'll make it perfect."

We spread the canvas out and divide up the sections.

We use markers, glitter, paint, and colorful construction paper. We cut up the construction paper into tiny pieces and glue them onto the canvas to fill up the large spaces like the waterfalls and the mountains. The pieces of paper almost make our banner look 3D. In Art Forms, our teachers always tell us to add texture to our projects. I wish they could see this.

While we work, Seraphina asks us what we want to wear for the Opening Ceremony. "We don't have time to make costumes but you should all match."

"I guess we could wear our green New York Shirts," says Jillian. "At least we'd match the Statue of Liberty at the top of the banner."

"That will work," she says. "Besides, you're not judged on your costumes during the Opening Ceremony. That part's just for fun."

I color orange and yellow swirls of fire onto the torch and stand up to get a better look. Seraphina's right about our costumes. I just wish we had more time to make something better. Our solution is so good and now so is this banner. Everything would be perfect if we had really cool costumes too. I kneel back down and add some red to the fire. That's not true. If Gregor were here with us then everything would be perfect. He's a big reason why we made it this far in the competition, and now he probably won't even get to watch us.

SPINNING THE GOLDEN LIGHT BULB

THE EARLY MORNING sun filters through the blinds of our bedchamber. It casts a glow on the star bed where my green New York T-shirt. I trace the block letters. They feel soft but look strong at the same time. I put it on with my khaki shorts and wrist band. I know I should feel nervous about today, but I don't. I know if wishing with my whole heart could make my dream come true, we'd place in the top five of the Piedmont National Finals, but wishing is only *part* of the solution. No team in this competition has worked harder than us to get here. That's the real reason we're going to place in the top five today. I know it.

I sit on my bed and brush my hair into pigtails. I don't even need a mirror anymore. Jillian stands in the bathroom. Mare sits at our work table. Each of us gets ready on our own. We don't talk, but it's not because we have nothing to say. Our thoughts are too big to spit into words.

The air purification machine kicks on. The room fills with sparkles. One lands on my arm, shimmering in the sunlight. I look at it real close and know right away why it landed on me. The magical dust of the Colorado team is sending us good luck.

Mare, Jillian, and I open the door and head out together. We're not even halfway down the hall when Swissa and the boys turn the corner. She's carrying a plastic bin with a tray of drinks on the top. "Hold on, girls. Go back."

"Go back where?" asks Mare.

"Into your chamber."

"Why?" I ask.

"Seraphina said so." She smiles and winks at me. "Go on."

We walk back and Swissa sets everything on our work table. "These are protein smoothies—mixed with kale. Seraphina sent them up for your breakfast. No dining hall today."

"Kale?" asks Ander as we examine the glasses full of purple goop.

"There's blueberries, bananas, and vanilla yogurt in there too."

"You could've left out the part about the kale," says Ander.

Jax tries it first. "It's good."

I try it too. "It is good, but where's Seraphina? We were supposed to meet her at the dining hall."

"She'll be here in twenty minutes. As soon as you finish your smoothies, she wants you to open this." She takes the drink tray off the bin. The top is clear. I see a large envelope inside. We slurp down the rest of our smoothies and give our empty glasses back to Swissa.

"Have fun with your package . . . and have even more fun today at the Finals. I'd wish you luck but I don't think you'll need it."

"Thanks, Swissa." I say. "I'll let you know how it goes."

"Oh, I'll already know. I'm coming to watch you. I saved my days off so I could watch the opening ceremony and see your team compete. I may even be able to watch the awards ceremony tomorrow night."

I walk over and hug her. "Thanks, Swissa. I'm really glad you're coming."

"Me too. Now you better open the bin. Seraphina will be here soon."

The door clicks shut behind her and we lift off the top. Ander picks up the envelope and pulls out a piece of paper. "It's a letter."

"What does it say?" I lean in to read it over his shoulder but the writing is small.

"Here," he says. "I'll read it aloud."

Team,

I'm sorry I missed your final rehearsal yesterday. I have been allowed to continue as your preceptor. I can't change my actions but I hope to make it up to you. Inside you'll find your costumes for the Opening Ceremony. See you at Gate 2 of Piedmont Coliseum at 9:00 a.m.

Gregor

Goosebumps shoot up my arms and a smile spreads across my face. My teammates and I just look at each other. I guess we don't know what to say. Inside the bin we find five plastic bags. Jillian opens her bag first. "Look at this," she says, holding up a blue dress with wings. She spreads out the wings, shaped like long fingers. Names of each of the Finger Lakes in New York have been embroidered into the fabric. Otisco, Skaneateles, Owasco, Cayuga, Seneca, Keuka, Canandaiqua, Honeoye, Canadice, Hemlock, Conesus, and Cazenovia.

"Wow! That's pretty," Mare says.

"Awesome," says Ander. "Look at mine." He holds up long pants with a wide shirt. It's stiff across his shoulders and drops to his knees. The fabric shimmers in silver, green and blue. "It's Niagara Falls!"

"That's so cool!" I say.

Jax holds his costume up next to Ander's. The top is covered in mountains, valleys, tents, horseback riders, skiers, and canoes.

"That's awesome too," says Ander. "You're the Adirondack Mountains!"

"These costumes are perfect," I say. "Mare what's yours?" She pulls out a pair of black tights, a black skirt, and a black sweater. The sweater is a collage of pictures kind of like Jax's. There's a Broadway theater, the Empire State Building, the Freedom Towers, lots of shops, a bakery, and a delicatessen. She even has a cap with the letters NYC across the top. "I love this!" she says. "How did Gregor know I'd want to wear the New York City costume?"

"Maybe he knows us better than we thought he did," says Ander. "KK, what's yours?"

I open mine and pull out a cloud of green fabric. Sitting under it, looking like it belongs to a princess, is a crown and a flaming torch. My heart takes a second to catch up to my breath. "The Statue of Liberty!"

"These costumes are amazing!" says Jillian. "I can't believe Gregor did this."

I smile. "I knew he'd come through for us."

At exactly nine o'clock, we rush up to Gregor, standing outside Piedmont Coliseum at Gate 2. He looks like a guard dog or a maybe a superhero. We try to thank him, tell him how amazing our costumes are, and ask him what Andora and Master Freeman said, but he holds up his hand. "No thanks are necessary. Your minds should not be focused on me anyway. You need to think about the task at hand. Lining up for the Opening Ceremony."

Seraphina skips over to him. "Oh, you big lug, I'm happy you're back. So are the kids. The costumes are a fabulous touch . . . and that's all I'll say about this subject. Now team, Gregor is right. Let's line up how we practiced."

We arrange ourselves behind the banner. I stand in the middle with the girls on either side of me. The boys stand on the ends. Seraphina and Gregor stand behind us and we await our cue to march in.

The team from New Mexico lines up in front of us. I turn around and see North Carolina behind us. A girl on the end waves to me. She's wearing a pine tree costume. Two boys next to her are dressed as the Wright Brothers, the ones who invented and flew the first airplane.

A voice from beneath my feet startles me. More hidden speakers!

"Welcome to the Opening Ceremony for the Piedmont National Finals. It is an honor to welcome each of our teams, their families and friends, and our entire Piedmont Organization to this event. In our audience today we also have the teaching staff and administrators from Piedmont University and the Piedmont Inventors Prep School. Now please sit back and enjoy the procession as we welcome the thirty-two teams from across the country who have qualified to compete here this weekend."

The Piedmont theme song thunders through the speakers. I bite my pinky nail and also my thumb.

An usher dressed in a purple suit with a purple and black top hat motions for us to move along. We follow New Mexico into a tunnel. It winds and curves underneath the Coliseum where concrete walls are covered with drawings of inventions and words like *imagine* and *leap* and *believe*. I hear the names of states being introduced: Alaska, Arizona, California, Colorado, Connecticut, Georgia, Hawaii, Idaho, Maine . . . New Hampshire . . . I look at Jillian walking next to me and at Ander standing next to her. I quickly face forward as we emerge from the tunnel and step into the roaring, dimly lit coliseum filled with twinkling lights. When New Mexico reaches the end of the path, the usher with the hat motions for us to proceed and we step onto the golden carpet. Master Freeman's booming voice thunders again, "The State of New York!"

We walk together—with our banner—through the stadium that holds about twenty thousand people. I know it's amazing even though I can't see faces because it's so dark. Lasers flash in every direction and I wonder if one of the lasers is flashing near my family. I have no idea where they could be sitting, but it's okay—I know they're here watching somewhere.

We reach the end of the carpet and a different man with the same purple and black hat motions for us to follow him. He points to a row of seats labeled "New York." We file in together and watch the rest of the teams walk down the golden carpet.

After the team from Wyoming reaches the end of the path, Master Freeman steps up to the microphone. He taps it twice and the stadium goes silent. "I now officially open

the Piedmont National Finals Competition!" The crowd roars
to life all over again and I have to remind myself that this
isn't a dream. I really am about to compete in the Piedmont
National Finals.

"This weekend's competition will be full of inventive ideas
and creative solutions. For those of you in the audience, you
are in for a splendid treat. You will be witness to the unpar-
alleled thinking of our youth. Today's idea makers will be
tomorrow's inventors. For those of you competing, on behalf
of the entire Piedmont Organization, we wish you well. May
you find the courage to be everything you are meant to be."

The applause fills the stadium and my butterflies wake
right up.

"Sixteen teams will compete today, and sixteen teams
will compete tomorrow. Tomorrow night we will gather here
again for the Piedmont National Night of Brightness Awards
Ceremony. Do your best, your very best. We of course look
forward to seeing just that."

It takes an hour for all the teams to file out of the stadium.
By the time we get back to the Prep Room with our sets and
props, we're starving. Lunch is waiting for us but we don't
have much time to eat. We need to report to the competition site at two o'clock. I take a bite of a sandwich, but
that's suddenly all I can manage. I get up and walk over to
our Circle Spinner, set up in our corner spot. The wooden
circle, which started out as a coffin box has come back to
life as something really special. I grab hold of it and spin it,
watching the words slowly rotate over and over again. Be
Curious. Be Creative. Be Collaborative. Be Colorful. Be
Courageous. And when it stops, I grab my team and drag
them to the changing rooms. It's time for us to get ready to
compete at the Piedmont National Finals.

THE NIGHT OF BRIGHTNESS

THE NEXT NIGHT at exactly seven o'clock, we file into Piedmont Coliseum and sit in the same New York seats we sat in for the Opening Ceremony. I didn't think it was possible, but tonight the crowd sounds even louder than it did yesterday morning. I can hardly remember our performance at all. Maybe it's because I'm nervous. But I do remember the room. It was echo-y and gray. I remember the judges all wearing orange. I remember the Golden Light Bulb spinning really fast. I remember someone in the audience gasping as Ander's Great-Great-Grandpa Jim appeared across the Circle Spinner, but that's about it. That's all I remember, and now our performance at the National Finals is over already.

Tonight, I move onto the Global Championships, or I don't. I either get to enroll at the Piedmont Inventors Prep School, or I go back home for programming. It's already been decided by the Piedmont people. Their decision is hiding inside that golden envelope in Master Freeman's hand, and now I can't do anything more to win this competition. I can't try any harder. I can't wish any more. I either worked hard enough or I didn't. And if I didn't, I can't get mad at anyone else. I tried as hard as I could. If I'm not good enough to get into PIPS, then I don't belong there anyway. Someday I may invent the Underwater Bubble Bike, or the Baking Pants, or someday I won't. Camp Piedmont was everything I dreamed it would be, but this may be it for me. For all of us. But that's okay, I guess. Everything worked out for Swissa. Maybe it will be okay for me too if I get sent back to Crimson.

We're wearing our green New York T-shirts and shorts. We match, like we always have. We wear our wristbands like we always have too. And now we lock hands. Jax holding Jillian's. Jillian holding mine. Mine holding Ander's and Ander's holding Mare's. "Say New York. Say New York. Say New York." We whisper so quietly I'm not sure even Seraphina or Gregor can hear us, and they're sitting in the seats right behind us.

If New York gets called, we move onto the Global Championships. If it doesn't, we go back home tomorrow and get programmed at Crimson. We'll all be friends, of course—*always*. There's no way we could face Crimson alone, away from each other, ever again. I bite my ring finger covered in green nail polish. Ander looks at me. I hadn't realized I pulled my hand away from his. I lock it back in place, tighter this time. He gives me a look that says he's trying to be tough, but I know deep down he doesn't feel tough. I promise myself I won't cry if we don't win, but I don't think I can keep that promise at all.

The Piedmont theme song fades away for the last time. Master Freeman, dressed in gold, walks up to the podium a million miles away on the stage below us. It's easier to see him on the jumbo screen in the air. He taps the microphone twice. I'm sure I'm going to throw up. I squeeze Ander and Jillian's hands. They squeeze back really hard.

"And now the results you all have been waiting for. I have in this envelope, the names of the five outstanding state teams that have received the highest scores in the Piedmont National Finals. These five teams will represent the United States of America in the Piedmont Global Championships at the end of September!"

"If your team is called, please come down to this center stage for your team trophy, individual medals, and instruction packet for the Global Championships. I'm pleased to announce that this year's Global Championship competition will be held in the fair land of our Canadian neighbors, Quebec City!"

The crowd roars all around us but we don't even clap. We're too afraid to let go.

"And now, the team in fifth place is . . . the team from Maryland!"

I let out a breath. It's fine. It is. Maryland was probably really good.

The Maryland team runs down the stairs in the corner. That area of the stadium goes crazy. I hold my breath a little too long. "It's okay," says Ander. "We have four more chances."

"And the fourth place trophy goes to . . . the team from

Idaho!"

The section directly across the stadium jumps to its feet. The Idaho team races down to the stage. They look like little bugs.

I wipe my hands on my shorts. Then I grab back onto Ander and Jillian's hands.

Ander and I look at each other. I'm trying hard not to get my hopes up but it's not working.

"We have three chances," he says.

"I know!" I snap. "I can count."

"And the third place trophy goes to . . . the team from Texas!"

"That's it. It's not happening. We didn't win," I say. "I know we didn't."

"Don't say that, KK. You'll jinx it. We might have won. We have two chances still. Be positive. We have to be cool remember?"

"I remember. There's just so many good teams. We couldn't have placed in the top two. I just—"

"And in second place, the team from New York!"

"Oh My God! Oh My God!" We jump to our feet and Seraphina and Gregor shove us down the stairs. We run so fast I swear I'm gonna wipe out on the steps.

We get to the bottom and race for the platform. Master Freeman hands Jax the giant second-place trophy and Andora begins placing medals around my teammates' necks. The Coliseum is crazy loud, but still, when Andora gets to me, I can hear her crackling voice. "Congratulations, Kia Krumpet from New York. You have not disappointed us. You have overcome great obstacles to solve this task and you have solved it well. Your solution is inspired. We are honored to have you represent our country next month at the Global Championships."

I smile huge and grab ahold of the medal around my neck. My mind swirls like a tornado. Global Championship . . . Grandma Kitty . . . The Ancestor App . . . Quebec . . . The Ghost Gallery . . . The Bubble Bike . . . I feel dizzy as I jog with my team back across the platform floor. I don't try to control the chaos in my brain this time, though. I don't think it would work anyway.

"KK, are we really going to the Global Championships?" Ander yells as we climb back up the stadium steps. I can only grin at him as I follow behind. Jax and Jillian and Mare are way up ahead. People I don't know stick their hands out into the aisles for us to slap. Ander looks back down the stairs at me again. "Is this really happening?"

Witch Girl from Michigan glares at me as we race by and crosses her arms across her chest. I bet maybe now she wishes her team didn't make that computer kid do all their work. It looks like Master Freeman was right. The teams who form close unions do great things together.

Seraphina, Gregor, Grandma Kitty, and my parents come into focus at the top of the stairs. I blink and grin at Ander. "We're going to Quebec and PIPS, and we're going to build the Bubble Bike!" I skip every other step to reach my team, and when I catch up to Ander, we race for the top of the Coliseum.

"And in first place, the winners of the Piedmont National Finals . . . The team from Pennsylvania!"

I leap to the top step and my team scoops me into the hug. We grin and jump all squished together, just like on the Day of Brightness. Tonight feels like that day all over again, but way, way better this time. And in the chaos I realize Ander was wrong before. We don't need glue to help us stick together. We're all friends now—stuck together without it.

We may need some glue when we get to Quebec though, just in case our Circle Spinner needs fixing, or our costumes get ripped, or our Golden Light Bulb spins too fast.

Acknowledgments

Kia isn't the only one who's better because of her team. It takes an entire team to bring a story to life, and I'm so grateful to have all of you on mine:

To my husband Jim, my first reader, who has believed in me and supported me in every way possible. Thank you for showing me that writing, like running, isn't always a sprint, it's a marathon. I love you and wouldn't want to share this marathon with anyone else but you.

To my daughter, Danielle, who reminds me all the time that dreams do come true if you wish hard enough and believe in them. Thank you for inspiring me to wish and believe, even when this dream seemed impossible. And to my son, Adam, who has read every word of every revised version of this book. This story is as much a part of you as it is of me. Thank you for encouraging me to keep writing it, even when we weren't sure anyone would ever get to read it!

To my parents, Patricia and Robert Boothby, who gave me a childhood I'll always cherish. Thank you for teaching me that family is the greatest team there is, and that when you have love and hope you have it all. To my mother and father-in-law, Anne and Hank Yeager, who've treated me like their own daughter since day one. Thank you for believing I could do this and for making me believe it too.

To my sisters and brother: Terri, Brian, and Amy, who let me write all the scripts in our family and neighborhood plays. Thank you for indulging me way back then, and for your friendship now. To all my family and friends—my cheerleaders. Thank you for never questioning my dream of becoming an author, for listening to my tales of rejections and close calls, and for cheering when I finally got to tell you that I did it!

To my treasured critique partners: Melyssa Mercado, Beth Hautala, Joe Burns, and Glenn McCarty, who helped to make this story sparkle. Thank you for giving so much of yourselves to me and to this book. You're all gems. To the friends I made in my early critique groups: Erin, Tracy, Dan, Vicki, LuAnn, Deb, and Glenn. I'm a better writer because of all of you.

To my writing group, The Rochester Area Children's Writers and Illustrators group: Thank you for being a wealth of knowledge and support through the years. I'm honored to be a part of such a fantastic group.

To my agent, Rebecca Angus of Golden Wheat Literary, for seeing potential in this story and in me. Thank you for your friendship and endless work on my behalf. My book wouldn't be what it is now or have this opportunity if it weren't for you.

To Dayna Anderson, my publisher, and Jenny Miller, my editor, and the entire Amberjack Publishing team: You've spun my words into gold, and brought the story of *THE CRIMSON FIVE* to life. It's even shinier than I ever imagined! Thank you for being amazing to work with and for making my dream come true.

And finally, to the original Crimson Five kids: Kara, Adam, Meg, Jake & Julia—my Odyssey of the Mind dream team. Your creativity, teamwork, and antics inspired me in ways I can't express. I had no choice but to write this story! Thank you for the privilege of being your coach and for giving me an experience I'll never forget. PS. I hope you like the book!

About the Author

Jackie Yeager is a middle grade author whose stories inspire children to think more, work hard, and dream big. She holds a Master's degree in Education and spent several years coaching Odyssey of the Mind, where her team once-upon-a-time competed at the World Finals. She lives in Rochester, NY with her real life prince charming and two royally amazing teens.

When she's not writing imaginative middle grade fiction or living in her own fairly-tale world, she can be found conducting creative problem solving/writing workshops for kids and blogging at www.swirlandspark.com. You can also connect with her on Twitter, Facebook, and Instagram.

Spin the Golden Light Bulb is her first book.

About the Illustrator

Gabrielle Esposito is an illustrator with a passion for using art to tell stories, capture moments, and bring imaginary worlds to life. She earned her Bachelor's degree in Fine Art at the American Academy of Art in Chicago.

Her work includes illustrating *The Story of Snowy Bear and the Lost Scarf* by T.C. LiFonti and Charles "Peanut" Tillman, and the four subsequent books in the *Bear* series: *The Story of Pirate Bear and the Treasure Hunt*, *The Story of Beach Bear and the Sandcastle*, *The Story of Scary Bear and the Pumpkin Patch*, and *The Story of Lovie Bear and the Valentine's Day Card*.

She lives in Chicago, accompanied by an orange-and-white cat with a big personality, and when she's not making art, she loves spending time kayaking, hiking, gardening, or wandering through museums. You can find more of her art online at gabrielleesposito.com, and connect with her on Facebook and Instagram.